TO
KAREN
FROM ARWEN

HAPPY MOTHER'S DAY!!
5/8/05

I HOPE YOU LIKE THE BOOK!!
THIS IS MY FAVORITE WRITER.

Tarzan's Tonsillitis

PANTHEON BOOKS, NEW YORK

Tarzan's Tonsillitis

ALFREDO BRYCE ECHENIQUE

**Translated from the Spanish
by Alfred MacAdam**

Library of Congress Cataloging-in-Publication Data

Bryce Echenique, Alfredo, 1939–
[Amigdalitis de Tarzán. English]
Tarzan's tonsillitis / Alfredo Bryce Echenique;
translated from the Spanish by Alfred MacAdam.
p. cm.
ISBN 0-375-42143-2
I. MacAdam, Alfred. II. Title.
PQ8498.12.R94   A6513   2001
863'.64—dc21   2001031401

www.pantheonbooks.com

Book design by Johanna S. Roebas

Printed in the United States of America
First American Edition
2   4   6   8   9   7   5   3   1

OVER THERE IN THE U.S.A.:

To Lady Ana María Dueñas
Always.
Without ever forgetting.

Also to Claudia Elliot and Julio Ortega, generous friends
in time and distance.

And in the Lima of my tremors:

To Luz María and Manuel Bryce Moncloa
fraternally
With a Bryce-to-Bryce embrace.

With all my affection, my sincerest thanks to my cousins
Inés García Bryce and Alfredo de Toro, and to my niece
and nephew María Elena Harten and Alfredo de Toro
García, for the generosity with which they on several
occasions invited me to their hotels, the Victoria Eugenia,
on the Playa del Inglés, and the Reina Isabel, on Las
Palmas, in Gran Canaria. It was there I found the
tranquility I needed to begin, continue writing, or finish
some of the last books I wrote in Europe.

These ladies given to writing who think that with their
pens they can open new horizons.
—VIRGINIA WOOLF, *Diary*

You won't be here, because everything here
presages distance.
—NURIA PRATS, *Deep South*

Often, only humor allows us to survive horror.
—MARGUERITE YOURCENAR*

And I'm not going to write any more right now because
I'm feeling a little lazy in my kidneys, my slippers,
and in my bra.
—VIOLETA PARRA*

He had experienced anguish and sorrow, but he had
never been sad in the morning.
—ERNEST HEMINGWAY, *Across the River and into the Trees*

*Quoted by Nilda Sosa in *Esas damas dadas a escribir*. (Author's note)

Contents

Tarzan's Tonsillitis

I

▲▲▲▲▲▲▲▲

The Prehistory of Love

Damn . . . Having to admit after so many, so damn many years that when everything is said and done we were better by letter. Sure, life beat up our relationship the way the guards smack convicts around after a prison riot, but something extremely valuable and beautiful always existed between us, and that's the truth. And if you can compare reality to a port where packet boats from another century drop anchor alongside brand-new cruise ships of the dinner-jacket-and-long-dress set, Fernanda María and I were always first-class passengers each time one of us made a stopover in the reality of the other. I think that united us right from the beginning. And also not being able to do a bad thing to anyone, I guess.

So what was missing? Love? Hell, no. We had that, in all shapes and sizes. From the platonic, underage love of a pair of extremely timid people to the sensual, jolly, and crazy chaos of those who sometimes had only a few short weeks to make up for, as the song says, *the whole life I'd spend with you,* to the love of a brother and sister born to love and help each other eternally, to the love of a pair of implacable accomplices in more than one criminal affair, and even the love of a young couple in love with love itself and the moon itself, and finally the love of a pair of old-timers still capable of frisking about on some remote island under the sun, again, as the song goes, *it doesn't matter to me in what form, or where or how, but at your side.* . . . In sum, yes, we had love of all shapes and sizes, but always good love, yes, absolutely, for sure.

It's also true that our loyalty was always honest and absolute, although here we've got to recognize (why not?) that we often acted like two players on the same court playing different games with the same ball. And who could deny, at this stage in our lives, that the thing we were always missing was ETA, that is, what air, land, and sea navigators call "Estimated Time of Arrival." Because our great specialty, Fernanda María's and mine, over the course of some thirty years, was never knowing how to be in the right place, much less at the right time.

So the real pain in the ass, the absolute pain in the ass, is having to recognize that we were better by mail. Which means, in that case, of course, that the best of me has in large part disappeared forever. Okay, I'll explain: on top of everything else, a good decade or more of the best of me disappeared forever. And it's that I died, completely and for all eternity, that day when some fuckers mugged you in Oakland, California, Fernanda Mía, Fernanda Mine, as I like to call you, and along with the other crown jewels, they took off with about fifteen years of the least bad element there was in me, as you told me yourself, Mía, in this letter you sent me from Oakland, God knows when because you forgot to date the letter, because in that moment you didn't know what day it was, but to judge from the context, or (better) our context, it must have been in the early eighties:

Dear Juan Manuel,

The circuit has been completely broken. For various reasons. First, your letters were stolen. Stolen because I keep the entire collection in a huge bag, and some horrible gorillas attacked me on the street, grabbing the bag, my grandmother's beautiful diamond ring, some gold necklaces I was wearing, and a watch. Can you imagine such a thing? I was so mad I ran after them, and luckily, while they were running, one of them dropped my wallet with all my identification papers. At least I didn't lose everything. But they took quite a few things. I called the police, but they haven't been able to find anything. That happened months ago. The only thing they told me was that I was crazy, nuts, to run after them, and that it was lucky I didn't catch them. That's true, I wouldn't have been able to do much against three huge goons like that. But you know that when you're mad you don't think about those things. All I wanted was to take a swing at them.

Okay, so at least nothing happened to me personally, but I did lose a lot. Some people come out worse, meaning that besides being robbed they get beaten up or something. But in this case, I was the one who wanted to do the beating. That took care of the month of August. So, among the things lost were your letters. I was so bereft that I became mute, at least in epistolary terms.

Now, to begin again, I want to know if that volume of D. H. Lawrence's poetry ever got to you in Lima, the one I sent to you with a gringo couple. Judging by your silence, it would seem that the book is just one more lost item. A real shame, because it was a beautiful book, and somewhere in it, quite unexpectedly, it talks about us, as if Mr. Lawrence had known us since we were kids. Just imagine, he compares us to elephants, my dear Juan Manuel. And imagine, too, that he's really right, because he describes us exactly. All we need are trunks. How could he have known? And with such wisdom, although that word is best reserved for Don David Herbert.

How did your stay in Lima end up, and what was it like going back to France? What are you up to? I'm way behind on news. I'll tell you about me, though there hasn't been much change since I last wrote you, except for what happened to your adored, adorable letters and the last (I think) pieces of jewelry left in the catastrophic history of my family.

I'm still in California. I'm working now, and the kids are already speaking English, but I'm still having a really hard time adapting, and I feel so damn alone. I hadn't seen the pale face of solitude for so long that I'd almost forgotten what it looks like, but solitude always waits for you right around the next corner.

Even so, I don't have much time to think about all that. I'm running around all day. In the morning, I run to drop the kids off at school, then I run to the office, run at work, run to have lunch, pick up the kids in the afternoon, get them home, give them a bath, make dinner, clean up, well, clean up a little, put the kids to bed. And then I'm so tired that I run to bed to read and sleep. It isn't exactly the most exciting program, and as you probably imagine, I don't know how long this business of my Great Independence is going to last. It seems more like a Great Fuckup, but in a way I also feel calmer, and sometimes I have fun seeing new things and then, for a minute, I feel as terrifically well as Tarzan at the instant when he dives into the water.

But right now I'm seriously wondering if it wouldn't be better just to go back home to San Salvador, war or no war. Or even go back with Enrique in Chile, Pinochet or no Pinochet. Why am I the one who's always running away from everywhere? In Chile, the one on the left—though just barely—was Enrique, and in El Salvador the only right-wing rich guy—and he really was right-wing—was an uncle of mine, disagreeable and pretty much invisible as far as the family was concerned.

Enrique's still in Chile, you already know he had to go back when his mother got sick, she's still sick, and being treated. He had a show of his photographs a little while ago, and he says he's looking for a job at the university, but nothing's turned up yet. It looks as if he wants to get us back. Poor guy. He must feel lonely too, but at least there in his own country he's got his family and lots of friends and shows and respect. All of that counts, and I'm happy he's back in his own country, where things always have more meaning.

Please write to me. I'd really like to get a letter from you and see you if you come here again soon. You said that in February you're going to Texas. Is that trip still going to happen? Because you and your songs always end up in the weirdest places.

You should know, brother and love of mine, that I was in good shape and optimistic and then suddenly everything changed a little while back, about ten days ago, my spirits deflated and I can't seem to get out of what looks like a depression, and here I thought I was immune to those problems. I'd like to run and find a safe place instead of running and running always to be no place.

I'm living in Oakland now, where I was mugged, but I'm looking for a better place and hope to find it. It would be better if you wrote to me at the office, because if nothing else I'm sticking with this job. I only hope I can shake these blue devils soon.

Don't get lost on me now, please. A hug and lots of memories.

Fernanda Yours

That bit about Fernanda Yours comes from when she was a little girl and people would call her Fernanda Mía—or Fernanda Mine—instead of Fernanda María. And since I knew nothing about that, she became, in translation, Fernanda Mine, the only time we really belonged to each other, in Paris, when she instantly turned into "Fernanda Yours" instead of "Yours, Fernanda," at the end of every letter, and as she gradually went back to the open arms of Enrique and left mine, without the slightest *Estimated Time of Arrival,* of course, and without anyone's going away from anyone, really, although finally the three of us ended up absolutely alone and each one at a different cardinal point on the compass, of course. The mail and a few demented trips did the rest, and we're all still connected that way, spoiling one another, treating one another more and more like shipwrecked kings. It pisses me off, of course, that three Oakland thugs took off with those letters in which, no doubt, I was always much better than in real life, and I'm sure that they took them only so they could tear them to pieces and toss them into the first garbage can they passed. And the only thing saved from all that correspondence and love and friendship, from all the goodness and tenderness and the understanding I always tried to use when dealing with a woman as adorable as Fernanda María, Fernanda Maía, or Fernanda Mía, or simply Mía, the only thing that's survived is a kind of anthology of little paragraphs and isolated sentences that she'd underlined in my letters and written down later in a notebook—but with no dates and, what's worse, with no context. I have a copy of that notebook that Maía sent me once, which is like having someone say the way people speak where you come from is so beautiful, or only you could think up these incredible, funny things you write me in your letters.

That's how she was, even in the letter from her I've just quoted and which ended, as always, with her new telephone numbers and home and work addresses so I could write her—I don't know anyone in the world who's moved as many times as Fernanda María, no one who's changed jobs and

9

destiny as many times, yes: I said DESTINY. I could have quoted, now that I'm opening the copy of the famous notebook that contains the remains of someone who was always better by letter, this crumb of myself:

As if we had to write it all over again, that's how hope is reborn sometimes, Fernanda Mine. Remember. As soon as I can, I'll be crossing Atlantics to get to Pacifics to get into your tenderness and into your house (etc.), always with that love of ours that time is transforming into a wise man highlighted by the snows of "as time goes by." Don't be afraid, I won't overwhelm you. Actually, I'll practice that "yes to tenderness/no to assholeness" concept. I'm really sorry you lost (via the muggers) the best of my repertory. When things get bad, don't look sad, a saying that over there in savage Oakland would probably be translated as "You can't shit upwards."

Your D. H. Lawrence will find his way to me. Don't forget that we incarnate, as no one else can, the idea that "Everything comes in this life." By now, your gringo friends will have figured out that I've left Lima, that I'm back in Paris. Meaning to say they've probably sent it via airmail, Via Láctea, I mean Milky Way, so it's probably dripping milk or something milky.

Meanwhile, my affection rises and snakes its way across transatlantic horizons and reaches you to crush you (provisionally) in a powerful embrace. Order and calm, Your Majesty. Also: hug and kiss the kids as if they were mine. If that were the case, I don't think I'd have done it so badly. And by the way without alluding to the saintly man and most beloved Chilean friend, Mr. Henry Kodak. In any case, as the proverb has it, "Photography, like philosophy, develops in an extremely dark room."

Paris adores you. Ciao,

Juan Manuel

Since our history—or, rather, Fernanda Mía's history and mine, the two always entangled but almost never together—never had what in conventional human time is usually called a Beginning, nor has it ever had anything that would allow me to call it an Ending of any kind, much less a conventional ending, I'm going to begin quite a bit before the beginning, in a kind of Primeval Mist or Prehistory in which the first news about a highly educated and super-naïve, Salvadoran girl of illustrious family reaches my ears. The only thing I can do, in fact, in speaking about an objective, prehistoric Mía is to be extremely subjective—to treat her as legend, even myth—and in truth I say unto you, to relate almost all as hearsay.

I'm also sure that I'll have to end that way as well. In a kind of Post-world or Encounters of the Third Kind, in which a man remembers a woman who was very fine, always happy and positive, adorable, and very Tarzan, yes, highly Tarzan. Even though Fernanda Mía has far, far more value than Tarzan, who, after all, was brought up by monkeys and gorillas so as to behave as one, in a makeshift environment, while Mía was brought up to be a young lady of the upper crust in the what the exquisite Cuban novelist Alejo Carpentier would call an artificial paradise, that is, in a very expensive boarding school the Sisters of the Sacred Heart have in San Francisco, and later in its postgraduate, junior jet-set equivalent in the white, skiing, Swiss-chalet, neutral, extremely boring, and polyglot Lausanne. And of course no sooner did Fernanda María poke her aquiline postgraduate nose into the vale of tears and tear gas in which we live, than a series of things began to befall her for which no one, not even one of her diplomas, had prepared her, poor thing—she was still so naïve.

I'd just returned from Rome, in 1967, from an interminable road tour for which no one had prepared me, either, and during which, at first, I'd sung to applause and a few encore requests, food and third-class hotel included, but later, very soon later, I was passing the hat around, and then, at the end, without guitar or words, only a sad humming, I washed dishes and glasses in a Roman restaurant. But I was young, I was composing the most beautiful songs in the world—admitedly not understood—and I had a marvelous wife always waiting for me in Paris. Her name was Luisa, she was the daughter of Italian immigrants, from Lima, my hometown as well, and to her I dedicated each and every one of my oh-so-sad love songs, the fruit, no doubt, of that indispensable distance I had to maintain (hence my frequent touring) so my love stanzas wouldn't just *sound* but really *be* sincere and oh-so-sad. Luisa didn't understand me. I did.

She was studying business administration. Maybe that was the reason why Luisa didn't understand me while I did. I fell in love with her—with her skin the color of a tanned peach all year round, with her knockout figure, with her long golden-blond hair, with her very black eyebrows and eyes— in Lima, singing at a party at Catholic University, where she was Miss Undergraduate or something like that and I was Nat "King" Cole in Spanish, and to the rhythm of "come closer, closer, closer, no, much closer," I ended up bringing her close to me, to the point that I still haven't managed to get away from her yet, even though "more than a thousand years, many more" have gone by, for which reason I think I could answer the composer of that bolero that, yes, love does seem to endure eternity.

We, Luisa and I, were a couple of newlyweds in Paris the night when I first heard something that, let's say, delighted me tenderly, deeply, and movingly about a girl named Fernanda María. It was at a party at some Latin American embassy, maybe of some banana republic, I'll never remember which. I'd been hired to sing, and Luisa was there as my wife. And the thing that always happens with rich people happened there. They see you as an entertainer, singing for your supper, microphone in hand, and they feel free to put the moves on your woman, using my very own love lyrics, whispered by me and everything, at the same time they're asking her for her address, and Luisa gives them ours—poor but decent—and has them make tremendous fools of themselves, the bunch of dirty old men, can you imagine? Well, I can, and with some frequency.

Okay, that night the waters of the Seine did not overflow their banks, and there was a really likable young Salvadoran diplomat who made all of us laugh reconcilingly, about a little scene he'd witnessed just that very afternoon.

"Fernanda María de la Trinidad del Monte Montes, a name that, as you'll see, simply typifies our countries, the daughter of very important people from there, right from the capital, straight from San Salvador, you might say, graduated only a few days ago from the most chic boarding school in Lausanne, with five languages, the best manners, and knowing things as useless as, you hail a taxi like this."

The Salvadoran, whose name was Rafael Dulanto, bent over his left foot, stretched out his torso, neck, and left arm, hand, and thumb, almost to the middle of an avenue as wide as it was imaginary, and was finished with his explanation only when the taxi stopped completely and the cabby opened the rear door, just as Fernanda María de la Trinidad del Monte Montes had been taught in Lausanne.

"What would she do, one wonders, if faced with a bus or with the subway, the poor child?" asked a delicately aged Honduran guest.

"Why, she'd ignore them, of course. My dear sir, a young lady graduated from a school the caliber of Fernanda María's simply does not *use* mass transit."

"Ah, yes, I understand now, Rafael. Please forgive my *intruption*."

"No, all the better she *not* use them," Rafael went on, "because of the calamities that ensue when she does. Calamities, that's right. Just listen, ladies and gentlemen, to what I witnessed with my own eyes—as specifically ordered by no one less than my ambassador."

It was then that Rafael Dulanto related the saga of how Fernanda Mía arrived in Paris by train. And a good tale it was, though Mía says Rafael exaggerates a bit, though even today she blushes when she remembers the first time she arrived in Paris, totally on her own and freshly graduated and prepared for nothing, from Switzerland. Fernanda Mía descended from the train followed by a porter carrying her two huge valises made of the finest pigskin, although by then they were a bit worn out from so many hereditary comings and goings. She advanced down the platform without looking at a single soul, as is only proper, crossed without waiting a second in the waiting room, and nothing stopped her until she reached the Information window, lofted along by the security conferred on her by that education of hers.

The lady at the window must have been quite—no, exceedingly—surprised that the tall, red-haired, graceful young lady with green eyes and a perfect accent could be so insistent, but, well, what was she to do, she was paid to inform, not to ask questions. So she looked up the addresses for Residences for Young Ladies, thumbing past the Residences for *e, f, g, h, i,* etc., until she came to something we would call in French very Dupont, in Spanish very Pérez, and in English very Smith, meaning to say she arrived at an absolute diarrhea of *RESIDENCES FOR YOUNG LADIES.*

"Would you prefer one part of town over another, miss?" asked the Information Lady, almost out of pity.

"Any well-trafficked neighborhood will do," answered Fernanda María, with the smile appropriate to such situations and that education of hers.

Truly mortified by now, because "well-trafficked" can be taken several ways, the Information Lady of the French National Railroad Services handed Fernanda María a piece of paper with nine regrettable addresses and their tragic telephone numbers.

"I seem to have heard of this Piagalle place" was all that Mía said as she glanced at the paper with an appropriately thankful smile and a *"Merci beaucoup, madame . . . Et bonsoir, madame, merci."*

Then she shocked a Parisian porter with a tip—the first

and last of his life—before bending over and stretching the entire length of her spine (which gesture Rafael Dulanto imitated mercilessly in that banana embassy), although her effort was completely needless, as she was the first in line at the taxi stand and a taxi stood there already, at her feet, waiting for her, *jeune fille.*

And not unlike the lady at the Information window moments before, the old taxi driver, who had seen everything in the life of a night cabbie—*et à Paris on voit des ces chose, merde*—almost dies of sorrow when the *jeune fille,* so freckled and young and green-eyed and skinny, says, with the most pertinent insistence and a trace of amiable smile, yes, any one of those nine addresses will be perfectly fine—that was how she'd been taught in her long years at the Swiss boarding school.

And so, by then dead of sorrow, the old taxi driver leaves her, he who until that night swore he'd seen everything in this life, because all that business about a "residence for young ladies" seemed to him nothing more than a very cruel and euphemistic way of referring to what it really was and with a very scandalous address, where he'd just deposited, one might say, such a feminine and thin and redheaded and very young angel . . .

Eh oui, on finit jamais d'apprendre, à Paris, merde . . . Et on aura tout vu . . . Et vaut mieux prendre sa retraite . . . Ah, merde, ça oui, et ce soir méme, que je te dis—so concluded, after a while, the night driver to his wife, dying of sorrow while he asked her to pour him another very dry brandy and his slippers forever, *putain.*

And even though she says I exaggerate, but that, after all, she understands that freedom in art is like that, Fernanda

Mía has never denied completely the content of that very long protest song, with my music and ideas but with her experiences and words (the record sold quite well in Spain and Mexico, above all, and we shared the profits that on more than one occasion helped Mía just a bit in her thousand different moves), according to which it took her, because she was so pure and such a rotten little bourgeois as she should have been, an entire week to realize that the oh so dramatic place where she was living was something like a mixture of the Salvation Army, a repentant *ma non troppo* whorehouse, Amnesty International, and a not-for-profit Relapse Center for Juvenile Rehabilitation. And she was already beginning to make lots of friends who were rather exaggerated in their style of dress and makeup, now this is the truth, Juan Manuel, when the one with the worst taste of all, the one most daubed up, poor thing, when you think how good she was underneath it all, revealed to her a tremendous relapse into forbidden things, and right in the *Résidence de jeunes filles* no less, where she'd set up a white-slavery establishment for fetishists of the clandestine relapse, pious prayers and all. Fernanda María de la Trinidad del Monte Montes, just at that moment, thought that perhaps it wouldn't be a bad idea to call her embassy and consult them, just in case.

They pulled her out by the ears, of course, and it was Rafael Dulanto himself who, on orders from the ambassador, and with the strictest diplomatic-police reserve, set about picking up Fernanda María's luggage and installing her most comfortably in the embassy residence, where the ambassador's wife wept with grief and whatnot for Fernanda María's parents, people so like us, and personally took it upon herself to watch over the waif day and night, especially at night, so it shouldn't happen that, on top of what her education in the United States and Switzerland must have cost those people who were no longer in a position to make such economic sacrifices, and especially, if I'm remembering correctly, because there are four or five sisters, so that, counting her, there are five or six women and no male, and the fortune of the Monte Montes is already very divided, no, no, it mustn't happen that on top of all that Fernanda María should make a second mistake, which is what she says it's all been, a mistake between the French she learned at school and the up-to-date French of this up-to-date world, although sometimes I have my doubts.

A few weeks later, Fernanda María turned out to be so good and intelligent and diligent, and to have been so mistaken—but *so* mistaken—that all of Central American Paris knew the story of Miss Monte Montes in all its versions and interpretations, but always with a happy ending, as in the *Thousand and One Nights,* and completely expurgated since it was of course Fernanda María herself who repeated the shocking elements of her seven nights between good and evil, with all its charm, such that this ever so hideous situation in which she found herself on account of how stupid a good education leaves you would be tremendously amusing.

"Now, just put Fernanda del Monte period, sir. And between you and me, let's forget about all that crap about María de la Trinidad, as far as first names goes, and as for last names let's forget that Monte Montes stuff, which just makes matters worse, because that's how people are where I come from, and proud of it, although here we're somewhere else, and what I need is for my name to fit on official forms . . ." Mía said that to half the city as she looked for work in five languages, her reading and speaking ability so good you can't tell which *isn't* her native tongue. And everyone was delighted with what a redheaded and green-eyed, long-nosed cutie she was, this skinny, freckled kid, so bright and lively. What exactly was Fernanda del Monte period looking for, in terms of work? Well, anything in which she could be very useful and use her free time to ratify her Swiss diplomas and to study architecture but without costing anyone one more cent ever again, that's what I'm looking for, ladies and gentlemen, and it's called In-De-Pen-Dence.

And so, always among ladies and gentlemen, Mía went from one interview and test to another, and from one day to the next and again as in the *Thousand and One Nights,* though never expressed better in this case, she became editor in chief to Julio Cortázar, who worked as an editor at UNESCO; she also corrected the Spanish in broadcasts for Latin America for Mario Vargas Llosa, as well as drafts for UNESCO *News* for the poet Jorge Enrique Adoum, whom she adored, and for another poet whom she must not have adored, shall we say, very much, because she always referred to him with the epithet *Argentine to the death,* spoken in a rather sententious tone by a person who was always, in everything, so *per bene,* as Mía always was, and to what end I wonder, and that I did not like.

Because it was then that I met her for the second time, in what for me was literally a *weird world,* a world that was too big for me, too elegant, a world that ate and drank in the places where I, if I was extremely lucky, only managed to finish a song before they threw me out, and not even with a passing of the hat.

But it's high time I introduced myself, at least the self I was

then. Name: Juan Manuel Carpio, second-generation citizen
of Lima, Andean thorax, and the rest in Native American
style as well, because my paternal grandfather was from
Andahuyalas and his mother tongue was Quechua; my maternal grandmother could also speak Puña, though she was pre-
dominantly a Quechua-speaker. With their immigration to
the capital my grandparents also moved up socially, and my
father was on the Supreme Court and all that, and he sent
me to the four-hundred-year-old National University of San
Marcos, the School of Letters, major in literature, for which I
had a monstrous vocation, I'd say an almost Renaissance
vocation, because nothing human was foreign to me, insofar
as writing was concerned, so that from the Bible to the Latin
American boom of the sixties, which is more or less where I
was when I took off for Europe with my first guitar after win-
ning two singing contests and metamorphosing, my diploma
now in my pocket, into the young poet of the year, leaving
Peru for Paris, as César Vallejo did before him, but with a
guitar.

Because I also compose the music for my poems, autodidactically I might add, but with a spirit so open and with
horizons so vast that really, knowing French and English very
well, and also being able to make good use of my smidgen
of Italian and German, I've managed to absorb practically
everything I've encountered. To wit: from the *Song of Roland*
to the *Song of the Cid,* passing through Georges Brassens,
Noël Coward, Cole Porter, Frank Sinatra, Drunky Beam,
Tony Bennett, Dean Martin, Sammy Davis, Jr., Edith Piaf,
Yves Montand, Aretha, Sarah, Billie, Ella, and Marlene, Los
Panchos, Nat "King" Cole (bilingual), Jorge Negrete and
"Mexico beautiful and beloved," little Carlos Gardel, Lucho

Gatica, Daniel Santos, Beny Moré, Atahualpa Yupanqui, Raimon, Joan Manuel Serrat, Luis Llach, Paco Ibáñez, Pablo Milanés, Silvio Rodríguez, and a long etcetera.

And from my own country: as far as poetry is concerned, everything, from Vallejo and Darío and Neruda and Martí, and, once again, Vallejo and Darío, and the whole thing over again, because we're all one nation in poetry from Berceo and Quevedo and Cernuda (I'm talking about 1967, just in case I've missed something later) up through Felipe Pinglo, who, after work, would return to his humble home whistling traditional Peruvian waltzes like the one in which even God was a lover, and, therefore, *Love, being human, contains something divine, loving is no crime, because* . . . because, damn, think what would happen if God sinned, the times being what they are.

But Felipe Pinglo, in Lima, was at least a tailor, while I, in Paris, wore the same cap for the cold and the snow and the autumn and the rain, and used it also to pick up some change during an economic recession, the moment Luisa chose to abandon me on charter flight number 1313 on June 13, 1967, direct to Lima, Peru, one-way only, murdering me on the spot.

That night, like Neruda, I could have composed the saddest songs in my life. Actually, I did compose them. Again like Neruda, twenty in all, though I swear that was pure coincidence. They were so incredibly sad, my songs, that neither I nor anyone else could ever sing them. They're still around, as Fernanda Mía always tells me, because she tore them out of my hands one day in a fit of mortal jealousy, but even after she changed them a tiny bit (she's an incredible writer), putting herself and all her charm in Luisa's place, she's never managed to find anyone to sing them or, much less, a record company interested in them, then, these songs she now claims as her "acquired rights"—the result of escaping from the right wing and being deported by the left, and with countries, cities, and moves by the thousand, and always with my twenty oh-so-sad songs on her back, my Fernanda Mía.

And so, if instead of talking about love and Luisa and Paris, I'd spoken about Troy and Helen and Paris, Fernanda María de la Trinidad del Monte would have had quite a resemblance to Homer's literary agent, or something like that, because she's been carrying my poems around for so long that they've acquired their own little legend, to the point that people don't often bother asking about their real author anymore—as if those poems had come right out of the night of time.

So, if someone were to say that this unknown author begged alms like a blind bard wandering from minor court to minor court, he might be believed, and besides, he'd be right insofar as the blindness is concerned—blind from love—and in the bard part, and insofar as my cap is concerned, the cap of a really unknown man, I indeed, at least and unlike others, unlike the unknown soldier, for example, who, to me— I mean it—sounds like an extremely important and well-known person, because any head of state who visits Paris, France, the first thing he does is rush over to bring a huge bouquet of flowers to the most recognized of soldiers.

Me, on the other hand, I wouldn't even be recognized by my cap in those prehistoric back-thens, when, finally, Fernanda María de la Trinidad del Monte Montes and Juan Manuel Carpio would meet again, finally, and how and how much and even to what point and also to what end, well . . .

In truth, neither Fernanda María nor I deserved to meet ever in such a bad moment and place. When I didn't meet her the first time I saw her and she saw me. That was also a terrible moment, and excuse me for meandering this way. But remember, please, that I warned you earlier that the story of Fernanda María, of which I am a part, period, from Rome, February 12, 1967, or from Paris, December 24 of the same year, has a complete prehistory, and it also has industrial quantities of smoke in its eyes.

So let's begin with the chronological night of February 12, 1967, Rome . . . Highly elegant young ladies with multinational airs and unique fortunes, as you can see with a glance. She's tall and red-haired, between thin and almost skinny, eyes that are so green, and, again, tall and almost thin instead of being a little thin for my taste. And now, again: she's a redhead, thin, yes, very thin, but she's no longer skinny this time . . . She's got red hair, her eyes are green, how terrifically thin she was . . .

Her nose . . . (he was sufficiently drunk to be aware of those tiny details) . . . No, her nose wasn't . . . Her nose, what it was is that it belongs to the most antiquated and red-haired and elegant shit-ass oligarchy, perhaps in Santiago de Chile, perhaps in Buenos Aires . . . But your nose, my beloved skinny, enchants me, as if it reconciles me with life, tonight, and if you only knew how difficult that is, as far as today is concerned, skinny, beloved, skinny little girl.

He was completely drunk—how could I not realize that?—but how sweetly he sings, right out there in Piazza di Spagna in the *città aperta,* capital of the world, how happily, how happily, oh how wonderfully he sings, and now, how he imitates Lucho Gatica when he sings *The girls in Piazza di*

Spagna are so very pretty . . . It just happened that he made a mistake because he was staring at me and said *are so very skinny.* And later (how wonderfully he sings) . . .

What he didn't know: that within a few seconds those girls on vacation would have to go back to their hotel, because tomorrow, bright and early, they were going back to a boarding school in Lausanne.

What she didn't know: that the boy was married to a marvelous woman who simply and plainly refused to see the world as a big, very moving show, especially at night, and with a glass of wine and a good song . . . She also didn't know that recently things hadn't been going very well for the boy, and that at night he wept in Rome's nooks and crannies, always thinking about Luisa and muttering like an idiot, *I love Louisa, and Louisa, she loves me,* until he reached number 1,500, and with his cap held out to life itself . . . And that, very much in his own style, and, above all, surprising himself doing it, the boy had been observing her much more than she thought, and hadn't made any mistake at all, as she thought, when he sang that line about *the girls in Piazza di Spagna are so very skinny,* which he did quite intentionally . . .

What they both knew, only God knows why, given the circumstances surrounding that fortuitous Roman encounter, millions of which must take place every day: that from the first instant they were certain they'd end up meeting. And that, thinking about the future staring into a mirror, they would run into each other from time to time, repeating with a grin that very pretty song in which the two of them meet again after all, and as they look at each other it was also certain both their hearts would skip a tremendous beat.

The double skipped beat took place in Paris on December 23, 1967, in the house of Rafael Dulanto, the young, brilliant diplomat from El Salvador, mastermind of Fernanda María's rescue. Place: overlooking the Seine. Where on the Seine: Notre Dame. Position of cathedral of Paris, relative to location: opposite the apartment, with marvelous views, from which you emerge, from Rafael Dulanto's, that is, right onto the very *quai.* Heavyweights: a dead ringer for Don Miguel Angel Asturias, who turned out to be a spectacular, incomparable Peruvian musician, although with the excitement the presence of Juan Manuel Carpio aroused in her it was completely useless that Fernanda María de la Trinidad del Monte Montes . . .

"My, my, we have a Sacromonte among us tonight!" The spectacular, false Don Miguel Angel Asturias, deeply entrenched in another era, mistook her name.

With the result that Mía spent the entire evening saying Don Miguel Angel to none other than Julián d'Octeville, Peruvian to the marrow of his bones, fat, symphonic musician, unpublished author, gourmet, gourmand, and bon vivant. Other guests: women of all ages, pretty and very pretty, or who had been pretty. And Fernanda María, helping, doing everything in the kitchen, so that not the slightest detail would go wrong. All of the women extremely nice, because Rafael Dulanto was a great specialist in knowing only delightful people.

Among the gentlemen: Edgardo de la Jara, from Ecuador, born to be liked and to be free; alias: Dancing Master, because he'd danced cheek to cheek with Princess Paola of Liege, in the springtime of her youth, and he'd won the reputation of being a dearly loved dancer and a painter with the beard and heart of a gentleman. Latin American cosmopolitanism of the highest order. And one more unforgettable guest among so many others: Charlie Boston, the purest Salvadoran—and chief of protocol for the Food and Agriculture Organization in Rome—because there never was in this world a man who could drink whiskey with such magical and mysterious elegance, removing a full glass from his ring, which bore the shield of the Bostons of d'Aubervilliers, tossing the entire contents always into the same pocket of his extremely elegant jacket over the course of an entire evening, without ever wetting anything, without ever losing a glass, much less his composure as he crawled down the stairs on all fours.

The mood: a forced and obligatory joy combined with a very Latin American *we live here but we don't live here* and *on trouve tout à la Samaritaine,* my beloved Buenos Aires, my San Salvador, my Lima, my Santiago de Chile, my and my and me and Mimi, and this Christmas season is always like that, false happiness and shitty disquiet. The guest singer: Juan Manuel Carpio, loved, really loved, by Rafael Dulanto, Charlie Boston, Don Julián d'Octeville y González Prada, Edgardo de la Jara (alias Dancing Master), all of whom felt really sorry for him because of Luisa, his wife—man, you don't do something like that to this boy. So if he wants to sing, let him sing, but he was invited here as a guest. An extremely late arrival: the Peruvian—and skinny—writer Julio Ramón Ribeyro. His manner of arriving: like someone who'll be leaving soon.

Finally back from the kitchen, from helping with everything: Fernanda María de la Trinidad del Monte Montes.

Fortunately, no one did ask me to sing, and Rafael Dulanto was even kind enough to ask me for something which I considered a thing among friends, symbolic, noble, generous: that I hand him my worn-out overcoat and my cap for singing and passing around all over Paris. That, and my taking a few more steps to reach the center of the room to greet everyone, coincided chronometrically with the instant when Fernanda María exited the kitchen, and she was the girl I saw in Rome months earlier, the instant when for her I turned into the singer who made a mistake with the oh-so-skinny cuties in Piazza di Spagna.

"How wonderful," she exclaimed, but with such refinement that the exclamation point was imperceptible.

It's the wrong time and the wrong place, I heard someone somewhere observe in a very serious, melodic voice, as if he were singing to an extremely sad instrument.

"It's Frank Sinatra," Fernanda María explained, adding, "I put it on not knowing you were about to arrive, so if you'd rather I took it off, I'll do it immediately."

"Hi there, Piazza di Spagna." I smiled, walking over to kiss her among friends in Paris, on both cheeks etc., and telling her at the same time we all have to live with our mistakes, and there are, as Vallejo said, "blows in life or in Piazza di Spagna, so strong, I don't know."

"You're absolutely right, it was there," Fernanda María said, informing me of only that much of her name and taking advantage of the fact that we were all friends and that it was almost Christmas and Paris and Notre Dame and those things about Piazza di Spagna to put one hand on each of my shoulders, lean over, bathe me in her perfume, and marvelously bury her red hair and green eyes and her devilish nose in the cushion of my chest, left side.

It's all right with me, commented Sinatra, melodic and

grave, somewhere between the realms of resignation and good guy, and with a touch of Latin lover tossed in.

"How wonderful," exclaimed Fernanda through the mute of my lapel between her lips, adding, "You leave him to me, and you'll see how wonderful he is."

Then I started drinking, because of Luisa, one after another, every glass of whiskey within reach, while Fernanda María went on calling him Don Miguel Angel Asturias even though he was Don Julián d'Octeville y González Prada, very much the *limeño,* son of a Frenchman who came to Peru to found the Lima Stock Exchange and married the daughter of our illustrious Don Manuel González Prada, historic citizen and thinker who spent his life in a fury because of our infamous national habit of saying things in an undertone, who both consigned the older generation to the grave and the younger to their labors, and who sent his grandson Julián to Paris so he could compose symphonies, and while he was addressing her as Mademoiselle del Sacromonte, while again and again the Dancing Master tried to dance with Fernanda María, she, uselessly, tried to spend the evening next to the disaster that, at the time, was me.

We danced—once—with, of course, Frank Sinatra reminding us in his most serious voice that December 23, 1967, and Rafael Dulanto's apartment, with its marvelous view, were not exactly the most auspicious time or place for us to get to know each other, but, well, we'd have to play the hand we were dealt.

It's poignant, and it's sad, said Fernanda María, raising her red hair from my left lapel and piercing me with such a green-eyed gaze that it was only then I understood that *poignant* in English means bitter and something more, and sad and something more, and wounding and something more.

Since that night, for Fernanda and me, the song "It's All Right with Me" has been what people in love call "our song," the song they dance to until death does them part, even if they've become incontinent. So, that song, which, if translated into Spanish would speak of a shadow of hatred, or something like that, crossing the path of "two souls united in this world by God"—the song persisted, even after Frank Sinatra's voice disappeared, even after the orchestra that accompanied him marked the rhythm of our lives with its final beats, and both Fernanda and I agreed that for better or worse our story had begun, this time with first and last names. We also agreed that just as she had her Prehistory for me, I had one for her. Rafael Dulanto, going over the list of people invited that night to his pre-Christmas party, had said a few days before, as he showed her a photo of Luisa and me, "Look, I'm also going to invite this boy."

"And the incredibly beautiful woman next to him—who is she, Rafael?" Fernanda asked.

"You mean, who *was* she. Well, only the wife of this boy I'm going to invite, who walked out on him one day, just like that, and the poor guy's walking around . . . well, I don't need to tell you."

"How strange, Rafael."

"What's strange, Fernanda?"

"That I feel I could hate her with all my heart for as long as I live."

"But you don't even know her."

"Couldn't pick her out of a crowd of two, but . . ."

"But what?"

"Look, Rafael. Just listen to me, please. Listen to me as if you were the older brother I don't have. You know, like the man who rescued me from the lower depths."

"Come on, now, let's just say that . . ."

"God, what a nightmare. Let's pretend I never said a thing."

They were laughing themselves silly, remembering the Residence for Young Ladies, the two of them in the Old Navy café, Boulevard Saint Germain, right in the heart of the Latin Quarter, Mía and Rafael—and to think he's already dead—and:

"Okay, yes, older brother, this man in the photo with this de-tes-ta-ble blonde—I know him. Or I love him . . . Sorry, I . . ."

"Come on, now, Fernanda. Explain yourself, please, slowly and clearly. Because your older brother here is turning out to be more than a little stupid."

"What I mean is that I know this man, and I loved him even before I met him and fell in love with him. Come on, Rafael! It couldn't be simpler!"

"Couldn't be simpler. Yes, of course, now everything's as clear as clear can be. Except that I'm not understanding a word of it."

"Besides, I knew him already, from before. Don't you know Gertrude Stein's poem, 'A rose is a rose is a rose is a rose is . . .'"

"Stop, little sister, you're making me dizzy."

"I'm getting dizzy myself from this red wine, but let's have some more and drink to the health of . . ."

"Juan Manuel Carpio. Peruvian."

"And troubadour globe-trotter, the kind who passes his

hat around for change . . . Didn't I just tell you that somehow, somewhere, I've known him from the moment I was
born?"

"Let's get that wine right away, little sister, please."

It's all right with me . . . I remember, and tears of love still
come to my eyes, along with tears of friendship, brother-
hood, complicity, mystery, intimacy, because you and I have
some of all those things, some and more than some, Mía—I
told Fernanda María that on that dawn of December 23 . . .
no, that dawn of December 24, tremendously *jingle bells* and
sad, as we made our way, snuggled together because of the
cold and my drunkenness, along the short, zigzaggy route to
her house, which I thought pretty, a *weird world* for me, lots of
house, lots of Paris, lots of skinny, pretty girl for me, freckled
redhead of my soul, in number 17 rue Colombe, and crossing the Seine without looking at it, because the water passing
under its bridges had already carried Luisa away, it wasn't
just the plane . . .

Anyway, it was also *all right with me,* and we went up to
have a nightcap, as they say, and for some reason I've never
managed to come down from that fourth, fifth, sixth floor,
damn it, I can't remember, but I damn sure remember the
event, and will carry it in my soul forever.

And this, exactly this, is what I understand by carrying it
in my soul forever. It consists, to begin with, in feeling myself
truly loved for what I'm worth, which is to say, nothing, that
night in December, that shitty Christmas of 1967 in Paris,
when, as I sank into the most comfortable sofa into which
I'd ever in my life sunk my shipwrecked humanity, a girl—
by now I saw two girls—helps you out of your overcoat and
swears that this morning, as soon as she wakes up, she's

going to run down to buy you a new and very *Merry Christ-mas!* cap, because, my God, only you would think of walking around with such an old, old cap, yuck, disgusting, Juan Manuel Carpio, and now let me get you something, and if you want I can even heat you up something to eat, because you didn't eat a thing all night—and I should be deeply offended, now that I think of it, because I made almost all the food at the party.

"Okay, heat me up a whiskey on the rocks."

"Listen, I was the one who first said that it was *all right,* but . . ."

"*All whiskey,* please."

"Whatever the gentleman prefers."

I fell asleep after a half-bottle nightcap, but not before sinking half my snout into Fernanda María's delicious and, as it were, so delicate heart, half, as it were, sounding out that ever-so-strange idea that her nose delighted me, that in my entire life never had I seen eyes as green as those green eyes, with the Fernanda María gaze, never had I seen hair so red and so beautiful, not even in Technicolor and Cinemascope, nor had I ever been so movingly, terribly, totally, comfortably, sleepily, pathetically, and yawningly in agreement with the idea of falling asleep in that out-of-place and in the least appropriate moment, also, and while somewhere way up on the Seine, no, the Seine couldn't be that ugly, so it was the filthy waters of the Rimac, way upstream, crossing the Atlantic and reaching Lima, that Luisa was waving that ever-so-sad farewell but so red-haired and so comfortable . . .

"Merry Christmas," Fernanda María told me, were the words with which I fell asleep on top of her, for which reason

I woke up with my arm all cramped up, look what a thug you are, Juan Manuel Carpio.

"How wonderful," I remembered her saying, with no exclamation point, sweetly and tenderly, as she noted that something called glass was falling out of my hand and I'm falling asleep in a *weird world . . . all right . . . me . . .* too.

Two years later, everything was more or less the same, I'd say, although if she were in my place, I'm sure Fernanda María would counterattack: "No sir. No, Juan Manuel Carpio."

"For two years now I've been begging you—please!—to call me just Juan Manuel."

"And for two years now I've been telling you that the day I stop calling you Juan Manuel Carpio is the day I am fed up with you."

"You enjoy putting on airs about my humble origins and turning up your nose at . . ."

"Idiot."

"Oligarch."

"As oligarch as you like. But of course the one working around here is me."

"Bitch!"

"Forgive me, sweethert! Juan Manuel Carpio, please forgive me. No one, not Piaf, not Montand, not Aznavour, not Brassens ever sang as beautifully as you!"

"And that isn't working? And night and day, with no schedule and no union, like you? And besides, every day I run to the Sorbonne to attend, as a free student, every literature course that exists. Well, I used to run, because the other day I asked the asshole who teaches contemporary French poetry about Georges Brassens and he told me that if I wanted to talk about Brassens I should take myself off to some bistro, or cheap café, or alley. Which of course I did, after telling him to shove his shitty course up his ass. The Sorbonne is dead, Fernanda María. But all that stuff—is it working or isn't it?"

"Yes and no."

"What do you mean, 'yes and no'? Come on, let's hear it. Is that working or isn't it?"

"It's also singing to Luisa, and that, for me, Juan Manuel Carpio, is a pain in the ass."

"What about Frank Sinatra and the *all right*?"

"Well, yes and no, Juan Manuel Carpio, because a girl does like to feel she's loved."

So for all those reasons, or so I imagine, Fernanda María would counterattack two years later: "Everything's more or less the same, Juan Manuel Carpio, sure. But please note the more or less in there."

She had her reasons, after all, because aside from the fact that her salary—just one minute's worth of it—was the equivalent of the monthly income of my cap, including the odd embassy gig she got me, the odd Pro Victims of Always Something in Peru fund-raiser, where I'd end up having to pay admission to hear myself sing, or some gig dressed as an Indian from Guatemala, Mexico, Paraguay, Bolivia, or Peru, and other countries where the Indians of the Sun are synonymous with hope for the homogenized and pasteurized noble savage, hope for the future of humanity.

Between the Cuban Revolution and that movie *The Condor Passes,* Latin America was more present than ever in

Paris, beginning in that marvelous May of 1968, when, no matter how tired Fernanda María might be when she came home from UNESCO, every time I would take off, guitar and imagination in hand, to carry them to power, she would pronounce her eternal *It's all right with me* and we'd run off to the revolution. We found it more beautiful still at night than by day, with the bonfires and barricades and human chains to reach for the next anti–police power cobblestone amid the solidarity of the nations of the night, in the famous remark by Malraux, who was minister of culture in the government we were going to topple, well, what can you do, that was *his* problem.

At the same time, we can't forget that among the most important spiritual leaders of May 1968, Che Guevara (with his Basque beret, his Winston Churchill cigar, and his Latin American, that is to say sparse, beard) took the grand prize. And, finally, he was the only one or the only thing that survived in popular memory and the collective unconscious, thanks to a postmortem poster that I used as a backdrop to my metro or outdoor-bistro summer playing so people would feel doubly obliged to tip me, and feel that in addition to contributing to art they were also contributing to the most noble, the most defeated of causes, *e povrecitó le Shé.*

"Disgusting. What you are is disgusting, Juan Manuel Carpio."

"It's just that I wasn't born with hot and cold running water, like you, my little heiress."

"Perhaps you'd like to examine my pay stub, you rat."

"You're really offensive. The other day you went to bed with a really disgusting singer, don't deny it."

"I didn't go to bed with anyone, idiot. What I did was

practice free love and the teachings of May '68 with that Colombian singer, and your problem is you're dying of jealousy, you disgusting rat twice over. To exploit poor Che Guevara that way, when he died all alone in Bolivia. That really and truly is disgusting."

"Yes, but I sing songs in his honor from metro stop to metro stop, while you hop into bed with an abject, morally indescribable and perverse Colombian. And you think that's nothing?"

"I didn't sleep with anyone. I practiced free love and that's all. And I'll thank you not to bring it up again."

"Why is that? Are you so full of remorse? Your freedom didn't work, or what?"

"Look here, Juan Manuel Carpio. And listen very carefully, please. Fernanda María de la Trinidad del Monte Montes, the very person speaking to you now, got to be hot shit at UNESCO because she deserves it, so she can sit her ass down anywhere she likes and pull it out clean. Got that? Understand? Is that okay? If not, get out and don't come back, Juan Manuel, and that's final!"

After all that howling, an extremely long silence ensued. I'll take advantage of it to tell you that contrary to what I'm sure you're all thinking, I did not live in Fernanda María's house nor at her expense. I didn't even take advantage of her excellent contacts in highlife. Thanks to her, I entertained at a few parties singing my sorrow and sadness, true enough, but Rafael Dulanto also got me singing gigs in palatial salons with beveled mirrors and silent rugs (as in Felipe Pinglo's waltz), but that does not mean that I ever lived off of Rafael Dulanto simply because I accepted a friend's favor, just as it also means I don't owe anything to Felipe Pinglo except, of course, for the fact that I quote him for having attempted the maximum without achieving the minimum success, that is to popularize his ineffable little waltzes in Paris, with or without Vallejo's rainstorm, when in that '68 era what the world was demanding, and what even Simon and Garfunkel were singing, in an English also of '68, was condors that pass, comandantes we'd learned to love, that Joan Baez's preso número 9 was shot (bis), and other beautiful sufferings of peoples originally Rousseauistic and uniform called *Le monde andin.*

I slept wherever night caught me, because I never wanted to go back to the apartment where I had lived with Luisa. Even today, I don't have a single photo of her—much less the bed or an armchair we shared—in my obsessive desire to immortalize her only through my songs, in love poetry, because of which, I've been told, on more than one occasion she's complained that I've failed to recognize her on several of my return trips to Peru. It's that I've been told that she set about making a great deal of money administering businesses, which made her put on a lot of weight, something that delights Fernanda María, on account of what she calls the Lima Slap.

But the Lima Slap chapter in my story, in the story of Fernanda, comes later, and we were in the part where I was sleeping wherever night caught me ever since Luisa . . .

And it generally caught me—though why the hell this should matter to you, I can't say—in Fernanda María's pretty, *weird world*-style apartment. And why am I to blame that night caught her from time to time in my arms, when I would turn up all worn out and without having saved enough money even for a hotel devoid of stars, and I'd cross through the rear part of the *hôtel partculier* of the multimillionaire family who rented part of that mansion, which had an interior patio and everything, entering the grand entryway of that patio of, well, actually, English luxury, and going up those marvelous stone stairs that brought me to the "How wonderful, Juan Manuel Carpio" with which Mía always received me, red hair, freckles, delightfully skinny, with her huge, smiling green eyes, immediately getting out the whiskey and ice I'd earned by insanely scrambling up that tremendous staircase, to wake up once again in her arms. We went down those beautiful wide stone stairs with their colonnade quite happily, as well, in order to organize marvelous cocktail parties, because the multimillionaire family was almost never at home, and, moreover, they instantly became immensely fond of Fernanda María and lent her their patio, their white benches, their trellises, the million flowerpots, their tables and chairs in Finzi Contini terrace style, in sum, the most springtimely beautiful stuff in that palazzo of stone that Fernanda María insisted on calling very late gothic and which I called *weird world,* period.

I also want it to be absolutely clear that I never charged Fernanda María a cent to sing at her spring or early-summer parties attended by half the writers of the Latin American boom, many of them embarrassingly docile, and all because she was still the big boss of some very big-name writers, who also brought along others, because someone was always passing through Paris. And if you're me, you sing and sing the best of the sad beauty of your own lyrics, but the Boom Boom Boom never took any notice, not even of the fact that the Peruvian singer was one of their own, with his French visa expired, his difficult beginnings, his hard years, his mythic quest for illumination in the City of Light, his heart on the left, profoundly rooted in uprootedness, his lost steps, his magic realism, and his poor Third World face. But all for nothing, those gentlemen, they never realized that I, too, was an artist.

"All the better for you," Fernanda María consoled me, she at whose feet half the boom prostrated themselves, she who occasionally justified my staying and their not staying by introducing me as her boyfriend and in-se-par-able partner when all of them had to leave—it's time, gentlemen—and some Don Juan Boom who wanted to sleep with her would look me up and down as if to say, "And when will the little singer be leaving us?"

"How is that all the better for me, Fernanda?"

"It's that, with the most honorable exceptions, such as Cortázar and Rulfo and some others who aren't famous and who have little or nothing to do with the boom, I have to say that with each year that passes, I find these writers to be more and more nouveaux riches."

"Oh, please! They've earned it with the sweat of their brow and that of the left."

"I agree, Juan Manuel Carpio. But just look what life teaches us. My own family has fallen on hard times and can barely keep their heads above water anymore. Even so, and forgive me for being so brutal when I say these things, without any subtlety, you know, so brutally but so honestly: if there's anything left of what on the radio soaps and now the television soaps is called class—my God, excuse me for becoming so kitschy, so Corín Tellado, Juan Manuel Carpio, but I swear I'm almost done, I think the wine has gone to my head—it's simply and plainly that I can't stand anything that smells nouveau riche, not even the slightest whiff. It's possible to wake up a multimillionaire after falling asleep a beggar and still not smell nouveau. And yet, just when you least expect it, you detect a whiff . . . Understand?"

"And just what does the boom have to do with that? Does it stink, too?"

"My love, what a brute you can be sometimes. I was talking about a whiff, imperceptible except in a tie or a pair of shoes, in a way of entering this patio, or in a wife, for example."

"Come, come, Fernanda, please. Explain to the moron standing before you the difference between a tie that's expensive and horrible and one that's expensive, pretty, and nouveau riche. Let's see if I'm capable of learning anything, because up to this point . . ."

"Know what makes the difference, Juan Manuel Carpio? Well, all I want tonight is for you to sing me the most failed of all your songs. Even if it's part of the Luisa series, sing it to me, please. And I'll be happy and feel clean when I kiss and hug you when we go to bed, no matter that you're dreaming of other moments and other places. On the other hand, if I'd gotten into bed with that matinee idol who's been translated into every language, including Latin, I think, the one who made a play for me tonight, I'd feel alone, sad, lost, abandoned, oligarchic . . . disgusting."

This is where that extremely prolonged silence ended. I think I've taken sufficient advantage of it, insofar as my relationship with Fernanda María is concerned. And now it was my turn to cut loose with a few howls: "Are you saying, then, that you'd rather sleep with the most abject, miserable, and corrupt singer than with Juan Rulfo or Julio Cortázar? Look, even me, if I were up to sleeping with men, would sleep with Cortázar or Pedro Páramo! But this lily of the oligarchy wouldn't! For her only dirt will do! For her it has to be Colombian filth! For her, the mud, which, of course, she never saw in the houses she inhabited, or the schools or finishing schools where she was educated!"

"As far as I'm concerned, you're already out the door, Juan Manuel! And that's final! No one ever threw as much mud on me as you! And nothing has ever given me as much relief as your departure! So let's say that in this very second, it's been something like a thousand hours since you left, took off, whatever, Juan Manuel! And that's that!"

"It's all right with me," I concluded, picking up my guitar, taking the last sip of whiskey in my glass, and tossing, as if it were a towel I was tossing into the ring, the cap Fernanda María had given me three years earlier—three years already, damn, how time flies—one frozen, shitty Christmas. And after concluding that besides everything else I'd lost even my work cap, I walked for the straight line that took me, in the twinkling of an eye, to the door of my *weird world,* then to its elegant, wide stone staircase, then—now on the ground floor—to the shitty sadness of the patio, its benches, its flowerpots, its trellises, and, once again on the straight line, to the grand entryway and the street, and here I am, fuck it all, straight line and all the rest.

Ladies, gentlemen, young ladies, Che Guevara is dead. Long live Salvador Allende! That, at least for us Latin Americans in Paris, was the historical background. And through that background, Fernanda María de la Trinidad del Monte Montes would daily make her way to UNESCO, crestfallen inside and out in her bottle-green Alfa Romeo, which contrasted so nicely with everything in her that was red-haired, that is, almost everything, seeing her that way, as I did, through the windshield of her car stopped at a light, despite the fact that it was my turn to cross and I had just become completely color-blind with regard to traffic, and completely the opposite of color-blind with regard to red-haired Fernanda in her green Alfa Romeo.

It's purely hypothetical, but if someone, some critic or journalist, were ever to discover the quality, the exceedingly beautiful sadness of my art, and asked me for an interview and said, "Now, Mr. Carpio, speaking candidly, would you be able to pinpoint what was the saddest moment of your life?" I would respond:

"Yes, though it will give me both great pleasure and extremely great pain. The saddest moment of my life is a green Alfa Romeo and a red-haired girl, both stopped at a light without ever taking the trouble to realize that I, too, lived in Paris and that, therefore, I, too, might be stopped, in the role of pedestrian, at that very light."

"The girl's name was Luisa, like the Luisa in so many of your love songs, isn't that a fact, Mr. Carpio?"

"It is, and it continues to be in my songs, and, in a certain way, in my life. However, there now exists a difference between the Luisa in my songs and the Luisa living in Lima. Luisa's taking off one thirteenth day of the month, on a flight numbered 1313, is a shock, something horrible, it's being left dead in life, amputated from within forever, and it wouldn't even matter if you could be world champion in the hundred-meter dash."

"So Luisa is a trauma."

"To the degree to which a tragedy can be a trauma, yes, Luisa is a trauma."

"Then let's go back to the stoplight, Mr. Carpio, before it changes color and your sadness leaves you behind."

"It's there that you critics and journalists always get it wrong with us artists."

"How so, Mr. Carpio?"

"The light never changed color, sir. Likewise, the car, the hair, the freckles, the grimace of impatience on the face of the girl—because that light never changes, and the girl will be late for work—have never lost their eternal content of sadness, *full sadness,* sir."

"*Spleen de Paris,* would you call it?"

"*Spleen* of nothing, sir. Only a stoplight and an Alfa Romeo, forever. And only a Fernanda María trapped forever inside a paralyzed car. From that morning on, no city in the world ever had as many stoplights and, especially, as many green Alfa Romeos, as Paris. And just think, the Alfa is an Italian car, you don't see so many in France as you might think, not even on a holiday. But, anyway, you've never understood us, you . . ."

But the saddest, the most Italian Alfa Romeo in Paris, the one that stopped on my sadness forever, at that stoplight, never again passed by that corner at that time, nor never again passed any other corner. And the next time I saw Fernanda María, Maía, Mía, she was by then a lady married to a Chilean photographer, the mother of a seven-month-old baby. She was coming to Paris without a cent, as a political exile.

It was the winter of 1974, and there was the Chile business, and the Pinochet business. That was extremely clear. But this business about Fernanda María exiled in Paris, in the same city where I left her when she was such hot shit and so stupendously well connected? How and when could so many things have taken place? And how, in particular, could so many things have happened to poor Fernanda? For starters, where did she find that husband? In any case, that was the news Don Julián d'Octeville would give me that morning at eleven, himself just having been awakened and roused from bed by a long-distance call from Rafael Dulanto.

"My boy, as you know, I detest being awakened at such an hour. I'm a night owl, a creature of the night. I like to come home at dawn and sleep until noon."

"I'm sorry about the early wake-up call, Don Julián."

"As it turns out, it was a wake-up call of another kind, dear friend. It was a call I listened to with the greatest interest and concern, because it came from, of all people, our common—and delightful—friend Rafael Dulanto."

"Yes. He's working now in El Salvador's Washington embassy."

"And I'm happy for him, because it's a promotion. But I'm not happy about what he told me about our dearly beloved friend Miss Sacromonte, remember her?"

"Yes . . . i-i-in aaa g-g-greeeen Alfa Rommmeeeoo at a s-s-stoplight . . ."

"What's wrong with you, are you crying, dear friend? Well, what he told me about her is worthy of tears, and I see that you, shall we say, more than *remember* the young lady."

"Sh-sh-she d-d-disap-p-peared ooone week in n-n-nine-teeen s-sevent-t-ty . . ."

"Son, get into the first cab you can find and come over here. I'll pay for the taxi, and breakfast as well. Miss Sacromonte, her husband, and her child . . ."

"What!"

". . . are doing just fine. They're here in Paris. But they've had to flee from history and its horrors, and we must help them. So says our beloved friend Rafael Dulanto."

It was my fault even if it wasn't my fault, that's how complicated life is, what might not have happened to Fernanda María during the three interminable years when I never saw so many green Alfa Romeos without her inside them in each and every one of the many cities I rolled through singing, like a Rolling Stone that doesn't make a spring, like a solitary swallow, I mean, although there were some seasons when I actually ate less than one of those jolly little birds. I distanced myself from Mía's *weird world,* and I was proudly ungrateful for the affection rained down on me by friends like Rafael Dulanto, Edgardo de la Jara, Don Julián d'Octeville, Julio Ramón Ribeyro, and even Charlie Boston himself whenever he came to Paris and we'd all end up most cordially invited to dine in worlds as otherwise inaccessible to me as Maxim's or the Grand Vefour.

And, I imagined while I had lunch with Don Julián d'Octeville, something quite similar happened to that crazy Fernanda María de la Trinidad del Monte Montes. Though without owing anyone any favors, in her case, she decided to leave Paris and all those friends who loved and admired her immensely. There was also the matter of the validation of diplomas, which in Paris was practically impossible for her to manage—I was recalling that during lunch with Don Julián. Yes, the thing about the diplomas was something Mía had talked about angrily with me on more than one occasion.

"What I remember, my boy, is that Miss Sacromonte, advised by one of her diplomatic friends, a Chilean in this case, decided that at the University of Santiago there was an excellent architecture school and that her Swiss degrees would be more than sufficient to gain her admission."

"And when was that, Don Julián?"

"Please stop being so formal with me, my boy. Just because I'm from another century doesn't mean you have to bury me with the distance you create when you address me like that."

"When was that, Julián?"

"In 1970. I remember that very well, because that was the year my great friend Pablo Neruda came to Paris as ambassador, and how happy I was . . . Or was that 1971? In any case, it was most certainly the year we gave the farewell party for Mademoiselle de Sacromonte. I remember that very well, too, because it was at Charlie's house . . . No, at Rafael's house . . . In any case, my boy, you can believe me when I tell you that I gave Fernanda a few addresses in Lima, because on her way to Chile, she was very interested in making a side trip to our city."

"Fernanda María, in Lima? The idea never occurred to me, Don—excuse me—Julián."

"Not in Lima, you mad boy. Fernanda is here in Paris, and this is her telephone number. And Rafael is begging us to help her. How are you fixed for cash, my boy?"

"I'm in better condition, Julián. I work regularly in a place called El Rancho Guaraní."

"With or without poncho?"

"With enough money to pay the rent on a decent apartment and even to have the telephone you just called me on."

"You're right, my boy. How bad my memory's become. That must be the reason everyone addresses me as 'Don.'"

"May I ask an immense favor of you, Julián?"

"Ask for two, my boy."

"Call Fernanda María but don't say you've seen me or anything, just give her my address and my telephone number, and even the number of my bank account if necessary. Believe me, Julián, I have my reasons for preferring that she be the one to look me up."

"I understand, my boy. And I remember something now. You two left Paris more or less at the same time . . . I understand, my boy. And I'll keep you informed on a day-to-day basis. Yes, now I'm remembering better."

I didn't sing the night Fernanda María, her husband Enrique, and Rodrigo, a little monster seven months old, dramatically sleepy and not very hungry, as if he'd come into the world prepared for an extremely long exile, came over for dinner, quite early because of the baby, as, naturally, they had no one to leave him with, etc. And, quite naturally, we stuck that same Rodrigo into my bed as soon as we thought it convenient, and in the living room we sat like three sad babies, a trio of idiots absolutely predisposed to start kissing and hugging at any moment, although I must recognize that Fernanda María knew how to impose sufficient calm over the course of that interminable night in order not to wake up the child, and to respect him as well, poor thing, what does he know about all of us—actually, what does he know about anything, the poor little angel.

And the one who asked us to put on Frank Sinatra was Enrique, a kind of authentic Araucanian, with stiff hair, indigenous skin, and ferocious hands, although at only about six feet tall he was a little shy of the giant category. Fernanda María shot me a glance, as if to say, "Do you hear what Enrique chooses to request?" and then as if adding, "Didn't I tell you over the phone that I'd married a very good man?" I looked at Enrique the way you look at a very large, very strong, very good Araucanian, and Enrique looked over to where my records were, like someone in exile really sighing for Frank Sinatra.

No doubt about it, that was why he was completely oblivious to the million shades of meaning, of implications, of givens, of complicity, and of tenderness there were in the fact that before I went to look for the Sinatra—so we could kill each other in a fight, or by being good guys, or in a ménage à trois—Fernanda and I both blurted out in a most harmonious unison: *It's all right with me.*

We finished up the evening worn out, each one singing a solo. We never left our seats, and no big, bad wolf came in to eat anyone. It all began when Enrique grabbed my hand, as if forever, because Fernanda, ever since they'd met, had spoken of me with a great deal of tenderness, and also because she'd given him two cassettes where I sang the tragedy of my life, my eternal love for Luisa. And I didn't know, *you're not just making it up, old man,* how he liked my songs and my spoken passages of horrifying beauty, *you're not just making it up, brother.* All that resulted in his authorizing me to grab, with all my soul but dissimulating quite a bit, true enough, the hand of Fernanda, who, in turn, moved to the maximum by the tender goodness of her Caupolicán toward me, squeezed his hand for all time, thus configuring the circle to which Sinatra sang of sadder and sadder things, as if he were guessing the future or something, as more and more bottles of red wine were uncorked and Rodrigo went on behaving like a real little angel, asleep in exile.

And he was, and to such a degree that it was only when his squeals, of dying of hunger and poop and need to be changed, woke us all up at eight in the morning—though it seems the poor kid had been crying for hours, and it seemed to Fernanda that she'd heard something, in a nightmare now that she thought about it—that we finally dropped one another's hands, and I was left with the following information in my other hand: Fernanda María de la Trinidad del Monte Montes had, in effect, made a stop in Lima.

"You ask why? Well, this is why, idiot—no, you poor little thing, not an idiot. Well, because if that time, that filthy time when I went to bed with the abject Colombian singer Ernesto Flores—even today it disgusts me, damn it, but understand that I emerged clean, almost a virgin again, in point of fact—it was because your love for Luisa was killing me and I wanted to subject myself to a real sentimental electroshock to see if you would come out of your catalepsy and pay at least a tiny bit of attention to me, because of the really disgusting nature of that Ernesto Flores."

"But we were practically living together, Fernanda."

"But, begging Enrique's pardon . . ."

"My jealousy is never retrospective, darling," interjected the huge, extremely tolerant Araucanian. And possessing the sense of humor that he did, he added: "We all have a past, my dear Fernanda. A past, and even several pasts, as in my case . . ."

"Idiot . . ."

"Go on, my Fernanda."

"Look, I wasn't going to say it, but now that you tell me you have *several* pasts, I will. Juan Manuel Carpio, at least, has only one single past, so yes, I'll tell: yes, we were almost living together, little brother, but let's say that it was not incestuous in the slightest. Or just a tiny bit, in any case. Or, to paraphrase the saint, just look, Juan Manuel Carpio—and heed my words, oh husband and Chilean landscape of mine: we were *almost* living together, correct, Juan Manuel, beautiful and beloved, like Mexico in the song, but that *almost* meant you weren't living *in me.*"

Thank God, Frank Sinatra could always be counted on to take charge of moments of great tension like this, with one of his songs, and with that dead-end voice of his, the voice of impasse in which he intoned, almost reciting them to you, some of his saddest ballads.

And Frank Sinatra also had something to say about the next stage, that of dear Fernanda María's stay in Lima. In any case, he gave it nuance. Because only someone who had the strange idea of staying in a "residence" for certain kinds of young ladies, without even realizing, as she did not realize, what it was, can conserve so much purity of intention and so much naïveté as to make an appearance (no less) at one of the companies administered in Lima by the ruddy and irate Luisa. Flashing her identification card from UNESCO, which was still valid, she urgently requested a meeting, because, given that the filthy electroshock to which she submitted me with the abject singer Ernesto Flores seemed to have some effect upon my beloved person, Fernanda María urgently wanted to speak, woman to woman, with Luisa about these two subjects.

The first consisted in that, taking into account some ups and downs of time and place—I can understand that—Juan Manuel Carpio and Fernanda María de la Trinidad del Monte Montes (some name I've got there, right?) were born for each other over there in Paris; and since she, unlike *other* people, loved me so, but so much that she could wait calmly until he finishes falling out of love with you, Luisa, and, well, that he goes on putting up with me in the meanwhile, until someday he can't put up with me anymore and then begins to love me as immensely as I love him . . . The second subject comes down to this: that in order to put all this into practice, an expeditious divorce is absolutely necessary because . . .

And that's where Fernanda María's second subject remained, because God knows that even for the dead (me, for instance) there remains retrospective jealousy. And now the rubicund and quite plump Luisa rises to her feet and walks toward that girl who is so pretty—so much younger than I, so much thinner than I, so that makes me, what, a pig?—and she lands a slap that, according to Fernanda María, left her in a state of mortal hunger and sorrow until quite a while after she landed in Chile.

In some way, Luisa loved me, and that grieved Fernanda María right down to her soul. And in Paris the matter of her validated diplomas was never going to be resolved, so she could never study architecture there. So, in fact, that Lima Slap created a whole new destiny for her, a whole new future, a whole new man, even a husband, a whole new adorable baby seven months old, along with this shitty exile, and now it turns out that they claim not to know me at UNESCO, and they're completely right, you know.

"No one is irreplaceable, and here I am, you know, reappearing three years later, and I never informed them that I'd left my job. A decent person doesn't do things like that, so I got what I deserved. Of course, the bad part is that now we're starving to death. And the worst thing is that yesterday afternoon Enrique was offered a real job in Caracas, but we haven't got any tickets or anything, and now I'm three, and counting you, four, if you can work up the courage to swim your way to Caracas, Juan Manuel Carpio."

I worked up the courage to stay in Paris and to go through, once again, one of those little airport scenes in which someone sorrowfully takes a plane and leaves someone else . . . Well, leaves someone else sorrowful, the way Luisa had left me seven years earlier, that is to say, completely distraught, although now with a rather enriching nuance, or, which is the same thing, with the following pathetic addition, because, damn it all, this time it was going from the Badlands to the Worselands, seeing as how in the first instance, at least, Luisa was so happy to take off forever.

On this occasion, however, Fernanda María would have paid to stay behind. And probably her very husband and the little seven-month-old exile, her son Rodrigo, too. Yes, the three of them would probably have preferred the precarious stability I managed to give them during the two months they stayed in Paris, making do as best they could to sleep in my bed while I executed a wondrous balancing act on the extremely narrow divan in the living-dining room of my apartment, constantly on the verge of falling if I made the slightest movement. That was the same divan we normally used for our moving, though sedentary, sessions of nocturnal, meditative love opposite a few bottles of wine and some love songs, all just as desperate as Neruda would have wanted them.

Anyway, I'll never know if all that was the pure fruit of love, of the greatest, strangest, and purest love, or whether the historical moment and our age, when we could still tolerate all the discomfort in the world and even the lack of vital space (which nurtures aggression) didn't also help a bit as well. But the fact is that our platonic, not very conscious, and extremely circumstantial ménage à trois, with the little seven-month-old angel thrown in for good measure, functioned marvelously well.

I managed to get Enrique the Araucanian established as the official photographer of Rancho Guaraní, the pleasant club of darkness, drinks, Paraguayan harps, quenas, guitars large and small, and any other Latin American folklore the occasion might demand, where I worked with a regular schedule and salary, intoning fifty fucking thousand times that line about *We learned to love you, Comandante Che Guevara,* and also, rather as contraband and by now without feeling, or, more to the point, with quite a bit of resentment, some of my interminable love songs for Luisa. Though now I sang them thinking of Fernanda María and cursing the horrible moment when she didn't see me at the stoplight and I was incapable of throwing myself under the wheels of her green Alfa Romeo so she'd realize that it was for her I was ready to give it all, now, in that present moment in which fate had chosen to invade me, which was the same, night after night, while I helped Enrique to pick up a few pesos by bringing him with me to the Rancho Guaraní and to every party it fell to me to play in my portrait of the artist as extremely depressed and screwed up, singing the name Fernanda where I was supposed to sing Luisa, because the fact is I couldn't wait to get back to my apartment to find Rodrigo fast asleep for hours and his extremely loving mother with a bottle of red wine and three glasses ready for yet another of our sleepy musical evenings, where once again we would hold each other's hand and each would sing his song while the wolf was at the door, with ad hoc music on the record player, and furtive little glances bathed in tears, all of it always out of time and place, of course.

The wolf was taken care of the day when, thanks to the help of Don Julián d'Octeville, Enrique managed to get a France–Latin America Solidarity Committee to take a good ton of his stupendous photographs, which they would later sell off, little by little. The committee paid for the entire lot with three one-way tickets to Enrique's job in Caracas. Of course, Fernanda pointed out that the ideal thing would have been for them to buy four tickets, and of course Enrique agreed. Even Rodrigo sounded a tiny fart favorable to my departure, as Fernanda explained, with a tremendous knot in her throat. But the fact of the matter was that there were three tickets, and the only one with a job in Caracas was Enrique. Besides, even though I was much more than a brother to them, I was neither part of the family, nor Chilean exile, nor anything else of that sort.

Thus it fell to me to be exiled from exile, to remain in that no-man's-land, which is what airports are, to mumble nonsense like, well, at least you aren't leaving on the thirteenth of the month on a charter flight number 1313, the way Fernanda did that time—excuse me, I mean the way fatty Luisa did, excuse me . . .

"Eternal curse on her slap," Fernanda María slipped up even more just as she was boarding her Air France flight for Caracas, Venezuela, but just then we heard one of Rodrigo's tiny farts, and Caupolicán, king of the sensitive Araucanians, as if he wanted to share his life raft in that strange mixture of farewell and shipwreck, said *It's all right with me*. Then we could all come out of this feeling fine and sense that at least this was not our final farewell . . . This one could be the first of many farewells, or something like that, so there was, after all, a future, and the future always leaves a door open to God knows what, though a smiling God knows what, yes, for sure, and ciao, we'll be seeing you, brother, tons of luck, and, again, my heart and a thousand thanks from the four of us, ciao, my wonderful brother . . .

II

▲▲▲▲▲▲▲

Corresponded by Correspondence

I just couldn't endure green Alfa Romeos of the same year and model as Fernanda's. But automotive time passes as well, and the car of my greatest sadness was gradually replaced by other, more modern and quite different Alfas. One would always pop up when I least expected it and force me to run after it—if a stoplight appeared anywhere on the horizon—with the hope of stopping next to it, gasping for breath, so I could observe the vehicle's driver. Rarely would it be a woman, but if it was, I'd close my eyes instantly and cross my fingers with all my soul so that when I opened them again the Alfa Romeo would be green and not, say, white, and the woman at the wheel would not be that damned old hag but a redhead and young, and then, after another eye-closing and crossing of fingers with all my soul, she'd be Mía.

My system never worked, of course. But I have to say that in a certain way it was practically the only communication I had with Fernanda, for whom things quickly fell apart in Caracas. That was probably why she didn't write me: she didn't want me to worry, didn't want to give me more details about Enrique and his drinking, and Enrique's drinking and his violence, and the violence of such a good man, and the unbearable exile and guilt, the damned guilt of fate that had conspired to screw him up, with a child and a wife to support, and now she was expecting another, and nothing turns out well, and everything's a failure, total failure, everyone but me gets shows, everyone's work sells but mine, and teaching some shitty classes in a shitty university, and more wine and more violence and much more guilt, and now hints of irrational hatred, where are we, what's become of us, what the fuck am I doing in Caracas, and a slammed door, night, the street, another bar.

Only one long letter from Mía told me about the horror, which began almost as soon as they reached Venezuela, when for the first time Enrique faced the awareness of exile, or, what is practically the same thing, faced the astounding and crushing daily nature of exile. Fernanda María, the one you'd imagine eternally protected by that huge man with pitch-black hair, indigenous skin, and ferocious hands, suddenly found herself having to take care of everything and everyone, and even writing wonderful children's stories illustrated with photos which she took herself because Enrique never took any interest in the matter, but then he became furious, of course, because "you've ruined my reputation with this shit," and a short time later, he went nuts one night, even forgetting his own last name, and almost killed her when he smashed a bottle over her head.

A single, long letter from Fernanda brought me up to date about all that madness, although as always my oh-so-marvelous Maía managed also to include news about our common friends, Rafael Dulanto or Charlie Boston, for example, with whom she always maintained a Salvadoran contact, and then, also, she added amusing anecdotes, extraordinary events full of fresh air, radiating life, because she had that grace some people reenter the world with after walking away, unpolluted, from the filthiest, most abysmal situations, still able to see the blameless aspect and the badly sewn shirt-stitch that renders ironic the very hand that grabs you and smashes a bottle over your head, and completely incarnates these words by Hemingway that moved me so deeply the afternoon when I read them, because it was suddenly as if a green Alfa with Mía at the wheel had screeched to a halt next to me and had shouted my name, yes, and even my adored Fernanda María de la Trinidad *experienced the anguish and sorrow, but had never been sad in the morning.*

That's what her letters suggested, her sometimes short, almost always bubbly sentences, her words graced with a crystalline freshness, like stones just pulled out of a playful creek early on a spring morning, bright with joyful, welcome sunlight. Sometimes, while reading a letter from Fernanda María, I had the sensation of encountering the agile and seemingly stark prose of Hemingway at his best—that ability to suggest and invent a reality vastly superior to the one our routine-glazed eyes can see, that extremely expansive conciseness of telling us things without naming them, that jolly and magical trick of brevity and terseness. So, then, like a

Hemingway but in Spanish, and written, moreover, by a particularly female woman who, little by little, was turning into a Hemingwayesque Tarzan—*that,* for sure—but also (and why not?) into an Arabian citadel: stone and walls on the outside, garden within.

The buzzer in my apartment rang, just as I was underlining Hemingway's words and thinking about the ever-so-long time that had elapsed without my receiving a single line from Mía. I persisted in writing her and writing her, but one afternoon, a green Alfa Romeo, though of a much more recent vintage and totally unrelated to ours (only the make and the color were the same) informed me that Fernanda would prefer that I not persist, that my letters made her uncomfortable, that it might be very painful, for instance, for me to tell her that Alfa Romeos like our little green one smelled totally, Proustianly, different from the current models, because nowadays they practically don't make them with those leather seats you adored, remember, Fernanda? A period of silence would be better, seeing that we two had more than enough tenderness and confidence in each other, and also because of the bad period she was going through there. That was what was happening, that was the reason behind this postal void, of course, what a fool I am sometimes. And since Fernanda María was never sad when morning came, I received the mailman in a most friendly way and gave him a tip when he handed me a certified express letter that afternoon.

Caracas, October 14, 1976

Dear Juan Manuel Carpio,

You're right. I always thought it was Luisa's rage in Lima, but it wasn't. Everything was decided the morning I didn't see you, sweetheart, and you didn't manage to move at that red light. I vaguely remember it, as if it were hidden under the fog of a sad, dark Paris morning with me desperately trying to get to UNESCO on time and suddenly turning right instead of going straight ahead because I'd decided to go to Chile, making, of course, a quick stop first in Lima, just in case. Of course nothing came of it. That morning in Paris, Juan Manuel Carpio, each of us decided to plunge into whatever mess was handy.

The blame for all this, as usual, rests with our *Estimated Time of Arrival*, which you and I obey with such discipline, and which always makes us arrive at different times, if not different places. Well, just look at me here in Caracas now, having decided to collapse this Latin American tent and migrate with my tribe to El Salvador. At least it's my country, and that's something. And I'll be able to work. Because now I am four.

That's right, four, and all that was decided waiting at the stoplight that morning in Paris, because it's as a result of my departure for Chile that I'm writing you today from Caracas to tell you that on the Day of the Innocents, December 28th, Mariana Fernanda was born. Ferocious, hungry, with enormous feet and a respectable nose, a bit highly colored. She makes up for her nocturnal sins with a smile like a sad little angel that always makes me love her. You'll see her soon—here, there, or somewhere else.

A while ago, Enrique and I sent an answer to one of your letters in Mexico. Did that go well? Did you record anything? Did you sing a lot? Also, via a friend who was traveling there, I sent you messages along with some drawings I made. But it turns out that the address on the letter you sent from a Holiday Inn in San Antonio, Texas, was incorrect. What the hell were you doing there? You said you were singing—was that true? It's great your voice is being recognized! I hope this letter finds you on the way back to your flat on rue Flatters.

As soon as we're in San Salvador, I'll be in touch with you. Send a hug to Don Miguel Angel d'Octeville, such a sweet old man, and hugs as always to you, plus a little fart from Rodrigo and a smile from Mariana.

Fernanda María

P.S.: I forgot—my incredibly lucky sister Susy managed to rent that apartment on rue Colombe. The owner, a really nice lady, remembered me and gave it to her for practically nothing. Look her up, she's already there. She looks like a gringa and likes to laugh a lot. Anyway, you could have a look at the old apartment we had . . . Did we ever have anything together, Juan Manuel Carpio? I won't go on because my little green eyes can't take it. Go see Susy. Ciao.

Susy, it turned out, was as nice as she was unstable. For her, the world was one gigantic, permanent joke. Her life: an incessant coming and going from one country to another and from one little job to an even smaller job, but always, always happy. She spoke of her sister Fernanda María as a badly used goddess and about her brother-in-law, Enrique, as a drunk who was both irascible and touching at the same time. In a certain way, Susy made up for another long hiatus in Fernanda's letters because she brought me up to date about what was happening to Mía and her family in San Salvador. Nothing very good, of course.

On the other hand, like someone simply stumbling over gold, Susy practically appropriated, paying a few measly francs for it, that beautiful apartment, which I now remembered as the heart of what I was in the habit of calling the *weird world.* Susy would often be out of Paris for weeks and months, and since she never told me, I'd visit, only to find another one of Fernanda María's sisters or some friend to whom she'd lent the apartment. The truth is that among the six del Monte sisters—one redhead, two very dark with black hair and eyes, one with chestnut hair and brown eyes, and two extremely blond with blue eyes—the only common denominators (the last name aside) seemed to be the big, aquiline nose and their incessant globe-trotting, the sole exception being the oldest, Cecilia María, who was solidly married to an American and living in California, long beak and all, practically since she graduated from high school.

Anyway, direct reports eventually do arrive, and on the blessed day March 15, 1979, I received the following huge surprise:

Dear Juan Manuel Carpio,

I'M GOING TO BE IN PARIS FOR A FEW DAYS!!!! I really want to see you, even though I'm burdened with things to do, hugs, photos, drawings and children's stories of my own. I only hope I find some friends and that we all get together. I'll only be there a short time. The company I work for is sending me to take a course in Manchester. Brrr . . . But after England, I have the firm—and joyful—intention of escaping to Paris to see beloved people and places. I'll only be there a week. And just for good measure, it will be Holy Week. I only hope all my fine-feathered friends won't be migrating.

I'll be in your town on April 7 and leave on the 15th, Easter Sunday. If you're going to be away then, please tell me, since my tourism is exclusively senti-mental, and maybe I can arrange another time if I find out there's going to be an absence as huge as yours, and the week risks being exclusively holy.

Another thing: I don't have your telephone number. Send telegram, please.

I'm leaving San Salvador on March 25 and I get to London on Monday the 26th. In London, I'll be staying with my sister Andrea María: 370 76 40. Address: 47A Evelyn Gardens, London SW7.

Enrique will stay behind to take care of the abandoned children, though of course this will mean he'll have to protect himself from the aunts, grandfathers, etc., who will all be in a tizzy taking care of the children. I don't envy him his task. But I'll be packing a few strong hugs for you from him.

I hope to see you and the others soon. Send me that telegram, please. And tell me if you're going to be there or not. As you see, I've given you my ETA, this time under the illusion that Paris is where I left it, and you.

Hugs, which there will be more of, from
Fernanda María

We allowed ourselves to be captured by each other from the moment when the lips of one went directly in search of the lips of the other—no cheeks, no foreheads, but directly and anxiously to the mouth of the other, and from the very tight embrace, painful, escaped arms and hands that sought out other zones of the body, a breast, a heart, hips, a sliding caress along a thigh.

"Let's get the hell out of this airport, Juan Manuel Carpio. We don't have a minute to spare. Do you have a car, or do we take a taxi?"

"I've got a green Alfa Romeo. Yes, the same model. A 1970, with leather seats."

"Maybe it even still smells of me."

"I'd have noticed, honey. Besides, it was blue. I just had it repainted."

"How wonderful, Juan Manuel Carpio. How wonderful and how wonderful and how wonderful."

"Julio Ramón Ribeyro, Edgardo de la Jara, and Don Julián d'Octeville are in Paris. Only Charlie Boston and Rafael Dulanto are missing, but what can you do? Besides, you always know what's going on with them over there."

"Right now I'm not in the mood to see anyone but you."

"That can be arranged."

"Which apartment? Susy's is empty. The ingrate—or the one with a real sense of timing, now that I think of it—took off for Rome just in time for my arrival."

"You choose."

"Yours has less of a past, and if we turn into two wicked people, it might prove to have more of a future."

"Fernanda . . ."

"I have no idea how in hell we're gong to emerge spotless from this escapade, Juan Manuel Carpio. But emerge we will, you'll see. I see you keep staring at this scar on this tiny red head. Keep staring. Your great friend and brother split it open like a coconut. So it may well be that we have acquired rights. I think we do. Frankly, I suspect we have all the rights in the world, now that I think about it, Juan Manuel Carpio. Or does it seem to you I'm just overexcited?"

"What it seems to me is that we have a red light and a green Alfa Romeo."

"Kiss me and let the guy behind us kill himself blowing his horn when it turns green. Kiss me until I can forget that the one driving this time is you."

"A thirdhand Alfa Romeo."

"Kiss me, you jerk, the light's about to change."

We saw no one during those days, and we were completely right to hide out in supremely egoistic fashion. Besides, our friends understood perfectly. Those were our seven days, our little week that could hold us for the rest of our lives, our being together for once in the same place with both of us knowing exactly what we wanted and how and for how long we'd be allowed to love each other, and that for once in our lives our infamous *Estimated Time of Arrival* had worked, that what we had now was a completely new world, the old one—

65

in our case, called husband, children, dictatorships, exile, domestic difficulties—having appeared inopportunely on the maps of the universe and its navigational routes. In sum, we were like Christopher Columbus sailing against wind and tide to the Orient of spices and on the way tripping over the tremendous item called America.

So, no, we had no time for friends, and yet in an altogether gracious way Fernanda called each one of them to say hello and inform them that she was in Paris, at my house, *with my* Juan Manuel Carpio, and they, one by one, and also in an utterly gracious manner, said not a word after promising an extremely brief (and totally fictitious) visit to have a glass of red wine (likewise fictitious). The balance was consumed in three excursions to restaurants where Fernanda María had dreamed of eating with me and a very serious, very formal visit, with full protocol—and flowers—to the damned stoplight that sealed our fate completely, leaving it, however, filled to the brim with the things we were doing and which we dreamed we could go on doing, a fate without a finish, you could call it. But, even so, there was the stoplight, green and red, and once again green and red, irremovable on that corner, eternally in Paris, although one pretty spring day, for sure, this time, but it might be better just to leave the flowers and go back to my apartment, my new music, some charming children's story Mía wanted to read me, to some good cheeses and a very proper red wine, yes, it might just be better to go back, yes, enough of this stuff about the soldier who feels always compelled to return to the front, to the same battle where he was so badly wounded and with such profound consequences.

Never was there a couple who parted at an airport with so much faith in the future, with so many shared illusions and so many common projects as Fernanda and me. Was it merely good taste, the simple desire that our little week end with kisses and smiles, a week that turned into a dream we really lived and shared? Now that much of that intense desire belongs to the past, now that nothing we did turned out either completely wrong or completely right, now that only a mountain of letters from Mía remains, some bits and pieces written by me, and a few of my letters from after the Oakland robbery—so much tenderness and friendship, and the same confidence and complicity as always—perhaps the only thing Fernanda and I could say is that sometimes dramatic awakenings do happen, and that sometimes in our eagerness not to cause harm to third parties, we end up becoming our own third parties. And seriously harmed, that's the truth.

"Ciao, Mía . . . You'll see, things will work out in our favor someday."

"Not just *someday* but very soon, Juan Manuel Carpio, you're going to see that something will come our way. Because when I was little I was called Fernanda Mía, and you've always called me that, so I'll always be your Fernanda, my love. And ciao. I'll write you from London as soon as I get there."

April 16, 1979

My dearest Juan Manuel Carpio,
Tired and not really wanting to, I've walked around. A blind musician was playing "As Time Goes

By." The sun tried to come out a little. And above all, the streets feel sad. I really feel a tremendous need for your tender, caring, patient presence. Which is why I went into a café to be with you, the you who is always there, who is never there, who will always be there.

I don't like returning to this correspondence, because correspondence means distance, and words are bastards that if you're not careful take over the situation. Shitty bullies that overpower us. How I'd like your beautiful and sweet presence of love to overpower me. Within the simplicity and awkwardness of a morning cup of coffee.

I love you, I miss you, I don't feel well, I hug you, I adore you,

Your Fernanda

April 18, 1979

Juan Manuel Carpio, my love,

I'm on the plane. Nervous about getting there. Happy about getting there and seeing the children. And missing your hands that caress me and make me happy whenever you touch me. Sweetheart, darling, you've got the right to express opinions, to ask me for anything.

I've been remembering so many moments, always the two of us together, without saying it, without thinking it. Me sitting next to you, or at your feet on rue Colombe. You sad, Luisa always absent, there between us.

I'm happy the world finally, one day, made its crazy spins somehow in our favor, and we could be together knowing it, talking about it, living it. A couple of idiots. But today it's difficult. Both of us more loaded with responsibilities and things to wear us down. And manias—like that thing about the herbs, or whatever you call them, torturing my teeth in that restaurant I liked so much.

I hope everything, someday, will be okay. I'd like to know you're going to take good care of yourself. And I'll be very strong and good and wise. And someday my kids will be able to laugh with us.

For the meantime, let's try to be able to take on these responsibilities. I'm thankful I was able, finally, to hug you.

I love you,
Your Fernanda

San Salvador, April 26, 1979

Dear Juan Manuel Carpio,

In the horrible confusion of the past days, I haven't written this letter I know you're expecting to give you news about my return.

Return I did. A knot of nerves and sadness. Absolutely. And therefore, everything else turned out disastrously, too. Just as you thought, Enrique is in the best mood ever and acting better than ever, that is, loving me more than ever. Although at the same time the difficulties he's had here trying to move his career along are wearing him down. The result is that my stomach is noisier than ever. And now, the latest event: Enrique's started vomiting! He doesn't understand what's wrong with me, but he knows something is wrong with me. And he's desperate, both because of his career situation and because of his life, and because of the distance he senses in me. As you see, we're all together in the saddest way, three trapped tigers. I think you're probably in the same mood, though I hope that you can be more at peace because you don't have as many conflicts, that you can *transform hysterical misery into common, ordinary unhappiness.*

I'm dying. I just can't go on chewing glass and smiling. I can't, I won't, I must not hurt anyone fatally. Not Enrique, not you, not myself. We're going to try to be very good.

The last night I was in London I had dinner with Adolfo Beltrán, a great friend, and more than a friend to Enrique, who told me that no matter what, he plans to go back to Chile next July to have an exhibit. And he's got high hopes that Enrique will manage to get some kind of permit for the same period to have a retrospective exhibit of his photographs. Parallel, simultaneous, whatever. So Enrique will write the introduction to Adolfo's show, and Adolfo will write the introduction to Enrique's, and they'll stroll the streets of Santiago and Viña del Mar, drink their wine again together in their old haunts. Finally the possibility for a happy ending. Enrique decided not to make a business trip to Guatemala and will dedicate these two months to preparing work to bring to Chile. I hope I can calm down and stop being such a pain in the ass so these will be calm months of good work. And maybe in this way Enrique's trip in July will be more positive and things can be cleared up. I want to be cleared up and happy again, sweetheart, and not feel as upset as I do now.

I think about you a great deal.

I took your Trenet record by accident. I'll replace it with something you'll like.

I haven't been able to listen to your cassettes. It's like talking to you, and since I can't be talking with you, I feel uneasy with this musical speaking. Writing to you today has done me a lot of good. I feel strong. I feel much better. Like Tarzan when he dives into the water.

I think you can write me at the office: MANS-FIELD & CO., P.O. Box 524, San Salvador

I'm going to ask that everything be passed directly to me personally, with the hope that everything turns out well for us, my love. I love you, I have been happy with you, and more than anything in the world I want us all to be well.

A big hug.

Your Fernanda

San Salvador, May 2, 1979

My dearest love,

Another day passed without a letter from you. And just imagine, what with all the disturbances going on here, the center of the city is closed off, and there are twenty-four bodies in the cathedral— fortunately people say they're going to be buried today. The poor French ambassador is still being held by the Popular Liberation Front, and now he's starting to look like a jerk because the Costa Rican ambassador, who was also a hostage, along with his staff, managed to escape, a big hero, while the poor Frenchy—who knows what will happen to him. Buses are being burned, so no buses are running, because everyone's afraid more will be burned. And now, just to ruin everything, the railroad car with all of the day's foreign mail for the entire country was burned. And I'm thinking that in addition to all this mess, a letter from you might have burned. The situation is horrible. And so is my internal situation. Like those Russian dolls.

How would all this be viewed in your Paris? Today, our office—*the English, they die hard*—is almost the only one open. But the banks haven't closed, so as not to create a greater panic.

Without your letters I'm all alone, but even so, I'm hugging you in a corner in the Montmartre labyrinths.

Your Fernanda

Corresponded by Correspondence

San Salvador, May 10, 1979

Juan Manuel, my love, where are you?

Never ever does any letter of yours arrive, and now I feel as if I'm up in the air. As if maybe I didn't really see you in Paris, that I imagined everything. I need you. Everything is so much more wonderful when you're around. And it's always been that way. And now I'm getting sad in this jungle because you're not here, not even by letter. To make up for your absence, I've listened to your cassettes about a million times. I liked the most recent enormously, though, of course, I'm dying of jealousy all the time.

Tell me what's going on in your life. The way things are, who knows what might have happened on your side. Especially because on my side everything is so contradictory. Now that I'm leaving, Enrique is finally thinking of arriving. But you can't recover what wasn't enjoyed at the proper moment, no matter how much you'd like to. Enrique still plans to go to Chile in July, the thing may happen. I think he's happy about that.

Write and tell me how your house is, your street, your city, and you.

My family, what little remains, is out of the country. Only my mother is here. My aunt and uncle are in Europe, I think as a precaution. They left at the beginning of May for two or three months.

I need you. I love you.

Your Fernanda

San Salvador, May 15, 1979

Juan Manuel, my love,

YOUR LETTER CAME!!! I really liked the image of the two of us floating on the life raft. The most wonderful thing I've heard since I got here. Because in these parts everything's quite sad. The little country's quickly heading for the shit pot. Nothing but murders, kidnappings, property seized, cars burned. And since so many cops have been murdered, there are none to be found on the streets. When the police do come out, it's a complete pack of national guards with jittery machine guns. And on the other side, the huge disorder of the ultra-left, and the thugs who exploit every opportunity. With construction workers out on strike, there are many more people on the street, but there are no buses because people burn them. So, the whole picture is insane. And the poor French ambassador is still being held hostage in his embassy. It's not the right moment to be trying on ball gowns.

Amid all this, I'm always thinking about you, and that makes me happy and is good for me, and is not good for me, and is good for me again. Mentally at least, we're together. I assume you must be worried, because the press, as usual, is telling how badly off we are here. But don't worry. Nothing's going to happen to me, I swear. That would be the finishing touch. At my age and in my circumstances.

What a great thing your touring the Canary Islands for a few days is. I have a map right in front of me at the office, and I see you're going to be much closer. Almost halfway here. If you were an excellent swimmer . . . But being the way we are, I think we're already halfway to each other. No one's going to stop us ever again. At least not me, because I feel as strong as Tarzan standing on the bank of a mighty river where the crocodiles hold him in the highest regard. No. No one's going to stop us. *Irreversible processes,* as the politicians like to say. Well, they're always wrong, but I'm sure we aren't.

The personal picture here is still the same. Enrique still plans to go to Chile in July, with the intention of setting himself up there. I think there's no reason why we can't see each other this summer. The only problem is that it's harder for me to travel than it is for you, because I don't get any vacation then. Maybe you could travel to this magnificent *Pacific Paradise.* Don't think it's all machine guns and murders. The lakes and volcanoes are still here, and so is the ocean and its conches. There's still the odd lobster to be eaten. And we could go to Guatemala or spend weekends on the coast. Or simply be together and be able to talk. You would be able to work, compose, even sing, if you want. I can arrange all that, I'm a *facilitator.* Plus I think something beautiful could happen for us. Although, of course, this paradise of mine is not very tempting at the moment. But running away seems even more complicated. What do you think?

I won't write any more because I really do have things to do. I'm in the office because, as you can probably imagine, it's the only place where I have a little privacy to write you. Always, every second, I'm thinking about you. I love you, I kiss you a hundred times while we have a drink in some café on some Canary island,

Your Fernanda

San Salvador, May 24, 1979

Juan Manuel Carpio,

There's good news and bad news. There are good days and bad ones. The most constant thing is that I think about you all the time, and I think and I think about possible solutions for us. Finally, it's better I stop thinking so much and let myself be carried along by time and events, because, in any case, you don't fix things by worrying about them. The events are as follows:

The country is still crazy. Yesterday the minister of education was murdered right here, four blocks from the office, along with his driver. After so many killings, the government has declared a state of siege, to last 30 days. Between this disgusting military government, which you can't believe on any subject, and on the other side the fanatics of all kinds who go around killing people, it's hard to know what to think. Now a "White Guard" has appeared, which is killing "traitors to the nation," which is to say they're killing poor people, who in turn are killing those who collaborate with bourgeois corruption, which is anyone who crosses their path. And the government kills anyone it feels like killing. The common denominator is dead bodies. A sinister little Tom Thumb of a country!

With regard to my personal life: I stick to my regular routine. That is, in the office during the morning hours. Now, with all the problems, there are fewer orders, less work, and also a lot of worrying and skittishness about whether it's worthwhile to go on working. Of course we just can't close the office overnight. The children don't have school this week: a period of national mourning was declared because of what happened to the minister of education. Enrique is still on his best-behavior campaign. Now it seems he'll die without the children and without me. It's a low blow. But he screwed up royally: constantly complaining, hitting, slamming doors, every five minutes saying he's leaving, and the moment I decide that enough is enough, he decides it isn't, that from now on he's going to be as good as gold, and that yes, yes, of course he does adore me and the children and everything else.

I wouldn't be surprised in the slightest if out of the blue Luisa started adoring you again. What gets into people? It seems they only want what they no longer have, or what they can no longer have. The worst thing is that when a girl really gives herself she gives herself so completely that all that business about mystery and being difficult and who knows what other exotic stuff is ruined forever. And men can only recover that love when a woman turns mysterious again and wants to leave. The shitty thing is that in my personal life, when I feel like leaving, it's because I really do want to leave. There is no mystery. I DON'T WANT ANY MORE OF THIS.

I don't even want Enrique to behave himself—to be good, to be anything. What enrages me is that it's only now that it occurs to the jerk that I'm worthwhile and that he loves me and that he's going to respect me, and that in reality he's always adored me. Just look at what he's churning up now. I don't know what to do.

But there is also good news. Andresín, our lost dog and the love of the children's life, came home. Well, came home in a rather imaginative way. Because it isn't really Andresín. Beginning with the fact that this one is female. The thing is that a little dog of the exact same kind turned up, and Andresín's collar fits her perfectly. And now Andresín's name is Manolita. She arrived yesterday afternoon, and the children and I are all excited about this return. Mariana baptized him, and the funny thing is that she's very happy in the house. Today we're going to give her an anti-flea bath, etc., and take her in for shots, as soon as I get home from the office.

Another bit of good news. Yesterday I dreamed about an airport where each and every one of the passengers who arrived was you. Another Juan Manuel Carpio, and another, and another, all wearing different suits, and they took out their passports and I became happy a thousand times in a row with your arrival.

This letter will likely get to you when you return from your long, previously announced trip to the Canary Islands. I hope that trip and the sea, which always settles things, make you optimistic, and that you feel well, with a hot little body, the way we are when we come back from the beach. Just think, here I haven't gone to the beach even once since I got back from Europe. And it's because you can't go the beach alone here, because the Pacific isn't pacific. And Enrique doesn't like the ocean. But then one of these days he'll pretend that whatever it is, it's always delighted him. And how good and helpful he'll become. Yes, well . . .

I hope to have your house flooded with letters by the time you get back from the Canary Islands, because I can't receive you there in person.

I love you and depend on you.

Your Fernanda

San Salvador, June 5, 1979

Juan Manuel, my distant and darling love right in the middle of all our troubles,

Charlie Boston arrived, apparently after having gone to France and seeing you in Paris before you went off to the Canary Islands. And with him arrived a beautiful Yves Montand record. And more than anything else, your love arrived in each word of each song. Thank you many times over. You're probably still on your tour through those islands, and I hope the sea and the sun fill you with strength and optimism. I know how slow the mail is, but perhaps this letter will be there to greet you when you return, as I'd wished.

I'd like to tell you how my life is, how my days go by. And I'd like to have something nice to tell you, but things aren't very nice at the moment. Judging by what Charlie told me, that he found you sad and dejected, I conclude that it's a universal sickness. At least it's reached your house and mine, and I call that universal. For my part, I, like Tarzan, buckle down against sadness and against interminable economic problems. I'm thinking about getting a different job. I'm comfortable here and only work half a day, but what I earn isn't enough for me to live on. I'm tired of this "put on a happy face" routine. I ran out of happy faces and would prefer a few material rewards. Just like you, according to the letter Charlie brought me, I need a time in my life when I feel very well, very loved, and not constantly on the edge of a cliff. That's closely related to Enrique's reason for leaving. In all the years we've known each other, we've never had a period of tranquility. If it isn't money problems, it's personal problems—aggression, alcohol, and when it's not those it's something else. Even though I don't feel tired and actually feel like doing a million things, Enrique is desperate. It may well be that for the first time in his life he really wants to offer me tenderness and material help, but right now he's got neither the ability nor the means. I don't think it ever occurred to him before that you've got to love a woman, or at least try to. It's funny, I've been happier and felt more like a woman and surer of myself in one week with you than in seven years of knowing Enrique. It's a sad thing, because, on the other hand, I do think he loves me, and I know he loves the kids a lot. But I just got bored. And more than ever now, I see that on top of everything else, he needs my strength to get out of the hole he's in. Excuse me, I'm sorry I'm unloading all my problems on you and that's going to annoy you. But I'm stuck in them, trapped, like Tarzan in times of danger, the kind we're all tied up in these days.

Aside from all that, an absolute pessimism dominates the nation, since we can see the coming crisis, and it's economic, political, human, and everything else. Very serious. As you might imagine, foreign capital has essentially disappeared, and so has a great deal of domestic capital. From now until the end of the year, we're going to see the economic problems get worse and worse, and with them everything else. I'm going to have to move quickly in order to get myself a salary that will allow me and the kids to weather the storm during this period.

All this is a bother and drives me mad, and this is a not very happy or romantic letter I'm writing you. Poor you, darling, to come home from a trip and find this letter. I'd like to tear it up, but if I do, how will you really know how I am? I'd like to be happy. But what can I do if I'm like a cornered animal. Sometimes there are pretty things too. I finally went to see the horses again, and it was wonderful to ride. So you see my pleasures are really simple. Even if my poor head is like an omelette.

The best thing would be to throw out this letter sent from the depths of my cage, from the depths of my family crisis, from the depths of my country falling apart, from the depths of my Central America awkwardly trying to be born into another life. And from here I clasp your hands and hug you.

The one who loves you,
Your Fernanda

San Salvador, June 7, 1979

Dear Juan Manuel, my love,

I received the last letter you mailed from Paris just before you went on tour, you who were so worried about the absence of letters you were going to feel in the Canary Islands. Don't worry. These aren't easy times. We're all going to need patience, strength, and the indispensable minimum of optimism to think that what should happen—and it will be good, you'll see—will come to pass. I say this to you because I say it to myself. And even though I'm very optimistic, I, too, lose my way and lose my confidence. I don't want to make you unhappy. Everything will have to turn out well.

I hope you put on some weight during your tour—you were very thin when I saw you—and that your house fills up with security. I need to know that.

I'm planting trees and flowers in my garden. And the kids are very, very well. As smooth as silk. Yesterday I inaugurated a serious program to shake off this sadness and pessimism. If I don't, I'll turn green and ugly. And that is unacceptable

I've got fifty saplings to plant. To you that must sound like a huge number, but behind my house, which is small, there's a ravine, which is big. I'd like to plant trees along the slope, so I can smell their aroma, and to stop erosion.

Enrique is getting ready for his trip. *What do we have to do before our guardian angels start working in earnest?* I think ours are the laziest anywhere.

I hug you with dirt on my hands and the hope for a pretty stand of pine. I'd like to see you happy.

Your Fernanda

San Salvador, July 3, 1979

Juan Manuel, my love on the other side of the sea, the clouds, and my dreams,

In this world we all try to protect what's ours. Separations are never easy, as you know only too well, and you don't wash off love with soap and water. You can easily imagine, because you know me, the situation we're going through. Just as you say: only after this storm will we know more clearly where we all stand.

And speaking of storms, the house that belongs to my aunt and uncle—the ones traveling in Europe—

flooded with the tremendous rains we've had. Some rugs were ruined, and everything's stained. I've been trying to find workers to fix things up.

There's also some possibility that I'll be going to Milan in September. A company we do business with is giving a course there, and if I can, I'm going to take it. It would only be for two weeks, but it would be so good. Please tell me it would.

I can't write much. My brain's turned into an omelette, but I hope these few lines bring something of me to you. At least that you know I'm not dead, and that I'm always thinking of you.

Fernanda

I open the copy of that little notebook where Mía copied out bits and pieces of my answers to her letters, and I confirm that the following paragraphs and isolated sentences may well be from that time. They refer, of course, to my trip to the Canary Islands—Tenerife, Lanazarote, and La Palma—and there can be no doubt that each and every one of these words speaks of the fear Enrique's departure makes me feel, especially (for instance) the part about "you don't wash off love with soap and water." What is Mía afraid of? That her kids will be left without a father or that she'll be left without that good man whose departure for Chile was imminent? "When our eyes see what they never saw before, our heart feels what it never felt before," declared Baltazar Gracián. So the only way for me to react is to play dumb, not to show I'm hurt by anything. No, nothing's wrong. All is well, Tarzan.

So you write as if nothing had happened. So I also write as if nothing was wrong. Or blurting out sentences of this kind: phrases like "It's just a tempest in a teacup." Mía, Mía, and Mía. And at the same time, or almost, I find myself adding:

> In the Canaries I was paid like a bullfighter. But I spent like a sailor. My agent (*yes, my lady,* you heard correctly, *my agent*), who knows you without knowing you, is still in love with Tintoretto's reds and suffers from a peculiar malady: every Botticelli, or Bottle-celli, he sees knocks his socks off, till he's passed out. My God! Never met a wine he doesn't like! And he sleeps without pills—unlike us, bundles of nerves— natural sleep. He lives on a utopian farm, something a bit like the Lima utopia for children, the City of God of my early childhood, but with a tavern. I should tell you that on the island of La Palma, where I'm returning from just now, I hung out with a group known as the Tavern Boys. One of them is so small he practiced baptism by total immersion, in brandy, of course, following the example of the early Christians and taking full advantage of his stature. He said when he was completely submerged he felt like Archimedes. It's also true he ran naked across half the island when he felt the truth of physics revealed.

I may also have sent Fernanda these sentences, given how long it took—as I afterward learned—some of the letters or postcards I sent her during that trip to reach her:

First things first: it's untrue that I didn't write you all this time. I wrote using all the images of a well-tempered lover boy. But your next letter, whose silence announces the imminent departure of the man you live with, reached Paris as late as the bubbles rising from a deep-sea diver. I only want you to know one thing, Mía or Fernanda María, or however your mood prefers to name you, from this point forward: I am neither against nor in favor of Enrique's or anyone else's departure. I am. I simply am.

Silence, but caresses, because I'm not going to sing you tangos or rancheras and ruin my reputation. And please excuse all errata, errors, and horrors. If you don't, the letter will get cold, and this one wants to run to see how it can be useful to you.

Paris, too, is. Simply is, and it still has stoplights. Ciao.

Juan Manuel

I must have been very afraid, in my eagerness not to show how aware I was of everything going on in that house in San Salvador, if I wrote so much nonsense. Although Fernanda does quote some bizarre words of mine, and I don't know in what context to situate them. They don't refer to her, to her and Enrique, to me, or to any of us. That part about *us* sounds pathetic, exactly because I'm living—and reliving now, so many years afterward—the hard sensation of being left stuck in Paris once again. Luisa represented a quick death. Was a slow death beginning now? I always loved, I always do love, and I always will love Fernanda María de la Trinidad so much that I still think that beginning back then I'd begun to prepare myself for an extremely slow and highly honorable road to the gallows. Anyway, here are my bizarre words: "Ergo, I see no failure. To the contrary, I see a beautiful and well-executed adventure." And its commentary in verse: ". . . that's how the rose is" (Juan Ramón Jiménez).

But I must have written her much, much more than these paragraphs and sentences, because Fernanda's letters that correspond to that European summer talk about totally different things.

San Salvador, July 15, 1979

Juan Manuel, my love,

I received your last letter, where you're anguished about my lack of words and about your nervous depression, or whatever it was you were suffering. For the most diverse reasons, the world is uninhabitable. Whether it's here or in your apartment or in Egypt. Look, today I received a letter from this couple, great American friends of mine, who actually *are* in Egypt—he's the cultural attaché in Cairo. And today they write: "Too much bitterness would filter through if I continued the inventory of the absurdities assailing us." That sentence surprised me coming from them, a couple who left the country when they were newlyweds full of adventurous illusions slightly less than two years ago. Now not even the most optimistic person can escape the sadness, anguish, insanity, and disorder that is our daily bread. They can't even catch a glimpse of better days to come.

The office, which was always a great emotional rest because of the way offices are, because of its impersonal and routinely easy way of communicating, is now in a state of perpetual disquiet. You've probably read that the two kidnapped Englishmen were released. But now ALL the English are gone, except for about a dozen, two of whom are in my office. And very, very sad. My uncle's partner and his son are both English and have received orders to evacuate. The son wants to leave, the father doesn't. But they both may have to. They can't go anywhere. They always have to be careful, and that's no way to live. The small dozen or so English people still here don't even have an embassy to watch out for them. New representatives for the English delegation may be sent, maybe. No one knows what's going to happen from one day to another. I don't know what my uncle will do if his partner has to leave, but I'm sure things will change a lot.

Last Friday, my other aunt and uncle came home from their trip to Europe. Too bad you didn't see them with Susy when they passed through Paris, and that you felt so ill during those few days. Susy, traveling as much as ever, is probably sad she didn't get to see you. She's very fond of you.

Around here, we're still trying to resolve things somehow, including money so Enrique can travel. I don't even know what to think. He adores the children, who are most certainly adorable, and they love him a lot, too. I don't know if he'll be able to stand being away from them. But someday soon he will make his trip, and being alone will help the two of us think things through.

Being alone, while we're on the subject, isn't helping you. I'm very worried about you, even though I realize that summer with friends like Charlie Boston and Don Julián d'Octeville will help you a lot. It's so good to feel the old and comfortable love of friends who know all your songs, and despite the familiarity there's always, as if by magic, the joy and excitement of seeing each other.

I haven't given up hope about the trip to Milan in September. Though sometimes we lose everything in this earthquake we're living through.

Big juicy kisses for Don Julián and Charlie.

And that goes for the Dancing Master too, if he shows up.

My love to you.

Your Fernanda

San Salvador, August 1, 1979

Dear Juan Manuel Carpio,

You're right—communications did break down because I didn't write anything during this past month of knowing and not knowing what's going on. So our complaints against the postal service, Central American disorganization, etc., can't be so vehement this time. Besides, it's possible that you'll be reading the letter I'm writing you today in September because of your vacation—which you need so badly, and which, I hope, will return you to Paris with lots of sun on the outside and lots of good times inside.

You can't imagine how much I regret the fact that Ernesto Flores made it to your territory instead of me. I suppose that filthy Colombian will be bringing with him, as usual, his heavy dose of delirious, giggling vulgarity and cynicism. But even if in his life and in his songs he's chosen to grab the world by the feet, by the armpits, and by the ass, why should that do you any harm? I'm sure that he respects and admires your contrary ability to touch life profoundly using less crude means, to know how to caress its windblown hair. It's simply a case of different passions, different styles. But I think—though nothing in this life is completely YES or NO—that Ernesto could be your friend, if there is a feeling in him that could ever take the name of friendship. Let's just say it's possible. Of course, sometimes his friendship is a kick in the ass.

As for me, Lima was about a thousand years ago, and Luisa and all that. You tell me Ernesto Flores was there when I passed through, but the truth is I don't remember if I even looked him up. I don't think so. Anyway, right now I can't think about Ernesto Flores. My plate is completely full. The truth is, I don't disdain him, and I'm sorry to hear what you said about him, that he stopped writing and composing songs—or at least stopped doing it well. What a pity that that excess of vulgarity, that enormous quantity of low passions and bad feelings, should go to waste.

Now about me. Enrique left on Sunday. Sad, and without knowing just what the future will be. I don't know either. This little country doesn't give you much to work with. As you so rightly put it: it's shit. It takes sweat and blood to live here, and there's no time for tears. Any of our Salvadoran friends would tell you exactly the same thing. Even knowing the ins and outs of the place, it's just so taxing to deal with the meanness that's waiting around every corner, the petty envy and mediocrity that characterizes this place. Of course you do find better people, and it's a pleasure when you do. But everyday life taxes you. Maybe it does everywhere. On the other hand, a person's country is a vice difficult to give up. I don't know if I could live anywhere else anymore. At least not today, which began so pretty. Perhaps some other day, my love.

The kids are great. But both of them have heart murmurs. They have to be looked after, not hovered over, just checked. Enrique was all broken up about leaving them because they really are adorable. He didn't think he could last more than a month without them.

Meanwhile, all of Central America is either exploding or not; and meanwhile, everyone is trying to secure his place in some private world: I'm raising the children, and I visit aunts in this town, which is pretty, ugly, horrible, insane, mediocre, explosive, easy, extremely difficult, dangerous, with a pretty, warm sea filled with delicious oysters and conch, with hellish heat during the midday traffic. Right now, today, this is my world.

How I'd like to know about your summer. I like talking with you so much. Always.

Always your Fernanda

San Salvador, August 16, 1979

Dear Juan Manuel Carpio,

Of all my girlfriends who live outside the country, Silvia was the only one who finally came home. Charlotte stayed in Paris, and none of my sisters have come back, either. Everyone's terrified of the country these days. You should see how many people are leaving. There's a huge sell-off of houses. I've had to get out of my own house, but not because I'm leaving. I had to have some major work done that'll raise lots of dust. The water situation became unbearable. We don't get water every day, and when we do get it, it's only at night. So we had to dig a well, with a pump and all. Let's hope this solves the problem. Of course it helps, because it's terrible not having water to wash in, etc. This week they finish, so we can go home again. The kids lose their bearings a little when they're not at home. Especially Marianita, who's very sentimental. A few days ago, Rodrigo slept at the house of one of his girlfriends, and Marianita was up all night looking for him. "Where's my brother, Mommy?" She was probably worried that he'd gone

away, too. Ever since Enrique left, she's been especially sentimental, lost, and weepy. Unlike Rodrigo,
who's the liberated man. He's more relaxed than
ever. And he's going into the first grade. My baby! It's
hard to believe he'll be six in January. And he's affectionate and very (I mean it) much in love with his
mommy. Still. Now that Rodrigo is going into real
school, Marianita will be left alone in her kinder-
garten. That will make her stronger, even if it will be
hard at first. Enrique's absence was hard for her. She
became very weepy and withdrawn, even if she never
mentions him. Sometimes she says—and it surprises
me—that she's going to the airport, that terrible place
that swallows people. Rodrigo's new school looks
okay. They give swimming lessons, and the teachers
are good. It's near the house, with a big garden and
trees. Later Mariana will go there, too. But in general
the lower schools are bad. Only good for learning bad
words and getting stomach bugs (Mariana's words).
Look what a reactionary mommy I turned out to be.
Actually, the school looks fine, with orange trees, a
big grove. The building itself is rather small, but with
lots of windows—it's almost all glass. They have lots
of classes outdoors—dance, theater, painting, swimming. They do all that outdoors on the grass. I want
to go myself.

Your Fernanda is a wreck. I've reached the most
complete bankruptcy. I owe money everywhere. The
car broke down and to fix it cost almost as much as
buying a new one. I owe someone every cent I make
and more. This just can't go on, so next week I'm

going to visit banks to see if someone will make me a nice long-term loan so I can get out of this hole and have a six-month break to look for a better-paying job. I've just got to become an executive woman. Unless we all drown here first. I mean, I even owe the gas station. And when you get to the point that you need loans of such tiny size, almost handouts, you're at the end of the line. Bankruptcy. But one thing's for sure: my situation can only get better. On Monday I'm off to make my pleas to several banks. I need about $25,000. It's neither a big deal nor a small one, but it will help me get back on my feet. Then I'll have to start paying it back, but with, as the bolero says, my *tropical path* all straightened out.

Greetings and a thousand hugs to our friends, and to you the memories of a thousand years of crossing bridges from your house to mine.

Fernanda

San Salvador, September 21, 1979

My beloved Juan Manuel Carpio,

I got your letter from Majorca and think you're right. My last letters weren't very pretty, or very tender, and that must have hurt you. Forgive me. I'm sure that today's, in which I have a lot to tell you, will wound you less because it's more real and more my own.

First of all, the September trip is canceled. They decided to send someone else from the office, a salesman who just got married and can take this opportunity to travel with his wife and spend his honeymoon there while he takes the course. I have to admit, it did seem a very human and very proper decision. No matter how much I really wanted to go. Maybe later.

Now I'll tell you about me, the mood I'm in, with the greatest honesty and tenderness, which I owe you and which I owe myself.

I've spent this recent time all alone. Recovering my places, my habits, my solitude. Maybe for that reason I kept you at a distance during those days, and that made me write you such cold letters. I really wanted to be completely alone so I could think and act in peace. And I got a lot done. To begin with, I myself am calm and happy. I've fixed my house up quite a lot, and it had a lot of things that needed repair and cleaning up. Now it seems like my own house again. I haven't seen much of anyone. I only went out a few times, because it's been so rainy. And the kids can't go out with all the rain. So, as a real lady of the house, I bought some good records, and by staying home I've recovered the peace of peaceful places. The place even looks bigger. Down at the office, I've asked for a raise, which means a longer workday. In October, I start working full-time, and I hope these ridiculous problems, which it's silly to have, will work themselves out.

As for Enrique. He's written a few times. It seems he misses us a lot, and that he really does love us a great deal. He's coming back, maybe at the end of September or in October, and we're going to try to straighten out all the misunderstandings we've had. I also sincerely think that's what we should do, because Enrique loves his children, and if we can work things out, so much the better. I think that now, protected by my new tranquility, which was so hard to win, I won't let my life be ruined again so easily. And that the two of us will be more careful about repeating so many terribly expensive mistakes in order to protect what little well-being we have. I'm sure you'll agree with all that, even if you're going to feel sad. I think it's the only honest way to go about things, the one most in agreement with reality.

Anyway, no matter what happens, you'll always find me your most admiring and faithful friend, who loves you enormously. Tell me, I beg you, what you think and how you feel. Hugs.

Fernanda

Of course, many more things, both good and bad, were yet to take place between me and Fernanda. And between Fernanda and Enrique, and even among the three of us. And even though the last letter speaks, at least between the lines, about something coming to an end, it also contains, for me, a dawnlike element, something of a profoundly threshold nature, almost like the entryway into a new reality and a new twist—perhaps sharper than ever—to our relationship, despite what the letter appears to say, and despite the things affirmed in it. Or it might be, simply, that no matter how I remember the brutal impact it had on me and the immense sorrow I felt reading and rereading it a thousand times, I always refused to allow the geographical and circumstantial distance between Mía and me to take on the slightest tinge of melodrama or guilt or error imputable to either of us. What failed us, as with so many other opportunities, the only thing that ever let us down always, right from the start, of course, was our *Estimated Time of Arrival.* But that hadn't ever depended on us but on some adverse gods, and there-fore, our relationship would someday find its way into a smil-ing and better future, in an outrageous optimism that would allow us to affirm, with greater and greater optimism, that the true miracle of love is that, besides everything else, it exists.

And here's the copy made by Mía of the notebook, com-pletely full of sentences that, no doubt about it, belonged to the letters where I commented on hers and which, inevitably, motivated the next letter I received from her. So I'll begin by quoting myself:

> I received your effusive . . . Hallelujah for your decisions! Hallelujah, because they reflect you! . . . Even though you don't think so, there are passages where your letter overflows with generosity, like milk in the old days, when the cream rose to the top . . . Besides, my dear overflowing Mía, we've got to know how to appreciate the quality of the molasses . . . Although, of course, I do recognize that all the beings it's fallen to me to love and respect in this life have several interwoven personalities, even personalities piled on personalities . . .
>
> The real truth is, Mía, that we all have our rea-sons for being sad, our disenchantments, our bitter-ness. Some because of their spouses, others because of alternating current . . . That's why those moments

when you can't count on anyone, even if you know they love you, to arrive as quickly as they leave, thank God.

A very objective fact. As soon as my *vacances,* which in your country are called, very singularly, *vacation,* almost as if it were something of a priestly nature, come to an end, I'm off for a few very brief days to sing in Mexico. Do you think we might be able to synchronize something? I await your answer with the doglike gaze of an Indian staring at one of his social betters, such as you can find in the novels of my genial compatriot José María Arguedas. Meanwhile, overwhelming effusions and glass in hand, in toast position, like, as the Mexican song puts it, the toast a playboy makes to a queen. Here I am with Don Julián, who, in pajamas and white straw hat, is thankful for your existence, and for that of Palma de Mallorca, and with Charlie Boston, who breakfasts toasting with Chivas Regal, all your fault he says.

The lines that follow, well, I expected all of them because they're a logical response, a very healthy, normal reaction to the oh-so-serene and jolly things I said to Fernanda when I commented on her letter. Indubitably, I had too desperately clutched at the lesson in the old admonition "Don't let your reach outstrip your grasp" for it to occur to Fernanda, for even an instant, to think that our relationship, even in its epistolary aspect, was finished. The only thing that surprises me in the commentary she makes on my letter is the part about *second best,* which doesn't ring true to me but which I must accept because I wrote it. Deep down, wanting or not, both she and I had been hoping that it would be Enrique who would make the false step, that it would be Enrique in a night of violence and drunkenness who would slam the door and take off for Chile once and for all now that he could so unexpectedly return to his country. But it turned out that the Araucanian giant with pitch-black hair had taken off *ma non troppo,* because, as he left, he declared he adored everyone in that house and could not stand being far away from his wife and children for very long, thus leaving *the rest of us* out of the game, in truth, though we'd have to recognize that my very naïve Fernanda had been as touched as an innocent little girl by the return of Enrique, something that sounded like a Trojan horse to me. Sincerely, I hadn't counted on his returning, and I'm sure Fernanda wasn't really counting on it either. But she ended up extremely touched by that great big guy, touched by the pure surprise that hit her when she saw him reappear so quickly, in such good shape and with such wonderful intentions. Life, who understands it?

Woe is me, my Tarzana, how naïve you still were then, from time to time, and how much you still retained of being the upper-class young lady with a Swiss and Catholic education and all that, how much longer it would take for Tarzan to become Tarzan in a real jungle, and with real muscles, and with a cry that would impose total respect, from the first to the last man, animal, or vegetable, in that tangled, demonic world where everything seemed to depend on anything except us.

San Salvador, October 20, 1979

Beloved and loved Juan Manuel Carpio,

Your letter came. More than good and generous. I've been thinking so much about you, and naturally have talked a great deal about you with anyone who'd care to listen.

At home: Enrique's already back, in much better spirits. He accomplished a lot in Chile, and that was very good for him. You are not *second best*. Just as I suppose I wasn't second best back then, when you were still dreaming, resting on my bosom with whiskey in hand, about Luisa's return and a reconciliation. What's happened to us is our eternal problem with time. When one is free, the other's married. And as you well know, being married isn't much of a bargain.

I imagine your streets are beautiful during these autumn days. It's the season I liked most there. From September to November. Afterward, Paris gets a little dark for my tropical eyes. Though there are people who like winter, *la saison du confort*. Delicious food and delicious wines that would kill us here with this implacable sun. I get hungry just thinking about the smells next door to your house. I hope I'll be able to get there again soon. We listen to your record *Le Paris d'Yves Montand* a lot here at home, and what reaches us are hugs from you, subway smells, wet raincoats, sausages in Pigalle, and simple Greek restaurants, the kind you like so much. Now, calmly thinking about all that with the tranquility and gratitude of your very generous words, your very jolly Lima expressions, your kindness toward me, toward my family, toward everything around me, it seems to me that when I walk outside I'm going to find the soft light of Paris as I slowly stroll the streets with you. And in my mind, I, with the same tenderness, mix up the time when you were the man who'd lost Luisa and the days when I was a totally happy woman at your side, but a woman who simply had to return to a country where children and a husband were waiting.

But as you always say, Madame Reality is the real grand winner in all our battles. And sometimes perhaps she gets even with us because we don't worship her with the same fervor she demands from realistic people. Actually, it's as if we stick out our tongues at her, and Madame Reality is so, so proud.

Well, then, my love, I hug you and send you hugs from all your great old friends over here, even that great majority of people who only know you by sound—music or conversation. You're always with us whenever we get together. I don't doubt for a second that someday you'll come to see us, and we won't have to put on any cassette because you'll be among old friends and there will be a guitar somewhere.

Fernanda

Life, who understands it? Because I'd just returned to Paris, tanned, in good physical shape, and still in a frankly vacation state of mind after a couple of delightful weeks in Majorca, when I was visited by a fat woman, as blond as she was beautiful. I'm referring, of course, to Luisa—I was happy to see her, sorry to see her. And I can still remember seeing in her face, in her eyes, in the curl of her lips, that is, in all of her, the profound impression of disgust she got from finding me alive and kicking, and with a face thinking and dreaming about Fernanda María de la Trinidad del Monte Montes, night and day.

Wherever I went I'd heard people talk about how well Luisa was doing in business, but now it was she herself who wanted to inform me personally, so that once and for all I'd give up the absurd bohemian life I insisted on leading, so that I'd cease and desist writing all that poetry and all those love songs, protest songs, or whatever it was I was writing, in effect, that I'd abandon Paris once and for all, return to Lima, settle down, and give her the child we still had time to have, and take up some position of limited responsibility in one of her companies, in view of the fact that you were always a bit irresponsible, oh, and a bit more than irresponsible, my dear Juan Manuel, although it is true that I've loved you from the moment I first met you, I don't know why, really, but that happens to be the real truth, and I still love you a great deal, and what do you say we celebrate the whole thing by dining at *La tour d'argent,* I'll pay, of course, because you, judging by that sad little apartment you have . . .

The incredible thing, of course, was that it was I who poured out those huge tears of grief, all that stuff in the song about *where there was love there always remain ashes,* that night at *La tour d'argent,* certainly her guest, yes, but her victim as well, judging by the observations Luisa made about an apartment where Fernanda and I had been so happy, about those walls that spoke of my success or failure in the world of music, and in the world in general, period.

"But Luisa . . . without singing, without composing, I can't live."

"You'd always have a little free time for that, Juan Manuel."

"But for me it isn't a matter of 'a little free time,' Luisa. It's a vocation, a life."

"No, it isn't, Juan Manuel. It's a matter of the day you finally grow up."

"Luisa . . ."

"Juan Manuel . . . I've come all the way to Paris to see you and tell you that it's high time you came home."

"Home? What home?"

"My home, you dope. Isn't it enough I offer you the chance? Or do I have to go down on my knees and tell you I miss you enormously?"

"Luisa, that isn't true."

"What isn't true, Juan Manuel? Explain, please."

"The simplest explanation is named Fernanda María de la Trinidad del Monte Montes and . . ."

"That freckled piece of spaghetti with tomato sauce on top?"

"There's no need to insult anyone that way, Luisa."

Luisa called for the check, and even if the waiter had broken all the world speed records for restaurant check delivery, the process seemed to take an eternity. Time seemed to slow to an interminable crawl from the moment when, to defend myself from Luisa's attack, I attacked her merely by mentioning Mía's name and by using an expression like *the simplest explanation*. It was as if my right hand, which in this life I use only to play songs on a guitar, had suddenly found all the violence and precision necessary to avenge Fernanda, returning to Luisa the tremendous slap Fernanda had received from her almost ten years earlier, in Lima. And then Luisa counterattacked, but I again reacted with a rapidity that made her settle the bill in a heartbeat and dash out of the restaurant, leaving me with half a bottle of excellent Côtes du Rhône Gigondas, once more abandoned in Paris. But how different this occasion was from the earlier one, because now I suspected that a pair of big old tears were blurring her pathetic, bad loser's exit. Mentally, I began to write Mía a long letter, telling her everything, more or less as it takes place in that tango: *She came back one night, I'll never forget it, there was so much fear in her eyes,* well, that was more or less the tone I used to tell Mía, sitting opposite a delicious glass of red wine, which Luisa, poor Luisa, you can't imagine how fat, how silly, how awful, Maía Mía . . .

San Salvador, December 3, 1979

My always beloved Juan Manuel Carpio,

I received your letter about Luisa's coming to Paris—untimely, self-confident, with a sympathetic smile, etc., etc. What a shame a person like that shrouds herself in so much mystery and self-satisfaction when she's with you, you who could do her the most good. Yet I'm sure she projects that mystery and tightness with all her friends, too. That way she won't let herself be touched, either by a butterfly or an aircraft carrier. Which means she has to take care of herself, and only according to her own personal and haughty criteria, which have not exactly proven to be the clearest, much less the most effective. I remember

Luisa with a great deal of tenderness and respect. Perhaps it shouldn't be that way, but it is, so there. Although I tell you, both seriously and joking, that her Lima Slap still hurts a lot sometimes, especially because of what she did to our lives without gaining a thing, after all is said and done.

The horrors here are coming closer to home, as close as the homes of the people I love most. Imagine, Rafael Dulanto's brother was kidnapped. Rafael had just landed in San Salvador, accompanied by a very pretty American girlfriend named Patricia. And for a moment things got even more complicated when a third brother who was over at the Ministry of Finance trying to arrange the ransom payment got taken prisoner along with 300 others and was held for two weeks. So for a few—*long*—days, the two brothers were deprived of their freedom, and Rafael, who is now a delegate to the United Nations, had to dash back here, with all the risks that entails. Now, fortunately, the ministry has been liberated and the hostages set free. But we still haven't a clue about the kidnapped brother. The kidnappers think people like us have millions and millions just sitting there in the dresser drawer all ready. I suppose Charlie Boston is still making his quick trips to Paris from Rome, and that you're probably more up to date on these terrible matters than I am.

This week I hope to take a short vacation, to go to the beach for a few days with the kids. It would do us all good. Rodrigo has had tonsillitis on top of tonsillitis. But Mariana, who's skinny like her mom, is in perfect health. Now she's very happy with her ballet classes. She just began and likes it a lot, even though she can barely walk. But it seems to be a good form of discipline for her powers of concentration, physical and mental, something my pretty little bird needs seriously. I've also been tired and nervous with all this kidnapping, and a few days breathing sea air would be good for me.

Of course you can write me at home, the only thing is the letters have to be general and expurgated, because Enrique would be very curious about reading them, as he adores you, as you know. He's always talking about you. You're always here, under an armchair or behind the plants, and you can pop up in any conversation. Well, as we know only too well, matrimony is a funny thing, and its rules will always remain a secret from me. I don't know if Enrique will be going to the beach. He doesn't usually like the beach, and if it's for several days, even less. So I end repeating that he'd be delighted to receive letters from you too. And I, of course. You're done for: separately and together, we both love you. What luck. *Madonna mia!*

But I love you more than anyone else, even if those words come to you in a chorus.

Your Mía

As you can probably see, I'd been transformed into a little angel, one who even wanted to write to Enrique, that's how eager I was to be present in that San Salvador house, morning, noon, and night. But this was perhaps not the best time to be worried about the niceties, as the blackest storm clouds were visible on the horizon.

San Salvador, February 8, 1980

My dearest Juan Manuel Carpio,

This place is getting too rough for my tastes. Even I, always the most optimistic in any situation, even I am getting worried. We've received three threats in a row from people saying they're going to kidnap my sister, Ana Dolores. I don't want to scare myself, and I don't want you to be frightened either, my love, because I insist on believing it's a tremendous evil rather than a tremendous reality. My sister, of course, is leaving the country. But who could be so badly informed in a country as tiny as this as to demand money from a family that, ever since the premature death of my father, lost all its sources of income and lives only on memories, friendships, and the few pieces of jewelry that still remain?

Even so, storm clouds the size of twenty aircraft carriers are beginning to appear. For us, I think, the most dangerous development is the formation of an "Army of Central American Liberation," made up of veterans from Somoza's National Guard, everyone who fled Nicaragua, the superreactionaries from Guatemala, the rich from El Salvador who went to live and invest in Guatemala, and the government of Honduras, which also seems to be collaborating.

Even Rodrigo Carazo Odio (if he were English, he would be Mr. Hate), the current president of Costa Rica, delivers reactionary speeches, although at least he's not supplying weapons or men. All these fine people are determined to "stop the Communist advance" here in my little country. Just imagine what that confrontation will look like. I can only hope the boys and the comrades are well prepared. No matter what, it's time to dig a hole and find a hideout. Of course, the comrades have weapons and troops, though I think they're at a disadvantage as far as arms are concerned, even though they've got the masses rather well organized. The People's Coordinator demonstration was enormous, the biggest ever seen here—200,000 people in San Salvador. Just imagine. In this city, until just a few years ago, a hundred people in one place was a crowd. And whenever someone missed Mass or didn't show up at his usual bar two Sundays in a row, people would conclude he'd taken off for the hills as a guerrilla fighter or as a member of a death squad.

Even though I don't want to be terrified, I fear for my sister, my children, even for that drunk Enrique, who faces everything with a glass in his hand. Right now I want to close my eyes tight and feel only the existence of that total confidence I have in you. Then everything would work, Juan Manuel Carpio, because you're like me and you wouldn't abandon me even for the Luisa of way back when, and definitely not the one from a few letters back.

Well, then, this is how life is: I can't even dream of

that "synchronization" with your tour you mentioned in your last letter from Majorca.

Think of me, trips or no trips.

Your Fernanda

I did travel to Mexico. I also made a quick trip to Lima, where I even had time to break my left hand—a very slight fracture, thank God. There are references to all that in a few sentences taken from the photocopied notebook Mía always jealously guarded.

In Mexico, my damned agent is so dedicated to absorbing the national alcohol supply that he barely got me enough to pay my room and board. But I'm just getting started with the calamities, because I also got a case of Montezuma's revenge which, if it hadn't been bacterial, would have ended up being, in my opinion, psychosomatic, and given the kind of lunacy I'm prone to would have probably led me to shit a grand piano. If you'll pardon the expression.

So I ended up fleeing Mexico and making a quick trip to Lima to say *bonjour* to family and friends. My success was complete: right in the airport I made the slip of a lifetime and fractured my left hand, though with no ill consequences for my guitar playing or my troubadour vocation. I looked like a politician in that city, where all the politicians have a broken (some limp) hand.

Effusions like whale spouts. I miss you and love you TO DEATH.

Juan Manuel

I still feel ashamed for having written those things when I reread the following letter I received from Mía.

San Salvador, February 26, 1980

My most beloved Juan Manuel Carpio,

You always try to make me laugh—I just received your short letter—though I'm very worried about those of us who are here, and worried about you in Mexico, Lima, and now back in Paris. It seems that no matter where we go, the risks you and I run seem in a way always to be the same, at least at the internal level. I think it's the internal demons who give us flat tires, burn our boats, tear our sails, and at times leave us shipwrecked smack in the middle of a sunny morning in the most beautiful Paris. Which is why we get along together, with a most continuous tenderness. By the way, we've been talking a great deal about you, all of us concerned about your life, your always being alone in Paris, and your solitary travels to earn a few cents. And at the same time we all love you a great deal, and we're proud, as well, to be part of the world that surrounds you in your apartment on rue Flatters or wherever you go.

Twice now I've made the trip to Occidente, as the Santa Rosa zone is called where Rafael Dulanto and his girlfriend, Patricia, are staying. Rafael's family has a very pretty house on the shore of Lake Coatepeque, and we got together with them there, along with Virginia Corleone, who also met you in Paris and will never forget you, plus Enrique and the kids. The whole family in other words. There were other friends who've only heard about you and who also live in that neighborhood, and they, too, recall you or ask about you.

With regard to us: we're not at all calm. Ana Dolores has had her departure delayed, and those absurd but serious threats hang over all of us like a sword of Damocles. On the other hand, Rafael's brother was released. I really don't know what Rafael and Patricia plan to do now, but they'll probably be visiting you in Paris to take a well-earned vacation after all the tension and hard work. We're all very relieved now, and Rafael's family has also settled down, though I suppose they're quite a bit poorer. But it's much better at least to be alive. He's just the same. He laughs with his big, extroverted tropical child's mouth, falls asleep when he's visiting with friends, and, at the same time, adores his girlfriend. He's generous and good, as you know. But a bit out of sorts and, as always, a bit lost. I think if he comes to Paris you won't have any trouble recognizing him the moment you see him.

The business about his brother put our Rafael in a bad way, but now he's much better. The first time I saw him he was sad, pale, and incredibly silent. And so was Patricia, whose debut in this catastrophic little country couldn't have been less well timed. But now things seem to be going better for them. Even so, three days ago I saw them in San Salvador. They were in their car and wearing mourning clothes. So was I. And I assumed we were going to the same Mass, one being said for a friend who was killed, shot down as he left his farm—Walter Béneke's brother. You may have met Walter, or Rafael can remind you who he is. He was minister of education. He was also a member of our group. I was on my way to the Mass with Enrique and my mom, all of us in black, and we said hello to Patricia and Rafael, but then we didn't see each other. They probably had another death to take care of.

Now I hope to be able to see them before they leave, because getting together with Rafael is always fun, and Patricia is a charming woman. I forgot to tell you that they came to my house on Mariana's birthday. We had a good time, all of us, and we gobbled up a platter of tripe as if we were starving—washing it down with a good deal of wine. I think it was like a piñata party for adults, but the kids also had a great time because even though it was midsummer, it rained, and that caused a great commotion and made the day an absolute success for them. They were playing with umbrellas in the muddy garden, what fun. Meanwhile, we adults were overdoing it with the wine. And we toasted you and played a ton of Frank Sinatra while we commented how much we love you and how little (or not at all) we love Bernardo Rojas, a compatriot of yours who lives here and is Virginia Corleone's brother-in-law. The consensus was that we should send this Bernardito Rojas off to live alone and that you should come to join us. It seemed logical to all of us.

Want to have fun, drink a good glass of wine, and eat a dish of the best lasagna—all in pure contentment? Well, I may be in your city again. I'm seeing if I can go there in July, though this time I'll have the children. As soon as it's confirmed, I'll tell you. Naturally, there will be three of us, and I'll have to stay at Mariana's godmother's house—she's got a house there, space, and children. I'd be there for three weeks. Anyway, I'll write as soon as I know.

Cross your fingers and don't ever forget me.

Fernanda María

But once again Fernanda's fate would be different. And once again nothing depended on her. She'd left Chile six years earlier for political reasons, because of some nonexistent left-wing militancy. And only because Enrique, her husband, who taught in the same humanities division where she was studying architecture, was accused of sympathizing with some extremist groups when in reality the only real sympathizing he did—and in that specific case this excellent man and great photographer *was* a militant—was with good whiskey and red wine. And now, Fernanda María de la Trinidad, whose only stigma was that she had the last name Monte Montes, which meant that somewhere in her family she had some fervent believer in the extreme right, had to flee from her own country with her two children because her name, which was also Rodrigo's and Mariana's—was found on the blackest, the darkest, of lists of the powerful, kidnappable, and murderable right wing. A telegram interrupted the joy of the two last paragraphs she wrote me from El Salvador.

SAN SALVADOR. JUNE 6, 1980. JUAN MANUEL. THE CHILDREN AND I ARE LEAVING IMMEDIATELY FOR THE USA. PROBABLY CALIFORNIA. OUR LIVES ARE AT STAKE. ENRIQUE WILL FIGURE OUT WHEN AND HOW HE'LL FOLLOW US. WE'RE LEAVING WITH WHAT WE HAVE ON, BUT WE'RE OKAY. I'LL WRITE AS SOON AS I CAN. CROSS YOUR FINGERS. A HUG. YOURS.

III

▲▲▲▲▲▲▲

Tarzan in the Gymnasium

When I go back to a letter like the one that follows, when I again confirm her naïve joy, her tremendous strength, her almost irresponsible elegance, and that—how to put it?—outrageous optimism based on a total love of life, when I see that Fernanda María again wakes up happy to see a new day, in another country, in another world, facing new and very different problems, when I imagine her sitting down, writing me as if nothing had happened, as if nothing had happened *to her,* as if she really weren't feeling the slightest anguish, the slightest pain, and as if she'd never, ever received any death threats, I still want to run to her, take care of her, pamper her, love her and protect her as I've never been able to do, except by letter, of course, and God knows that by letter I always seem to have been better.

But of course she's been Tarzan, always was Tarzan, and now Tarzan's just discovered the total voraciousness of every living cell in the jungle. Now it's as if Tarzan were beginning to mature, once and for all, in order to take care of her babies amid the foliage and its inhabitants—devouring like hyenas, or poisonous like tarantulas. And now it's as if Tarzan had become fully aware of a thousand horrible and perverse Rambo-style ambushes, and when she confirms that her shout in the jungle no longer projects enough energy, enough ferocity, or whatever you like, she ends up joining a gym.

And from that moment on, surrounded by a load of weights, ropes, and pulleys, after a million abdominal crunches and three million dorsal flexes and four million leg lifts, from that moment on it seems Tarzan breathes softly and harmoniously while she gives me an account, or rather takes me into account, or—why not?—while she sends me the most beautiful battle report ever written from a war front, this letter in which a happy, complex genius seems to have managed once again to make Fernanda María de la Trinidad del Monte Montes happy that morning as she writes:

Trinity Beach, California, December 27, 1980

Beloved Juan Manuel Carpio,

You'll be happy to know I got out of San Salvador with the kids. We're in opulent California, in my sister María Cecilia's house, which is right on the beach. The beautiful California coast received us with brilliant days and tranquil nights, far from the bombs, the constant death, and more and more serious kidnapping threats of the kind I told you about. After the death of so many friends, my nerves and spirit are beginning to fall apart, although all of us keep up a genuine and credible optimism about the final results, which will be both difficult and costly to achieve. Right now I'm happy to be here. And I hope to be able to go back at the end of February or the beginning of March. Enrique stayed in San Salvador. Maybe he'll join us here later. Excellent friends and comrades have fallen, but there are still many of us left, tough ones. So there's no reason to faint. To the contrary, it's as if you protect yourself with a new skin that, without losing its freshness and beauty, also has a side to it that can be armor, lances, cannon, and even aircraft carriers.

If you want to write, or if you need anything, here's the address:

c/o María Cecilia Weaver, P.O. Box 372
Trinity Beach, California 94901

The truth is, I couldn't stay in San Salvador any longer just now, but soon we'll be able to go back. Sometimes I think about you, while sitting here in a Berkeley café, with the delightful California sun warming my hands and nose, a very cold nose. Or while I'm walking around San Francisco. Or in Santa Cruz, which is a beautiful place. Luckily, the weather's been wonderful. Yesterday, the kids swam in the ocean. My sister has children, horses, dogs, cats, and the beach right next door. The perfect retreat.

Write and give me all the details on how you're doing. Your friendship is always one of the shiny treasures I count on even at the bottom of my most beloved sea.

A big hug, and I wish you all the best for the new year, as always.

Your Fernanda

Sometime during the thirties or the forties or the fifties— what do I know, and what difference does it make, anyway, if their voices still invade me?—the Ink Spots recorded a song that goes, *Time out for tears, because I'm thinking of you* . . . That's all I have to say about Fernanda María's letter, the first one Mía wrote me from California. And, judging by the date when she wrote me the second time, it makes me happy to deduce that I answered her very promptly, making her a little happy.

California, January 30, 1981

Dearest Juan Manuel Carpio,

Your letter was, of course, a bomb! More than anything else because I was thinking so hard about you as soon as I got to California. I went with my sister to Berkeley, where we sat on a sunny terrace to watch all those people there. And you were so present that I was smiling more because of you than because of the sun tickling my cheeks that beautiful day. So the most logical next step would have been to see you in Berkeley at that very instant.

You don't know how happy it makes me that you've decided to go home to your country, though there's no reason to rush things. Paris, and you're right to say it, is often a party, but only for the invited guests, and it can fill up with sadness and fatigue, just as it can also get so cold. And you never know, and you don't choose the moment when you stop being an invited guest in that beautiful city, but the day comes when there's no more party and the most sensible thing is to leave. I'm happy you've made that decision and that you're now in a place as pretty as Majorca, writing, composing, singing, and meditating on how to carry out your plan to return to Peru when the first good opportunity turns up and without having to depend on anyone's self-serving offers of help. All that makes me happy, just as it made me happy to receive your letter and your "I love you a lot, Red." I felt very strong and very much a woman, understand?

As for me: *my most charming hands* are dedicated to painting and making signs carved on wood for stores, restaurants, and all kinds of other places. At the moment, I'm making a sign for a bakery. It's fun, and I earn a little to survive. Fortunately, being in my sister's house, I don't need much more. Poor María Cecilia has to take care of all the hard work in her house, we all know that. But I try to help insofar as I can and try not to be too much of a burden. I really don't want to go back right away. Now that I've thought about it more, I don't want to go back as soon as I thought I would when I first arrived. I left many, many things undecided. Also, the sadness of the killing that was taking place in El Salvador was making me crazy. That doesn't simply disappear here, although life does become more possible. Also, in addition to all the other pressures, my job there had become very boring. I guess I'm just not all that inclined to return.

They called from the office to ask me please to come back by mid-April at the latest because my uncle is traveling to Europe at the beginning of May and wants to leave someone in charge. Personally, I'd prefer to spend a year away and let things clear up. We'll just have to see how things work out. I don't like the idea of having everyone expecting me in April and then I don't turn up, but I can't decide yet. The only thing I do know is that for the time being I'm staying here. Besides, there is the possibility of traveling again to England in March for the office—to take another course like the one I took the first time. But if I accept the office's offer to go, I would leave from here and would also return here, until I see things more clearly. The kids are already in school and trying to learn English, and with my sign business I'm sort of beginning to function normally, so there's no reason to leave and run right back into the tiger's jaws without at least getting a little in shape beforehand.

One part of the idea of leaving was to push Enrique to leave and get on with his work. No one can stand his neurotic inadequacy about the failure of a career that only he can revive. His great friend Adolfo Beltrán called him from Mexico, where he was having a show in the Museum of Modern Art in Chapultepec Park, to put him in touch with people there, but for mysterious reasons he never managed to leave. Now I suppose he's trying to arrange his visa to come here. I haven't received any letters from him in quite a while, and I'm afraid he must be drinking like mad. Well, this time I don't want to help at all. I promise you I'll be the most passive woman and hope the young man can find a way to get back up on his own two feet. Ultimately, we're all extremely weak, fragile, sad, failed if we let that side of our personality dominate us. On the other hand, we're strong, able to resist anything (that's a fact, even if sometimes we need some outside help). I do believe that in Enrique's case, neither he nor anyone else will put up with him weeping his way through life. Just think how huge he is, and with all the talent he has—he could at least get a grip on himself and try to be a little happy. I think and hope that this trip, if he brings it off and doesn't just hide out in the patio of the house, drinking, could be highly beneficial to him. Of course, time will tell.

As you can see, what I need most, and luckily what I have most now, is time. My sister is very sweet to me, and we help each other and do things together a lot. I can stay here with Rodrigo and Mariana as long as it takes for things to clear up. I think that's what I need most urgently at this moment in my life. Also, it's quite wonderful being in beautiful California.

I'm sorry you can't come in February. And as far as April's concerned, if I'm still here, it's likely Enrique will be here, too, which will make it more difficult to enjoy long, tender chats on my sister's beach.

If by any chance I travel to Europe, I'll let you know, but if I leave the kids here in California, it would only be for the shortest time, plus I'd be in Edinburgh. But even so, I'd probably escape for a couple of days to London to visit my other sister, Andrea María. Luckily we have an international mafia of sisters, as you see.

A kiss and a hug with my carpenter hands.

Your Fernanda

California, June 1, 1981

Dearest, beloved Juan Manuel Carpio,

So many days have passed, but I finally received a letter from you. And just look, I'm only writing you today. But this mess I live in just keeps me so off balance. I can't even write to my mother. This is how things stand: first we moved into the house of some friends in San Francisco, and then to another house in Oakland, hoping to find another place to live God knows where. Enrique's been talking with his Caracas friends and managed to get them to give him his old job back at the university. But he can't decide whether he should leave or not, and besides, he doesn't have a visa yet. I've had enough time to lose control completely over this matter, so every day I just limit myself to solving the problem of the day, and that way I manage to stay afloat. If I start thinking about what I'm going to do even next week, I get desperate, because it's impossible to know what's going to happen from one day to the next.

I'm working as a teacher in Rodrigo's little school, which gives me some time with the kids. That makes me very happy and gives me lots of stability. The kids at least are having a better time than the rest of us, and before I never had much time for them because of the insane work schedule I always had. But there's no way out, and it looks as if I'll have to work forever, and for the time being the solution's perfect: all three of us work together. I don't know how Enrique spends his days, but I imagine he spends them worried and drinking, which seems to be his answer, his only answer in this life.

I only wish I had more time and could write you a well-thought-out and good letter in the happy spirit that's always been with us when we're together. But the spirit with me today is a disgustingly nervous one, and I feel all the time that if I miss my wave I'll drown, so I sail rapidly with the accelerated rhythm of the waves of the Pacific Ocean, which is, as you know, the least pacific of oceans, and luckily I feel I have a lot of strength to swim in these currents and cut my way through this jungle.

This week I plan to start looking up my old schoolmates. A few days ago I visited the nuns, who were very happy to see me, and who promised to do everything they could to help the kids and me. I spent almost ten years in the Sacred Heart over in San Francisco, in a beautiful building on the hills facing the bay. And it's always a pleasure to see those tranquil, cool marble halls again, to smell those waxed wood floors and find some of the nuns who taught me twenty years ago. They still remember me, just as they remember my older aunts from about twenty thousand years ago. So that's still one of the old pleasures I can find in the city. The nearness of a beach is great, but I can never have the same feeling for that San Francisco I strolled through so much and lived so completely in when I was a student. Those years leave a big mark on you.

I can't tell you anything about myself or what will become of my life for the simple reason that I just don't know. I've spoken very clearly with Enrique, but he won't let me go for love or money. Just as you say, there doesn't seem to be any way out of this situation. I don't want to hurt him, but someday I'm going to need someone who'll love me and back me up. But I do believe everything will work out and things will be fine in the end. One step at a time, and after a while a path will open up.

Meanwhile, I love you, think a lot about you, and hope everything's okay with you.

I hug and kiss you.

Your own Fernanda

Well, in the best military style, I suddenly had an atrocious desire to set some tanks and a couple of batallions of troops on Fernanda María's latest considerations regarding her Araucanian giant. Remarks such as *But I do believe everything will work out and things will be fine in the end* were bringing us to a state of immobility, to a long and true period of deep, sentimental swampiness. Because, well, let's see: there's Enrique, in San Salvador, that's the worst part; plus me, forever running to hell and back to sing a few songs, though finally and once and for all expelled from the Paris party; and there, in the mythic and jungle-like California, Tarzan María de la Trinidad del Monte Montes with stained hands full of calluses and splinters from so much painting and carving signs for third-rate restaurants and two-bit bakeries, to mitigate the hunger and education in English of her two prides and joys. This meant that neither everything nor nothing in this life would be done, except for each of us staying put, one more nailed down than the other.

Which meant that according to my healthy judgment and understanding, the time had come to take charge of Enrique and to discharge him. Because it was one thing for Mía to be incapable of hurting him, but something rather different that every time the guy gave himself another alcoholic, self-destructive stab there in San Salvador, his indigenous, savage blood would make a tremendous leap and flow over Mexico and the Atlantic and end up splashing and staining the two of us from head to foot, both inside and outside, and in places so far from each other and so different as Berkeley, Oakland, Trinity Beach, and San Francisco over on the American side, and Majorca or Paris on the European side. The truth: enough was enough with this bloody Araucanian.

And well, since it was time for action, I acted. And in June of that same 1981, as soon as I found out that the giant with the pitch-black hair was hot on the trail of a probable visa that would allow him, doubtless very soon, permission to visit his wife and children in California, I paid a visit to the U.S. Embassy in Paris to get my own visa for the U.S., with travel dates and times that would allow me to fly the Atlantic and land at the Oakland airport in plenty of time to toast— hey, wait for me!—Enrique's arrival in California. Which is to say, I got off my plane barely one hour after he did, and in this happy, coincidental, and altogether fraternal manner, I could be received by the entire family, and, moreover, without their having to make the trip between their Californian exile home and the airport twice in one day. And while Fernanda Mía, more mine than ever, took advantage of the jolly natural confusion, with all the ease in the world, to ask me to sing that song in which a mule driver says that *you don't have to arrive first, but you do have to know how to arrive.*

After all that, we woke up the next day still happy on all sides but confused, really, about the vision of what those days would bring us. Only one thing was very clear, and it was that we had before us a week when the kids could miss school and the best thing was for all of us to head for Trinity Beach even if it was quite chilly and overcast. There I could at least get a room in a little motel next to the house that belonged to Mía's sister María Cecilia, her husband, a huge, slightly dumb gringo who was also a good person, and their children, horses, cats, and dogs. Plus there was the beach, extremely important so that Mariana and Rodrigo, almost dressed for snow, the poor things, could have lots of fresh air and be free in a place where they could run around and get lost among the dunes and coastal mansions. Above all, there was lots of noise from the waves in the distance and lots of shrieks from deafening seabirds so those selfsame kids would hear nothing even if war broke out in Aunt María Cecilia's house or in the bar of the motel across the way, what with the happy arrival of our daddy and the Peruvian singer about whom Mommy always talks with a knot of joy in her throat and who every so often writes her letters that make her laugh and cry a great deal, Mommy says, because there's a lot of ingenuity in the way they tell things and also because they contain words called archaisms and others called neologisms and still other things called Peruvianisms.

Like Susy, the sister who'd set herself up in Paris, here in Trinity Beach, María Cecilia, the oldest of the six del Monte Montes sisters, thought, with all the sincerity and love in the world, that her sister Fernanda was simply an ill-used goddess, a genius of terrible luck, and the most noble, purest, the best woman in the world, though for the time being it was as if she'd fallen asleep inside a nightmare, from which no one except time and she herself would ever succeed in helping her escape someday. And the almost blessed Paul, that is, María Cecilia's husband, the owner of María Cecilia's house, restricted himself to thinking in monosyllables and smiles, both in English, that it was all the same to him whether we killed ourselves or not, or whether we were good or evil or perverse or poor or rich or Vanderbilts, but for the simple reason that it was all the same to him whether the San Andreas fault and California and the entire world ended that very morning, as long as, seriously now, he could enjoy the last instant, before the apocalypse, of the presence in this world of horses and dogs and cats and ducks and chicks and seabirds in the naked distance in which the Pacific waves furiously broke.

In short, the guy supplied all of us, but especially Enrique and me, starting at breakfast, with red wine and Frank Sinatra, restricting himself quite hospitably, to showing us how to work the record player and the corkscrew before continuing his monosyllabic and smiling gringo march toward the animal world there in the depth of the coastal landscape, amid immense dunes and moist sands. Actually, to this day I don't know what to think of that Paul, better known as María Cecilia's big gringo, at least when he wasn't around, although I suspect that even his wife referred to him that way, with something between total tenderness and absolute indifference, which was nothing more than the result of his own attitude toward us, his silence with tons of music by Frank Sinatra, his way of drinking only iced tea even though he left a trail of whiskey and red wine wherever he passed, his loving animals so much that the first thing he called to mind was a California version of Saint Francis of Assisi, although in the very next moment he could shoot his wife and children a crushingly brutal glance, accompanied by a face so vulgar and so homicidal that you'd think you were hallucinating, for here was the poor little saint from Assisi reincarnated as Rambo in Vietnam, or was it CNN's First Gulf War, but then he suddenly seems to return from the world of chemical and nuclear weaponry, fully televised, and he is retransformed back into María Cecilia's big gringo as something, something extremely clean and good reflowers in his face, and from deep within that Stallone everyman, the poor saint from Assisi who cohabitates with him surfaces again, and then, at that moment, I swear, the very habit of Saint Francis would fit his soul like a glove as the humble and ever-so-simple gringo marches, monosyllabically and smilingly, through the living room of the old mansion on the immense beach, opening new bottles of wine and offering more whiskey.

But none of that was serious, or even important. It was all banal and natural, it was all about California and the U.S.A. with us stuck in the middle like pelicans out of season. Not even the kids were serious, because when the moment came—and it came from time to time—Mía, perfect mother and Tarzan in the gym, would take care of them delightfully, perfectly, and tenderly. So it wasn't important that Mariana and Rodrigo would spend hours and hours, day after day, making up games between a brother and sister who adore each other but who sense that something's rotten in the state of Trinity Beach. Mom, of course, is always Saint Tarzan. And Daddy finally turns up, and you and I adore him, and, wow, does he love us, he always drinks more and more wine, but even as a falling-down drunk and exile he idolizes us. And our aunt and uncle in the U.S.A., María Cecilia and Paul, are the way they are because of living here, for good or bad, yes, *they are different, they are like that,* that's how you say it, Mariana.

"And what about this Juan Manuel the Singer, Rodrigo?"

"Juan Manuel Singer is a good friend of Dad and Mom, and before you were born, Mariana, according to Dad, I spent my life sleeping or howling or drinking milk, or poop-ing, including yellow poop, way back then, when you're such a little baby that you can't even remember coming into the world, which is another way of saying to be born, Mariana, Juan Manuel Singer was already such a friend of Mom and Dad that when we had to run away from Chile and had no place to go, we did have one place to go. And that place was Paris, because that's where he has his house, his guitar, and his songs, this man from Peru who delights Mommy when he sings to her."

So none of that was serious, or even important, but what is, is the brutal intensity with which I want to do all the good in the world for the woman I love, while she does not want to cause the slightest scratch on the body or heart of a husband whose only idea is to move the piece called wine or the one called whiskey with words by Sinatra in that explosive chess game that begins almost at breakfast, which is when I come over from the motel across the way in search of the truth in this love. To drink and to let others, in Sinatra's voice, think, play, feel for us: that's all Enrique desires, conscious as never before this time that there is no trick, but that there is a love that seems to exclude him, a profound love that has grown, even by correspondence, while he was slamming doors or splitting red-haired heads with bottles, a head, nevertheless, that the friend who stayed behind in Paris and who has now come here would never do anything to, apart from combing, caressing, and kissing again. Enrique wants melodies, but reality demands dialogues and words. Enrique wants to elevate the moment to the level of poetry when truth requires hard words, plain words, prose.

And that is serious. Serious because Juan Manuel may understand that Mía is silent because she's good, because she's delicate, because she's dumb, because she's well-mannered, because she's an idiot, because she's affectionate, and because that man is the father her children adore. And that, too, is serious, very serious, because Juan Manuel, since he arrived, has not fallen into the easy trap of whiskey or wine plus music. And so, without drinking a drop, he waits like a chess player who sees that what's staggering is not a king, a queen, or a rook but an entire strategy, the total conception of something that a while ago ceased to be a play of melodies and their lyrics. Juan Manuel's silence does not signal acceptance, and that is obvious in shouts.

And in shouts it's also possible to note that there is something in him that has reached its limit, that might explode at any moment, on this night when no one in the huge house will dare to turn on the record player, which, suddenly, with no explanation whatsoever, Juan Manuel turned off during the afternoon, once, as you might say, and for all. And now a tremendous night weighs on Trinity Beach, and outside a strong wind is blowing, and somewhere upstairs there must be an open window or a badly fastened shutter, something flapping in the wind from time to time, in an enervating way. Fernanda María has collapsed onto the sofa, and at her side a lamp is burning, and even though her hair is a mess and she herself is a total mess, she's beautiful. Juan Manuel doesn't want to hide it from her, so he's repeated three times in thirty seconds, You're beautiful, my love, really beautiful, Mía. And now it's been an interminable ten minutes since he stood up, poured himself his first glass of red wine in five days, sipped barely a drop, and walked over to her. He slowly bends over, kisses her forehead, caresses her face, and for a long, expansive time caresses her shoulders, and when he goes back to the armchair where he's been seated every day, every morning, every afternoon, and every night, he begins to tell her how, day by day and hour by hour, with words that seem carried by the wind from the darkened sea, from the invisible breakers, the way in which he's begun to love forever, the irrepressible intensity with which he is living that love this night.

"In sum, nothing none of us didn't already know," he interrupts himself, from time to time, as if expecting a commentary.

And it is terribly serious, for it is 2:00 A.M., and that commentary has not come. Or should he have taken as a commentary the tears, the runny nose, and the hiccups of weeping with which Fernanda María managed to silence him once or twice? Enrique, too, has proffered the odd desperate and drunken sob, but then he's completely hidden himself in the total silence of the fugitive who knows that the slightest false step will reveal him. Juan Manuel glances at his watch at 2:24 A.M., stands up, again approaches the sofa where Fernanda María is raising her face to look at him, to try to figure out his intentions, to make him understand simply that, yes, she has read those intentions in his eyes and that, yes, let's go, and here I am, yours, Juan Manuel Carpio.

"Let's go to the motel, my love."

"Yes. I want to go, Juan Manuel Carpio. But it seems I'm not strong enough yet, so I'd prefer you carry me, that you carry me in your arms, tenderly and happily, like the happiest brides in movies."

"We were brothers, Juan Manuel," stutters Enrique painfully, sunken in his armchair and his life.

"Believe me, Enrique, none of this is against you. Believe me when I tell you that everything has always been against us, against Fernanda and me, for a long time now, for simply and plainly too long a time, suddenly, tonight."

"I know, man. But it's also been against me. And it still is."

"But Enrique, let's be honest, you haven't helped things to change very much."

"That's true, Juan Manuel. I didn't know how to help. Or I've only helped with more sadness and anguish, with bigger complications and problems. That's the truth, brother Juan Manuel. And I've also been a beast, a savage."

"That has to be judged by Fernanda, Enrique."

"Fernanda? Judge? There wouldn't be a guilty party in the history of humanity, my brother, if Fernanda were named judge for even a quarter of an hour. You and I know what a silly idea that is."

"In any case, right now I'm going to the motel, and I want her to come with me. And you just heard her yourself. Fernanda wants me to carry her in my arms, tenderly and happily, like the happiest brides in movies."

"Tomorrow I'll disappear, Juan Manuel . . . So just wait until tomorrow, please . . . And you, too, Fernanda, just wait, please . . . Wait . . . Wait . . . Wait even though I can't think why or for whose sake, but wait."

Extremely serious were the words Fernanda María said then. Because she said that, as always, in the most brutal and absurd form, but also in the most concrete form in the world, that the three of us would end up parting ways. She would go to Oakland, or some other, better, place in California until the day came when she could return to El Salvador, and Enrique would return to San Salvador until the day came when he could permanently return to Chile.

"And you, Juan Manuel Carpio, my love, have you decided to return to Peru or not? Maybe it's because you aren't
waiting for the most favorable moment to do it?"

"I want to leave Paris, that much is true. But I could wait
there and meet up with you in El Salvador the day when you,
Fernanda, can go back and Enrique leaves the field open to
us. But I wasn't talking about any of that a moment ago, Mía.
Or have you already forgotten my invitation?"

"No, Juan Manuel Carpio. This is the moment when Fernanda María de la Trinidad del Monte Montes doesn't forget
a single word, good or bad, that's ever emerged from you,
from your life. Sung or spoken, let that be understood."

"Well, then?"

"Well, let me explain to Enrique that I can't wait until
tomorrow to go to the motel with you, because you are you,
and not him—the one who's leaving tomorrow. And let me
say to him as well that I also love him and that he should wait
for me until tomorrow, please, because there are two children
who've spent whole days playing on the beach, virtually
abandoned, almost numb from this cold and damp, and it's
high time they returned to their own home and to some sort
of order. And believe me, gentlemen—because I'm saying
this to you, too, my ever-so-beloved Juan Manuel Carpio—
that it's high time the trio of poor jerks that we are return
to their habitual discord. What are we going to do, when it
seems it's the only thing we're fit for? Or do you two see
another solution to the problem? In any case, I'm open to
suggestions . . ."

"I've been suggesting the motel now for hours and hours,
Mía. And I really don't know at what point things got twisted
around and everyone began philosophizing."

"What a bastard you are, my love! But, after all, I love you for that, too, and that's why you charm me so, Juan Manuel Carpio."

"Well?"

"No, nothing, my love. But I was hoping you'd give Enrique a say in all this."

"The three of us in my motel?"

"Whatever Enrique wants, but let it be understood that I only have eyes and ears and lips and arms and legs for you, my love. And that to Enrique I can only say, Cheers, comrade."

"Agreed, comrade, cheers. Cheers and to your health. I tell you, I need a good night's sleep, because all the time that I have left in this shitty country I want to dedicate to being with Rodrigo and Mariana. Hours and hours, every day. I just realized that's what I should have been doing from the beginning, and now I have an immense need to recover the days I've lost drinking. I'm leaving behind locking myself away in this room, the wine, the whiskey, the music, the drunk daddy. I mean it, comrade, so for the last time, cheers."

"So turn on the record player and leave with something happy playing. Any song that doesn't talk about good-byes, Paris, or airports. A song that absolutely does not talk about anything that concerns us, please, Enrique."

Listening to three or four songs and drinking a glass of wine was an elegant way to wait for Enrique to disappear into the upper reaches of the mansion, by now almost completely darkened, locking himself up in that bedroom to which Fernanda would not return until after my departure, one week later, because I couldn't get an earlier flight. Truth be told, I couldn't conceal from Fernanda a certain admiration for the bravery and calm with which her husband had witnessed the preparations for our brief voyage to the motel across the way. Considering how ferociously violent Enrique could be, especially when he drank too much, I had feared that at some moment during our first night he'd jump on top of Fernanda or me and try to kill both of us.

"Right now, he's completely incapable of anything," Fernanda explained, telling me that Enrique didn't speak a single word of English, and that she knew him well enough to know very well that no matter how surrounded he was by his family, he felt totally helpless in California, and that in no time he would adopt the attitude of a lapdog, even with his children, in view of the fact that both of them could make their way fairly well in English, never felt lost anywhere, and acted with all the independence and ease of a united brother and sister, eight and five, respectively, but with a quantity of experience for which even some adolescents would envy them—in certain practical matters.

"Poor Enr—"

"Do me the favor of listening to me very carefully, Juan Manuel Carpio. One more word about my late husband and there won't be arms enough in this world, not this night or any other night, to carry me to the motel across the way."

"Cheers, my love, and let's be gone. By which I mean, come over here so I can carry and adore you once and for all. To the motel, James, and don't spare the horses!"

We would go back to María Cecilia and Paul's mansion only for lunch and dinner, and sometimes not even that, and the truth is that as far as the semi-simple gringo and his wife were concerned, nothing could have mattered less to them in this life than the behavior of Fernanda and her singer during their long disappearances and brief appearances in search of food and news of Rodrigo and Mariana, both happy to be able to spend hours and hours conversing and strolling the beach with their daddy. Mía and I also would bundle up every morning and go out to take a delightful walk on the beach, and without fail we would run into that huge man with pitch-black hair walking in the opposite direction tightly holding the hand of a little girl and a little boy in each of his savage paws.

The fact that it all seemed so natural to us, that the world seemed so incredibly natural now that each of us had found his proper place in it, now that Enrique was everything for Mariana and Rodrigo, and was only for them, in the same way that Mía was everything for me, and I for her, directed by Divine Providence, at least for this little week in Trinity Beach, to be exclusively for one another. It even happened one day that we got into Mía's car and without telling anyone disappeared for the entire weekend and went all the way to Monterey and Big Sur, from beach to beach and motel to motel, loving each other and laughing all the time and really managing to forget that all of it would have a new, though familiar, ending, and very soon. But in those moments not even that familiar ending mattered to us, although I know very well that Fernanda was suffering as much as I was every time we abandoned a motel, every time one more door was locked behind us forever, one more of the doors we had left to pass through in those new seven days that, this time for sure, seemed fallen from heaven. After all, they'd arisen in the very heart of her family, and right before the eyes of a husband for whom I suddenly was feeling a brutal affection and sorrow.

Mía, on the other hand, seemed to hate him for the first time in her life, and never stopped explaining to me that as soon as I left, she would have to pay a high price for all this freedom, humility, and generosity. It would be then that Enrique would screamingly throw in her face the horrible suffering his sacrifice for us had caused him, that from now on he would cling to the bottle, completely abandon himself, not make even the slightest effort to contact some American photographers whose addresses he had in his notebook. The reality I had to accept was that the time between the day I took the plane for New York, and then Paris, to the night of horror, when, without knowing a thing about where he was or how or with whom, Enrique might split her head open again with a bottle, could be extremely short.

"Mía, if I could only stay . . ."

"It would have to be forever, my love, and that's impossible."

"But listen, now Enrique knows everything."

"Don't forget that the children are his, Juan Manuel, and that they adore him. And the one who possesses the love of those kids has me."

"It seems incredible, Fernanda. I've never felt your love so strongly, but even so, it suddenly seems as if you've never been less mine, so completely not mine."

"Just remember always that everything went wrong for us right from the start, my love, except our loving each other this way."

I spent the last afternoon sitting with Mía in her sister and Paul's mansion. We also ate there, so I could say good-

bye to the entire family and thank them profusely and everything. Later, she and I crossed over to the motel for one last
night of the kind when neither my hands nor my words ever
tired of caressing her, when my advice never stopped offering
her a security and protection in which Fernanda believed
blindly, in the least realistic fashion in the world, yes, one
hundred percent and blindly, as she believed in few things, or
perhaps nothing, in this life. And that was the result of my
letters, of those long folios crammed with every bit of nonsense that passed through my head, but all intended to make
her feel strong, beautiful, desired, missed, extremely valuable
as a woman, folios that also very often corresponded exten-
sively and profoundly to doubts and anxieties and worries
that she revealed to me and which were so natural in a young
woman who'd been educated for such a superior destiny, or,
at any rate, a destiny so completely different from the destiny
that had been dragging her from one place to another, oblig-
ing her, twice now, to abandon a country where she was
comfortable, and with two kids besides.

And yet a day never dawned—I'm absolutely convinced
of this—to find Fernanda María sad, thanks to Rodrigo or
Mariana, nor was the little toy boat the three of them sailed
through the real storm of their lives ever adrift, and all because of that extremely pure mix of an all-powerful capacity
to see the good side of things, and an innate joy in living
and enjoying everything, and that strength and astuteness of
Tarzan that Mía kept on developing without even realizing it,
in her eagerness to make sure her children had at least something of the great portion of good she had in her own childhood, and that, later on, in their adolescence and maturity,
her offspring would have more of the same as she moved

them forward, as if the road of life, no matter how many traps and trips it set for her here and there, was formidably destined to carry her, always with her adored Rodrigo and Mariana at her side, to a much better world than this one.

Of the next morning, at the airport in San Francisco, I remember only an extremely long silence, coffee that was quite bitter, terrible orange juice, and Mía's eyes occasionally focusing on my own while her hands wandered along my thighs under the table in a horrible cafeteria.

"I love you, Red."

"But I'm going back where Enrique is."

"I couldn't care less about your Araucanian, skinny. As far as I'm concerned, he can tie his balls into a bow tie."

"My very great and beloved and authentic Juan Manuel."

"I'm with you one hundred percent, Mía, you know that."

"My well-tested friend for many years."

"Even if the next few months are tough, let's hope they're battles we win, right, Mía?"

"Count on it."

"Ciao, my love."

"We'll see each other in our next letter, Juan Manuel."

"Right, my love. Letters should be portraits of the soul, or something like that, because you and I are as photogenic as can be, speaking in an epistolary sense."

"And that's one more brotherly link between us, Juan Manuel Carpio."

"What you just said is a wonderful farewell. Even if it is an honor I crave, I don't deserve it."

Berkeley, June 30

My most beloved Juan Manuel Carpio,

Finally, with some tranquility, I can answer your last letter—which came like a much-needed embrace in the middle of many complications I don't even know how to begin to tell you about.

Okay, the first is that Enrique (the same day you left, he embarked on an interminable bender) left for Chile, leaving me in peace for the time being, in spite of the fact that circumstances here are a bit difficult. But I'm sure that they'll have to get better soon. As I told you, I was working for a while in Rodrigo's little school. When I quit to come over to Berkeley, it turned out they had to charge me for Rodrigo's tuition, which left me totally bankrupt and in debt— this is all on top of the cost of Enrique's flight.

But all that will take care of itself, and it's stupid to tell you about it. Besides, inside I feel that none of it is of the slightest importance, because, bankrupt and all, I'm calmer than I've been for months. I'm living in a house that belongs to an old high school classmate of mine. She has two kids, both grown up and very sweet. And she is helping me a great deal in moral terms, so I think I'm even recovering a little security in life.

I'm writing you today from the peace of her garden. Her carpenter husband is having a siesta, and the kids are playing. She's working. She's a librarian. It's funny, but I ended up in the house of the poorest of my classmates. Or maybe she's the only poor one.

The others all live in California mansions and palaces, sometimes of a taste, well, you could either die laughing or break down in tears. But, well, as we all know, my beloved Juan Manuel Carpio, with money you can buy everything, or almost everything. Horror, to be sure, you can buy with a mine, an entire bank, or an oil field. But here, in the house of my poorest friend, all squeezed together, I've been happy, and I haven't felt so much pressure. I hope this tranquility lasts.

Enrique, of course, never tried to get a job. And he never called the photographers whose names he was carrying around in his notebook. Luckily his parents helped us a little from Chile. And then suddenly we got an urgent call that his mother was seriously ill and he had to leave the next day. He feels fine about the trip, which was something he just had to do, so he didn't have to think or drink about it much. Poor lady, his mother. I barely got to know her in Santiago, but she writes me, and it makes me sad to think she doesn't know her only grandchildren. No one knows what's going to happen to her.

On Monday, yesterday in fact, I went to Rodrigo's school to pick up my check, and they informed me they only owe me $200 for a whole month's work since they had to take out for Rodrigo's tuition. It's my fault for not having a clear contract. But there's nothing to be done. Luckily, Anne, my poorest friend, is a woman who's fought a lot, so she's a placid and benevolent rock whose house breathes strength and sweetness.

And now with regard to you and the memory of your visit, Juan Manuel Carpio. You can't imagine what the certainty of your affection for everything mine has always meant to me, amid all the tough situations that have come up. Just by existing, and because of the existence of your affection, you've always given me a great deal of security. I love you and your songs, which are getting more tender, more beautiful, and finer every day. They're always with me and fill me with courage and make me smile as I walk bravely through the streets of Berkeley, even feeling that sense of health and optimism typical of the moment when Tarzan dives into the water.

Yesterday, I ran into a couple who said they were going to Paris, so even though I know you've been dividing your time between Majorca and the City of Light, I sent you a book with them, because they seemed like serious people, nice, and formal, the kind with whom you could send a present without their losing it. I hope it works out that way. I really like D. H. Lawrence. And if you can't figure out the dedication I wrote in it, just look up *elephants* in the index, and you'll see a title, "Elephants Are Slow to Mate," and I'm sure you'll instantly think of us when you read that "elephants, those mastodons, are slow to domesticate." But at the end it turns out that elephants are very good, the most docile and noble of all animals. Very slow and very sure. Doesn't that remind you of someone? Or a pair of someones? And I hug and kiss you again, Juan Manuel Carpio, as I walk and smile in Berkeley.

Today I was out looking for a job. I went to the university, and there are lots of good jobs, but the only professor friend I have there is on sabbatical in Buenos Aires. We'll wait and see. We'll be patient.

I reread this letter and it's a jumble, like a conversation on a ferocious summer afternoon with flies everywhere. Write me here, please:

c/o Anne Gotman
1893 Londonderry St.
Berkeley, CA 94710 U.S.A.

I hug you, kiss you, and love you so much.
Your Fernanda

A few notes remain in the copy of the notebook Fernanda sent me. They probably belong to my stolen answer to this letter and even to some of those that follow it. I thank her for sending the D. H. Lawrence book, which luckily found me in Paris and not in Majorca, where things were going better and better for me. I was working more, both performing and composing, so my stays there were getting longer and longer. Anyway, I'm bringing together some of the sentences from the notebook, because in doing so I again feel the marvelous illusion that the correspondence between me and Mía never stopped, never slowed down until it disappeared, I am tempted to say, like everything else in this life. Finally, these are sentences that delighted Mía. That's why she copied them out. Only for that reason. And by way of thanks, she sent me a copy of that notebook, which I'm using today to respond, even if the response is imaginary, to the love of a great friend and the friendship of my greatest love.

Paris, July 1981

Ever so beloved Mía,

Infinite thanks for the stupendous book. And I extend that infinite to include my parallel thanks for the tender way you deal with me. In an interminable earlier letter from Palma, which you don't seem to have received but whose truthfulness I swear to—giving my word as a gentleman—I speak to you of the complete love I feel for you. Perhaps now, as I write to you this time, I won't attain the same affectionate warmth, but it isn't necessary. Because right now you're the one with all the warmth, and you just give it away.

With regard to your personal economic program, which right now seems more like prestidigitation, it would seem that divine grace will have to illuminate you very soon. And I can say such a gross thing because of that old saying that goes, "In the house of the poor, God will always provide." Also because I want you to know and count on the fact that if God doesn't exist, I'll step in.

I'll dig my heels in deeper: if you stand firm a while longer, this whirlwind will pass you by. And you're hearing it from someone who escaped a whirlwind of his own—of a different magnitude, granted, but it was a whirlwind nonetheless. I'm no model to be emulated, but I'm certainly no worse than my fellow men. Besides, like you, deep down I'm a timid soul who fights, though in my case the matter is getting serious, because for some time now I've been noticing that, though it's rather premature, I've got gray hair on my balls.

Forward, my beloved, open a path as you move ahead. Don't give up, and at the same time receive a landslide (but completely clean) of hugs and enormous affection. And like Valle-Inclán's character Tirano Banderas, I'm always at the ready.

Juan Manuel

P.S.: Very soon, at least insofar as my desire is concerned, I'm off to Majorca. So don't write me in Paris, unless I'm left crippled or I get warts along with the gray hairs on my balls, something that would keep me from flashing my charms when I close in for the kill.

Furthermore. I forgot to tell you in my previous letter (it's a sign of love, the fact that once again our letters have crossed paths) that when I got off the plane that carried me from San Francisco to New York I caught an air-conditioning cold, the kind that makes you piss ice cubes. I survived thanks to millionaire doses of antibiotics and vitamins.

Okay, now your most humble servant hugs and cheers you. And more hugs (oppressive) from your old buddy.

Juan Manuel Singer (I heard your kids say that, back there in *Remember Acapulco*, when it was cold).

Berkeley, November 12, 1981

My adored Juan Manuel Carpio,

It's been so long that I haven't seen you, that I haven't felt your nearness, that it's almost like a lightning flash to suddenly feel a desire to be with you, to talk and listen to you, and to walk together. I adore your letters filled with love. Besides, as much as they help me for what they say, they help me just as much for making me laugh.

Anyway, all that for two things, or three, or four, or a thousand. A few days ago, Rafael Dulanto called to tell me he'd been with you and with Don Julián d'Octeville in Majorca and that in your house in Palma the first thing people see when they walk in is a huge photo of the two of us, which led me to conclude that in some corner of your heart I'm always present in some way, as you are in me. Even though I know just how limited the two of us are, and also how unlimited the two of us are—we're simply useless and lost when it comes to this love thing.

And today, thanks to the long embrace that goes around the world of the people who love you, Charlie Boston called me from Rome to tell me he's going to visit you and that he's bringing you a series of new musical concepts which, he thinks, may well be very useful for your work.

The rest you already know. I always love you so much and get so excited whenever someone's just seen you or is just about to see you. That's how it was with Rafael and Charlie. They spoke about practically nothing else but you, and I went so wild that I couldn't control myself anymore. So I telephoned you and was talking to you for hours. And now I'm dying of shame that I had to reverse the charges on you, but here I'm fighting like a cat that's flat on its back, and it seems my salary covers nothing. Well, that seems to be a very common problem, a kind of pandemic, though it seems things are going much better for you now. There's nothing to be done, as far as the call is concerned you'll just have to pretend you took me out for a heavenly meal and we ate excellent oysters washed down with Dom Perignon, and we laughed and had the best time ever. Because that's how happy I was to hear you.

I understand that even though you're very comfortable in Majorca and despite the nice house you could buy for pennies in Minorca, you still insist that you want to go back to Lima. With each day that passes, it becomes harder to live outside our own customs. It's terribly hard for me to speak English (even though I'm supposed to be bilingual), and every so often I start talking with a hideous accent, just to feel comfortable, to know that after all is said and done it isn't my language and that I won't have to speak it for the rest of my life. It's funny, I always liked speaking English more than French, but right now I get no pleasure from it, and it actually seems a cold and ugly language to me. I don't like to say bad words, because they sound horrible to me. And the good ones just won't come out. I think I'll have to leave or start com-

municating with people through notes, or sign language, as if I were mute.

Well, then, Juan Manuel, I'll tell you once again:
it was fun, joyful, amusing, intelligent, grand just to
hear you. And even though it shouldn't be up to me
to tell you this, watch out for the blessed telephone.
Those bills can shiver even the biggest pair of balls,
and put holes in the pockets of the richest man,
which is what I read somewhere: Paul Getty, the
millionaire oil man, protected himself by having an
extremely complicated pay-phone system installed.

And now I'm waiting for that letter of yours,
which never arrives soon enough.

Your Fernanda

San Francisco, November 24, 1981

My most beloved Juan Manuel,

Your letter finally came, so full of real tenderness
and such kind wishes for us that I was very moved. I
imagine you've been worried about the kids and me,
and we really deserve to be worried about, here in
these parts, like children of the storm. But time,
though these are hardly the best of times, is very useful to me. Little by little, with a great deal of happiness, I can feel the anger and hatred I've felt coming
to an end, along with the sensation of fraud in my
relationship with Enrique. The kids, even though
they need me a lot, also help me, because they're so
good and so pure. The mere fact of having recovered

my serenity is worth the price of all the sacrifices I've made, which aren't even sacrifices because there wasn't much else to be done, and all the effort expended until today was the only possible way.

To feel the strong ties of friendship and love with which you support me has been like having an angel at my side. I hope Enrique, now in his own country, has found his old friends and has calmed down. He hasn't written me in quite a while, and I can only hope the time has been well spent for him. He's had two shows of his photographs. That will give him strength, to see his work appreciated, just as feeling myself loved and respected has done me good.

It's really sad, but with Enrique I always felt rejected and at the same time used. For my little woman's ego, it was a real disaster. I think I'd even forgotten that I'm also a woman like other women, and that I don't have to take being treated like dirt, without any respect. Poor Enrique, I don't think the problem is a lack of love, but what a terrible way of loving me he has. Now, right at this moment, I don't have any idea what he's feeling, because, as I said, he hasn't written me lately. But I do hope that like me he's recovered some serenity, so he can see things with respect and love, thinking of what's right for both of us and the children.

Only time will have the last word, but today I'm thanking time for the peace I've gotten back. I look at myself in the mirror, and sometimes I smile. I fix myself up, and sometimes I even feel pretty. I play with my kids and enjoy them. This timid progress, step by step, slowly it justifies being far from everything I know. Besides, in reality no one can be in El Salvador right now, and, as you say, running back to Chile doesn't make sense without first slowly looking things over and thinking it out carefully. We're not in any shape to be running around the world only to end up with nothing but bitterness.

Write me. Did you know that very often I take my best steps after reading one of your letters?

Love, kisses, and hugs from

Your Fernanda

San Francisco, December 10, 1981

Dear Juan Manuel Carpio,

They've got me trapped here in an enormous office with huge windows that overlook the bay, on a beautiful blue day with little sailboats under the bridges. And opposite me, a secretary who's so efficient that she answers telephones, types, takes dictation, all at the same time, while I'm sitting at my typewriter, turning out a letter full of love.

It seems they've placed me in the office of a vice president in this gigantic company, Rogers and Brooks. And his secretary is so territorial about her work that she won't even let me answer the telephone, nothing that would cause her to lose an atom of her prestige. You can't imagine how annoying she is. And when you answer the telephone, you've got to be incredibly careful, because it might—God help us—be Mr. Brooks himself or Mr. Rogers himself, or Henry Kissinger, or George Shultz, or Reagan himself. And you might say any dumb thing into the phone. An enormous shame that the job is so tedious, because if it weren't I'd sign on permanently, since it would mean more money, and, no doubt, some measure of prestige of the kind that doesn't matter to me. But a bit more money wouldn't hurt. Even so, I'm not going to accept. I'm not really such a good secretary, and I don't think I would survive very long in the midst of such efficiency. I can't even figure out why they put me here.

Last night I was thinking about how much time people spend talking about music, remembering music. Your last letter was almost exclusively about music, songs we've danced to together, records you need, records that are filling up your apartment. And seeing where we both live now, all the photographs Enrique took related to music. I have one of a pianist and another of some tango dancers, and a poster from his last show. I'm sending you one, because I think you'll like it. The show is all about solitude and music, its title is "Sentimental Beauty Parlor," because all the poor and vulgar beauticians have their heads stuck into enormous Victrola horns, completely forgetting about their clients who are also lulled into sleep by the music. The poster is from a whole series of photos with Victrolas, and I don't know if you saw any of them when you were here, though I wouldn't say we had much time left over for art.

The kids and I are getting ready for Christmas. We're going to see *The Nutcracker* at the San Francisco Opera. It's a really beautiful show. There are also ancient Spanish chants in a church and medieval Christmas music in another. We want to go see as many of those things as we can—things we really should take advantage of. Mariana is very excited, and Rodrigo, too, because she takes ballet lessons with the San Francisco company, and some of her classmates are going to be in *The Nutcracker.* Rodrigo swells up with pride about anything related to his sister.

As you see, we're talking about music again.

I hope you have a nice Christmas. And I hug and kiss you with the almost holy sort of mystical love that gets into you this time of year. And with music of the kind you like, of course.

Your Fernanda

Berkeley, December 19, 1981

My adored and indisputably indefatigable Juan Manuel,

I just can't tell you how happy it makes me that your new record has arrived and that you never get tired of me!

I'm listening to you, and every song is better than the last, and each and every one of them is and are my favorites. And the kids listen to you simply from listening to me listening to you. It even looks as if they're beginning to understand you and beginning to like your music, its melodies, its lyrics, your voice, which they recognize, Juan Manuel Singer.

Something's working just right, my love, something's just as true as true can be. If you go on gaining balance, you're going to turn out your best work. You're on your way up, Juan Manuel Carpio, my singer.

I won't write any more because I'm still listening to you, still adoring you. I won't write any more because no one can do so many marvelous things at the same time. But one last thing more: thanks for calling the album *Trinidad Motel,* knowing that the motel part exists only in our experience. But that's what you make me feel with so much grace and tenderness, that thing about how love can bring a person to the highest level of discomfort and the most sweaty and cold and happy sordidness. You're so deep, so sad, so funny that, whether you like it or not, I'm not writing another line to you.

Yours musically and absolutely,
Fernanda

The next is one of the very few letters Fernanda María copied in its entirety in that notebook she photocopied for me. I imagine she did it because she'd been robbed of years of our faithful and beloved correspondence and, fearing a new loss, she copied it from beginning to end in that handwriting which was so much a part of her, something between clear and ordered and fast and catastrophic. So here comes my answer, full of a joy as great as the one she felt about the reception of that new fruit of my travels and songs.

Palma de Mallorca

January of this happy new year

Fabulous and Grand Fernanda María,

I see my record was like the flag on top of Mount Everest for you, as it should be with a friend like you, who'd forgive me even if I married another woman and named you civil, penal, military, and even ocular witness. So if you dose yourself with tablespoonfuls of my *Motel Trinidad,* look out for what the gringos call ego—and which has made Argentina necessarily so large in its geography, as they had to make room for such a tremendous, Freudian ego-grove, stuffed, additionally, with psychoanalytic anguish, because, no doubt, farther south, from Patagonia down, you might say, there awaits them *le néant* of the frozen end of the world. In conclusion, my ego is dangerously huge now that it extends beyond the edges of the largest of the Balearic Islands and begins to project itself toward the Ibizas and Minorcas, the Cabreras and Formenteras.

With one arm I clasp you in a sustained embrace, while the other simultaneously squeezes and squashes your little thingamabob with all due respect and honor.

Juan Manuel

Berkeley, February 2, 1982

My adored Juan Manuel Carpio,

I don't know when this letter will reach you, with all your coming and going from Palma to Paris. But I'd like it to reach you quickly for two reasons. The first is that I'm going to have to travel myself soon. It seems that Enrique's mom is still seriously ill in Chile and demanding to see her grandchildren. So the trip has now become inevitable. I'll leave with the children at the end of this month. With a thousand fears that they're going to want to keep us there, but thinking that it's an injustice, knowing how badly off the poor lady is, to keep her only grandchilden here, tanning in California. The plan is to stay in Chile for a month, more or less. On the way south, we'll spend two weeks in San Salvador to see my family (the specific danger for us has completely disappeared, and besides, I'm curious to see with my own eyes how my poor little country is doing), so we'll be getting to Chile in mid-March. It seems right around the corner to me and sends shivers down my spine. Let's hope it's a good trip.

Okay, don't stop writing. If you can write before I leave on this horrible trip, it would be really great to find out how you are. We'll be here all of February.

Your record plays on and on and on in this music house.

I love you more and more every day,
Your Fernanda

California, for just a little bit more.
February 18, 1982

My most beloved Juan Manuel Carpio,

You're right, and I felt the same thing, that in leaving this beautiful, sunny, peaceful land, which has been good, calm, and solitary for me, I'm leaving, in a certain sense, your house, which is so much like mine, always full of music, nostalgia, and solitude. I don't know when we'll see each other again. I don't even know what I'm getting into, or why, to tell you the truth. But in some way, this rest period, which was so necessary, is over. It's been so good for me that sometimes I think that this solitude is the real air of my life, and that in this air I'm fine. Being so awkward with all the old connections.

But now we're on our way back to all the old connections. Giving in, at last, to the pressure. And I think that's why you and I aren't together. Both of us have respected everything in an incredible way. Neither of us would allow the other to be pressured. Out of fear, respect, love, because of everything you are and what I love in you, like a presence that is so near, like a mirror that only knows my most beautiful me. And it's for love, as well, of that beautiful me that I've never put pressure on your life in moments when perhaps a tiny weight would have tipped the balance in our favor. Neither of us has ever dared to be that weight.

In any case, I love you forever, and that at least is something.

I don't know if I'll see you soon. Believe me, Juan Manuel, there's nothing in this life I'd like more than to see you very soon, to be with you even before this letter is in your hands. I'm asking the impossible, I know, and I'm not going to make a fuss, or else I'll get so desperate the kids will notice.

Even so, I'm going on: I think because of that mysterious date I'd like to have with you I'd be capable of postponing my arrival in Santiago. Is all that pure insanity? What do you think? Will it be possible that the two of us will always find hands more pressing than ours, more possessive, and more demanding?

I think life will tell us that. Luckily, I still have faith in life, and that faith saves me from a lot.

Besides, I firmly believe that everything that happens between us will be good, and that makes me very calm.

I hug and kiss you, good night for today and until I don't know when.

Your Fernanda María

That time, luck was with us, Fernanda and me, lots of it, because just when I was reading her letter about the trip to Chile with the stopover in El Salvador, I received a very handsome offer to sing in a hotel in Mexico City. So there could be nothing more logical than to improvise a side trip there, children and all, so as not to complicate Fernanda's affairs needlessly. My beauty, Mía—I think she guessed what was going to happen the second she picked up the phone over in Berkeley and heard my voice.

"You're a genius, Juan Manuel! A genius, a genius, a genius! And the most wonderful thing I've heard in many, many moons!"

"Know something? I'd like Enrique to know about this. Present it to him, if you like, as a four- or five-day picnic— with tents in the Zócalo, tamales and tacos, Coca-Colas, and hard-boiled eggs. I would feel better knowing that he's been told, especially that he's told that the kids will make this stop before the stop in El Salvador, and that all of this will slow down the arrival of the del Monte Montes clan a few more days."

"You know, Juan Manuel, I like your idea. It seems correct and honest to me. But I don't know how Enrique's going to react, especially since his mother is so sick."

"I tell you, Mía, despite all the tenderness and respect I feel for him, all that stuff about his dear mama's serious illness sounds like a trick to me, like a trap he's set for you and the kids to drag you to Chile to have you at his side. Anyway, I don't know what to say, Mía, but I'll bet you it's the least serious serious illness you'll ever see in your life. But time will tell. In any case, I'll be waiting for all of you starting on March 1, in the Gran Hotel del Centro. I think it's on a street called September 17th, which is only a few steps from the Zócalo, and any taxi will get you there. But please tell Enrique."

"How do you think he'll take it?"

"He'll act the way friends should act with wives who love or loved their friends."

"I'm in the first category."

"In this and in everything else, Mía. So, we'll see each other in, as the song says, *Mexico beautiful and beloved,* in two shakes of a dead lamb's tail. I'll have everything reserved and ready."

"And the children will be happy to see Chapultepec Park and the Anthropology Museum. And me, listening to you sing every night."

"And I'll be happy every night too, but only when I finish singing and the kids are softly snoring in the next room."

And that's how it went in Mexico City. Just as perfectly as the unforgettable weekend we had with the kids in Cuernavaca, singing them old Spanish lullabies and flying kites, stuffing ourselves with tacos and enchiladas and laughing our heads off at the clowns in a circus that was so poor that the Black Magician reappeared in a blond wig, transformed into the German King of the Trapeze, Herr Boetticher, and then, a few minutes later, he was also a Russian lion tamer, Vladimir Popov, and at the end he went so far as to trade his race, his gender, and his nationality to turn into the terrifying bearded lady of the circus—a true circus of poverty.

Later, back in the capital, and heading for one more airport, for more farewells, Mía and I lived the only non-sad good-bye of all those that fell to us in so many years of seeing each other and having to stop seeing each other. The fact is the kids were delighted with me and I with them, and now, for them, the trip would go on just as happily in El Salvador, where they were going to see grandparents, uncles, and aunts, and just as happy, too, when they got to where Daddy was, in Chile, where, well, unfortunately, their paternal grandmother, whom they were going to meet for the first time, was not in the best of health. All this made Mía and me say good-bye—why deny it, when it speaks so well of us?—

you'd almost say delighted with life. And there you have it—
the couple of idiots we always were with regard to our love
and in everything regarding proper respect for others, their
caprices, their feelings, virtues, defects, exiles, binges, slammed
doors, and even their smashing bottles on heads. And so,
yes, definitively, so, Mister David Herbert Lawrence, elephants, those gigantic beasts, those tremendous mastodons,
are domesticated very slowly.

San Salvador, March 15, 1982

Juan Manuel Carpio, my love,

How much I've needed you these past days!
The days in Mexico were so beautiful and filled with
things. They've left my entire memory of you so
strong and huge that I smile to myself feeling you still
near.

My family here is fine. My immediate family is
still loving and welcoming, the sea still warm, the
oysters delicious, the air delightful, the shell necklaces still touching. My trees have grown. I have an
offer from people who want to buy the house. I just
don't know. Anyway, we're going to stay the whole
month of March and then see. I'll be needing your
letters. If you can, write to: 189 Pasaje Romero,
Colonia Flor, San Salvador.

As always, in everything there's something that
works out and something that doesn't. Seeing my
family was excellent, but my friend Charlotte and her
husband abandoned the country last week and with

them Fabio, one of my dearest childhood friends. So I practically won't be seeing any friends. Besides, the bombs and murders are still a fact of life. So going out is hard. Without Charlotte, her husband, Yves, Fabio (my buddy, remember?), and Clara, my best friends, going out's no fun.

But something much worse happened inside me when I came back here, my love. Something I want to tell you, because you've always helped me feel as strong as Tarzan, but suddenly it's as if there's been a disaster in the jungle and Tarzan finds himself all alone and surrounded, afraid, not daring to swing from a vine, unable even to dive into the river out of fear of crocodiles, which, besides, are in the streets, the houses, the eyes of people lurking in every corner of life in this country.

Everything happened like this, my love, my Juan Manuel Carpio, my beloved friend: I took Rodrigo to see a Tarzan movie, one of the classics with Johnny Weissmuller, a real oldie, from when you and I were kids. And I don't know why, but I felt so much fear when the lights went out. I felt a fear that was so, so strong that I think I'll never get over it.

I couldn't even have fun with the childish adventures in the movie. I could only feel fear, lots of it, too much.

But the worst, my love, came when we left. Because I was trying to keep Rodrigo from noticing anything—that I was trembling, that I was dying of fear of being in my own country, with him in a movie theater, or in just any street in the city, and in broad daylight. Yes, I was making a really enormous effort to keep Rodrigo from noticing anything at all, when I heard him ask me if Tarzan had tonsils. And the more I didn't answer him, because my tongue and throat were all twisted up, because my entire life fighting here, there, and everywhere was all twisted up in my tongue and throat, the more he asked me, once and for all, Mom, answer me, does Tarzan have tonsils?

From that moment on I've locked myself in my living room, I've stopped eating, and I only listen to your *Motel Trinidad* record, which I carry with me wherever I go. And I only think about one thing as I listen. Going to Mexico to meet up with you, no matter that we told Enrique, was cheating a bit. Could that, then, be the magic? To know how to cheat a bit and to know how to do it at just the right time? In any case, today, under the bower that completely shades the picture window in the living room, under this sun I sense outside, opposite that sea I neither want to visit nor am capable of visiting without you, and with that sad black breeze that's come into the living room, I hug and kiss you and, as in that Mexican song, *I wish I were a sunbeam to enter through your window.*

My country, my horrible, destroyed country. Anyway, never again call me Tarzan, because I'm not Tarzan. And if, thanks to a season of California serenity, when I never missed your love, privileged student in a gymnasium of Tarzans, today, as your venerated poet and compatriot César Vallejo would say, referring to his humerus bones, today my tonsils have gone bad on me. And know only too well what tonsillitis can do to Tarzan there in the jungle: a lion might eat him alive—and so, his honor, his pride, and some very solid convictions, all lost forever.

In my new life as a weak woman, one thing remains strong and immense: I love you, Juan Manuel Carpio, singer and friend. Comrade. Thanks for Mexico, and forgive me for abandoning the gymnasium, but realize it didn't prepare me for my return to my country, not even for a visit, what with so many bombs, so many friends dead or disappeared, by the right and by the left, and by the front and by the rear and by the north and the south, the east and the west of my oh-so-fragile Salvadoran identity.

Rodrigo, who had tonsillitis a little while back, taught me a tremendous lesson. A single detail from him was enough for me to learn a million things about myself. The most insignificant and infantile of his questions raised a huge, full-length mirror before me and made me see myself so skinny and emaciated—but all of a sudden, because in Mexico I was neither skinny nor pale, and I felt very pretty. Anyway, all that made me remember that this child (!?) is going to be ten years old.

I'm not saying good-bye to you in this letter, Juan Manuel Carpio.

I find myself too weak, and besides, I have you on your record taking care of me so strongly.

Santiago, April 12, 1982

My most beloved Juan Manuel,

We finally reached Chile last Tuesday. Despite everything, despite so many worries, it was really hard for me to leave El Salvador. And even though I don't know yet for sure, it may well be that I was wrong to come. We've only been here a week, and already I feel both enormous depression and a tremendous sense of waste. To have traveled so far to not want to be here. I feel like a jerk.

Just as you suspected, Enrique's mom isn't seriously ill at all. She'll probably become seriously ill when we leave.

All this, and I've only been here for a week. I haven't found out anything about my friend Gaby Larsen. I'm going to try to call her. I'm dying to see someone who can buck up my spirits. Now, while I'm writing you, I'm with the kids in the Plaza de Armas, in the center of Santiago, horrified of this life I manage so badly.

I don't know where you could write me, but your words would do me so much good.

Fortunately, in El Salvador my relationship with the family, with the few of them left in the country, was excellent. You just can't imagine how marvelous they were when the tonsillitis thing hit me and I locked myself away in the living room to die listening to your last record. They understood me perfectly and acted with a discretion uncommon in our countries. Simply put, they guessed that I wouldn't be capable of screaming again in this vortex I call my life, that I had just fled in terror from the jungle and its animals, from its trees, its rivers, and its vines, and that I loved that gentleman whose voice incessantly poured from a record to which I'd turned the way a shipwrecked sailor clings to a buoy.

And now I don't understand why in hell I had the obligation to come to fix I-don't-know-what in order to achieve a friendly and amicable separation, something almost always impossible.

Please, hug me in your thoughts. I only wish I could feel your embrace, which always does me so much good.

As soon as I have an address, I'll send it to you. Maybe Gaby will come soon and I'll be able to use hers. Anyway, sometimes I think I'm the dumbest woman in the world.

I hug and kiss you,
Your Fernanda

P.S.: Juan Manuel! You can write me at General Delivery, Central Post Office, Plaza de Armas, Santiago, Chile.

Here I was, sitting in front of the building, and I didn't even realize it. Isn't that a brilliant idea? I'm already feeling happy.

Santiago, Plaza de Armas, May 3, 1982

My most beloved Juan Manuel,

Today I came to the post office and found your letter, whose mere existence cheered me up a lot. And when I read it, I was even happier to know you're okay, after your Mexican tour, recovering strength and peace.

I'm still listening and listening to your *Motel Trinidad*. Every day it gets better and better, weaving with gold thread. The title of each song and the way it's integrated into the text is so smart, as if it provides an aura for the story in each stanza with magic punctuation. I think it's the best work you've done yet. And may Luisa forgive me.

As for me, basically I'm fine. The kids, luckily, are made of an unbreakable and rustproof material. It's incredibly lucky that with all the changes, they stay pure and beautiful, their eyes still full of the same stars you saw in Mexico.

I'll write again very quickly, now I have to go back to Enrique's parents' house. A million kisses from your

Fernanda

Santiago, June 10, 1982

Dear Juan Manuel Carpio,

There you were in the plaza, running, and out of breath.

I received your kiss, furtively, and then I'm running, too. Soon I'll write more relaxed letters from my mother's garden.

This week we leave. If I haven't told you much, forgive me. Believe me, my haste has been real, just as your words are also real. The kids are running through the post office hallways, so I'd better say good-bye.

Thanks for your haste and for always arriving at our dates on time.

Hugs and kisses,
Fernanda María

San Salvador, July 23, 1982

Most beloved Juan Manuel, always a little mine, luckily, miraculously,

I received your last hello in Santiago. There you were, running into the Plaza de Armas, and I was just able to receive your embrace before I ran off at top speed, promising you a calmer letter from my mother's house.

There's no calm.

First, the house itself isn't calm. Mom's been renting it for the last fifteen years, and it looked as if she'd be able to live there forever. Now, with the new laws, the economic crisis, etc., the owner wants to sell it, and his buyer is an engineer who wants to tear it down to build I don't know how many houses. We have to wait and see how this plays out. And if it does, I have no idea what we'll do.

Then there's the fact that I'm not calm. You know that, generally speaking, I'm not given to existentialist anguish, and that I've made my way through the world in a fairly carefree, even cheerful way, I'd say. But ever since my tonsils failed me, I'm afraid of everything, my love. Of the future, of the present, and of the past, which looks like a muddy floor to me. I don't even know where to begin. The country is horrifyingly sad, ugly, poor, with earthquakes and rains— and I feel the same way. Forgive me for talking about anguish to you. I don't like feeling this way. Much less talking about it like this. But I know you'll forgive me. Luckily, I still have a few things I'm sure of, a few convictions. Oh, how I'd like to feel just a little of the happiness we had in Mexico.

Our departure from Chile was extremely sad. Sometimes I think that only by dying can I straighten out this mess. Though being in San Salvador now and feeling this way has got to be the closest thing there is to dying—and not going to heaven.

I'm really happy you ended up buying the house in Minorca, where you can lock yourself away and listen to and compose music, which is what you've always liked and what's always helped you. You'll always be able to visit Peru, especially now that you're beginning to be recognized internationally. If you only knew how many people tell me about your last record, here in this bombed-out little corner of the world, people who don't even know we know each other. And every once in a while, one of your songs is on the radio. Which makes me so happy, of course.

Because of what I told you at the start, I almost wish this letter would get lost in the mail and that instead another, a better letter, a less sad one, would get to you. But I'm sending you this one because I like talking to you, and need to. Of course, I'd like to talk to you about more beautiful things and not annoy you like this.

There is one good thing I can tell you. None of us here was caught in the earthquake. I'm with the kids in the house of an aunt who's traveling in Europe, a huge house as solid as the Rock of Gibraltar—both the house and the aunt. Only a few mirrors and some pre-Colombian pottery broke—a pity. But the house and those of us inside were unhurt, apart, that is, from my internal earthquake, for which I have yet to prepare a damage report.

The kids are in school, and I suppose the first step I have to take will be to look for a job. But I haven't wanted to see anyone just yet. Maybe next week, when I'm really convinced I want to stay here, that I can do it, that one way or another I'm going to stay with my kids in my country.

It's hard, you know, to realize that all your sisters have gone with the intention of never coming back except to visit—and even that less and less. And the same thing applies to your best friends. Sometimes Mom and I don't even know where all my sisters are, though just in case, let me tell you that Susy still has that beautiful apartment on rue Colombe.

Okay, my love, what a strange letter I've written. I hug you and cling to you, your memory hugs me tenderly and lovingly, and I thank you for always letting me feel your great and sweet friendship and tenderness.

Your Fernanda

IV

▲▲▲▲▲▲▲▲

Just Flor, Letters and Years

*Could that be the magic? Knowing how to cheat a bit and know-
ing how to do it at just the right time?* I asked myself, the way
Fernanda María asked herself in the only letter she wrote me
after our marvelous meeting in Mexico, when she was on
her way to Chile, with a stopover in El Salvador. Of course,
that was the same letter in which she told me how Tarzan
was undergoing a profound crisis, a true *tonsillitis,* to use her
own word, and how, suddenly and all at once, all it took was
for her son, Rodrigo, to ask her a typical child's question
about the King of the Jungle and his tonsils for her to realize
she was totally defenseless, psychically and physically depressed, and unarmed in a jungle that was both internal and
external.

That was, definitively, the moment when I should have
acted, when I should have suggested to Fernanda that she
prolong her visit to San Salvador, which would have given

me the chance to make some changes in my work schedule and arrange, for real or just pretend, some concerts and recording sessions there in her country, my love, so that once and for all we can learn how to cheat a bit more and a bit better, so we can repeat the pleasure and the magic of our meeting in Mexico, but now more deeply and more clearly and brazenly and openly, Mía, meaning that there in your own city and among those family members and friends about whom you've told me so much over the years. Mía, believe me that everything, absolutely everything, is one hundred percent justified by the fact that you felt, that you feel, so ill, that you have an imperious need for rest and tranquility, anybody in the world can understand that, and I'm sure that all you have to do is inform Enrique that there's no other alternative and that you really don't want his mother to get worse again, so that despite this tremendous and oh-so-inopportune misfortune, you and the kids can arrive on time and . . .

However, I still hadn't finished imagining my complete strategy, my Mexican cheat plan, expanded and perfected, when Fernanda's first news from Chile began reaching me. Damn her. Once again our *Estimated Time of Arrival,* our famous ETA, had dealt us a low blow, and this time without Fernanda's even noticing it, and why bother telling her anything when she'd just abandoned El Salvador? Meaning that I tore up the unfinished letter and in its place I confidently wrote her one that was very different. I'm pretty sure that's what I did because of the news that came later, that is, from the two or three letters Fernanda María managed to send me from Santiago and the ones she sent me later on, back in San Salvador, although among this latter group there is one, dated July 23, 1982, that contains a knockout paragraph:

Our departure from Chile was extremely sad. Sometimes I think that only by dying can I straighten out this mess. Though being in San Salvador now and feeling this way has got to be the closest thing there is to dying—and not going to heaven.

So what the hell did all that mean, and so unexpectedly like that? What the devil did this sudden confession mean and why at that precise moment? Why, suddenly, this latter-day repentance? Did all those hard words include or exclude me? Exclude, I'd say, but even so, there they were, written by her own hand, and in the very first letter Fernanda María wrote me as soon as she got to Santiago. It was enough to drive anyone crazy, really . . .

Because now it turns out, just like that, that the blessed departure from Chile had been extremely sad. And on top of that with me in the world. Yet isn't it true that Fernanda had complained about how badly things had gone for her in Santiago, practically from the moment she stepped off the plane? Yes sir, she had complained, and not only that, but from the first instant she realized she'd fallen into the trap Enrique had set for her and the children, just as I had suspected and warned her, long before her departure. The big Araucanian's mother had never been gravely ill, not even slightly ill. To the contrary, the dear lady was overjoyed at having met her little grandchildren and, as if things were that easy and natural, she instantly decided that the only thing she wanted in life was for all of them to stay with her and live in Santiago. With or without the red-haired Central American skeleton who was, no question about it, a Communist, the bitch. So, the mess of the century had wound itself up there in Santiago, and now the only thing missing was for the Araucanian's mother to really fall ill, deathly ill this time, yes, from her rage and sadness on seeing her adored grandchildren take off again for Salvador, and from there to God knows where with that Bolshevik daughter-in-law of mine and things would be different if Pinochet were to find out, yes, you can believe that.

Even so, Fernanda María referred to that farewell as something extremely sad and even managed to think that her death would be the only solution to such a damned interminable mess. I, on the other hand, had been thinking, and only a few short weeks earlier, that the time had come to learn how to cheat big-time, which, in this case, meant recreating our Mexican time without any remorse, no matter what, and even if we had to lie to half of humanity—beginning, by the way, my beloved Fernanda, with Enrique. Or is it the case that at this stage in the game you still feel incapable of fabricating one or two little lies in favor of our cause? Sure, I believe the poor guy suffers a great deal, and not only that: I'm also convinced he'll multiply his daily dose of wine and whiskey a hundredfold. The truth is, alcohol is a very jolly friend, but only when we beat it at its own game, which, let's be sincere, Mía, Enrique is not about to do. Alcohol for him is a dark, nefarious monster that showed him its ugly face and beat him a long time ago. That's the only truth, my love, and believe me, it pains my very soul to be the one to sing it to you, and with all its pathetic words, but it just seems to me that it's high time you made a count of all the years it's been since Enrique fell into that hole.

Are you saying he wasn't always like that, Fernanda? Are you saying your dear husband hasn't, since time immemorial, been a true expert in bottled sorrow? Of course he has. To the point where, by suffering and drinking, he doesn't eat and doesn't allow anyone else to, because the truth is that the deeper he sinks into his dark forest, the less you and I enjoy life and the more we grow accustomed to old thorns. And look, my beloved Fernanda, yes, look and listen: I'm taking this opportunity to remind you, with your permission, that both of us are right on the brink of the famous *mezzo del camin di nostra vita,* the point when things become infernally twisted up for Dante Alighieri himself. So let's fool, lie, and cheat, my dear Fernanda, because either we react and find *la diritta via* or we end up totally immersed in *esta selva selvaggia e aspra e forte, che nel pensier rinova la paura* . . .

Wait, I'm remembering it clearly right this instant: it was exactly then when I had to close my Biblioteca Universale Rizzoli edition of the *Divina commedia* and give myself over completely to the new and profound sensation Fernanda's words had just produced in me while I was trying to read Dante and, at the same time, find a solution to our bullet-proof honesty. One inferno brought me to another, because just when I was trying to imagine, once again, real strategies to save our love, Fernanda María informs me from El Salvador that leaving Chile this time was very sad. In effect, a low blow, to put it mildly.

But hold on, maybe not. Maybe these words weren't written against me, words that don't even exclude me in the slightest from the life and most real, most complete, and most profound feelings of Fernanda María . . . That's right, the bullets are flying, no doubt about it: Mía's words, so hard and sad, could only be explained by locating them within a much wider, much more complex context, which I should have been able to imagine very easily and which included not only her. In reality, Fernanda María had virtually limited herself to describing, with very logical sorrow, the umpteenth separation of the kids from their father, adding to it, of course, a new separation, this one perhaps definitive, from their paternal grandparents, also another useless trip, insofar as their personal situation was concerned, and God knows how many other things.

Well, no matter how much someone tells us or tells himself, and no matter how much we confess, or vomit up, page after page, the person able to show us all his cards in a letter is yet to be born. Not even in the most extensive and intimate of correspondences. Therefore, no doubt about it, Fernanda María could express to me only partially and circumstantially the totality of her departure from Chile. By the same token, she and I were totally and essentially for each other, although at times the same letters that kept us informed impeded our telling any one complete moment of our lives— or two, or three, or a thousand. And of course let's not even mention the concise, faded, and blurred fax—which fades completely with time—where even what is peculiar to letter-writing is completely suppressed, beginning with the envelope and the many things it implies about color, geography, climatology, philately, distant horizons, memory, forgetting, sorrow, sadness, friendship, love, the passage of time. . . . After all, what do twenty years matter. We could have been nothing more than faithful pen pals.

Well. What more remains to be said about the fax, the guillotine for letters, actually the electric chair for the epistolary mode? . . . Well, wait, I do have something else to say— though more than anything because of an association of ideas about merely technological advances. Not writing letters is a shame. Letter-writing is elegance, tradition, and class. Fernanda María and I never had recourse to faxes, and the only time I sent her an electronic letter, only to test my new computer, she answered me in a fury from the office where she was working, urging me instantly to hang up that "light telephone."

But, well, I, who at the time still hadn't stated any of these things of life and correspondence and was really surprised and hurt about what Fernanda María said about leaving Chile, opted for a vengeful epistolary muteness that lasted for many months, I remember it, though I never told her anything about the real cause of it. Besides, I made up a story about an interminable concert tour through Equatorial Guinea, a notion that is, I think, really patently absurd. I remember all this clearly, but I also have in front of me her letters from those months, in case my memory fails me, since it had been a long time before then that Fernanda had lost all my letters in that mugging in Oakland, and the photocopy of the notebook she sent me had stopped forever in time with the pieces she liked best of my answers to her letters.

San Salvador, August 23, 1983

My most beloved Juan Manuel,

I still haven't heard from you. The mails are extremely slow.

It's like living in the days when letters went first by ship and then by mule. I hope that in some way and in some place my letters have reached you, especially now because with each day that passes, you become more international and more of a traveler. Perhaps you aren't in Minorca these days, though now that it's summer in Europe I'm surprised you haven't taken a rest from so much globe-trotting in your new isolated residence. How I want to know what's going on with you.

Today I was very happy to learn that Charlie Boston is here on vacation. On Tuesday I'm going to see him at the beach, where his family has a beautiful summer house. I hope Charlie tells me something about you, because he's certainly more up to date than I am thanks to our international band of pals. I'll continue this letter when I get back from Santa Ana.

August 28

I'm back. Charlie had no word of you either. Where has my love gone? Charlie says most likely you're on a summer tour through Spain and southern France, from nightspot to nightspot, and those things kill me with jealousy.

As the days pass, I'm getting more and more used to being here. It was really better that I didn't find a job right away. That way, I've had time to get used, little by little, to this rhythm of life that is so unlike the haste of other places.

My mother's affairs worked out fine, because she's going to spend some time in California with my sister María Cecilia, and when she comes back, she'll look for a new house to rent, one more in line with the times. Besides, Susy will be here around that time. In December she's going to have a Parisian baby and then spend some time here, her companion with her. As you see, these people never stop moving.

I hope you get this letter soon. Tell me about your summer.

A big hug,
Fernanda

San Salvador, September 28, 1983

Very beloved Juan Manuel,

I'm puzzled and sad because you haven't written me. I hope nothing bad has happened to you. Did you receive my address (34 Calle San Andrés 1106, San Salvador)?

Let me know how you are. Please.

Yours,
Fernanda

Only one comment, or, rather, confirmation, that I should have made sooner. I'm sure about it, but even now I find it surprising. I've never known anyone who moved as often as Fernanda María. The address books I've had over the years testify to it. And, well, I think I should also mention the shame and sorrow I still feel for not having answered Mía. I imagine that Chilean sadness of hers was still affecting me, but in any case here is her letter:

San Salvador, October 30, 1983

My most beloved Juan Manuel,

The days pass, and still I hear nothing from you. Sometimes I get worried and think something's happened to you. Sometimes I get mad and wish you'd go to hell. What could have happened? I can't believe I no longer have your love and friendship. It seems so horrible to me. Maybe you fell in love and got married, or you got sick, or maybe you're even dead. Whatever it is, your absence weighs on me. I only hope I find out something soon.

Things are going better for me. In January, I was offered the chance to teach at the university. For now I'm teaching English and French at a high school run by nuns.

Know what I found out two days ago from my mom? That when I finished secondary school in the U.S., the head of the school called her to say they had a scholarship available for me, for anything I wanted to study, at Berkeley, Stanford, UCLA, and who knows where else. She doesn't even remember anymore. But she didn't accept it, and never mentioned it to me until just now.

Shit!

When I think about that, and about the times we've been together, I think my life has been a series of missed opportunities, which this time have brought me here, almost to nothing. But I'll slowly have to get out in some way. Just think, when my mother told me that, I was almost certain that my relationship with you had gone down the drain. It seems that every time I get close to something good, it falls apart.

Shit! And shit again!

I've become a pessimist again. So maybe the best thing would be for me just to curse you out once and for all. That should buck up my spirits, don't you think? How strange this is! What could have happened that you don't write?

I hate you.

Fernanda

San Salvador, November 10, 1983

My dear Juan Manuel Carpio,

God bless the boots of the mailman who brought me your long-awaited letter this morning! If you only knew, my beloved friend, how indispensable you are, even in black ink. You can't imagine how much I've missed and hated and missed again and hated again. And now I beg you to forgive me my lack of faith and confidence in you, but the truth is that only you could come up with the idea of giving a series of concerts in a little African country, which probably doesn't even have mail service. Well, a performer's life is that way, and I understand it very well, and even congratulate you because more and more people know who you are and listen to you every day, but I would think incarceration—excuse the pun—would be better than risking your neck in one of those World

War I planes. Frankly, I think I have the right to be informed about these things.

During your absence, I really needed your tenderness, which I've always felt surrounding me. Your disappearance left a void in my life. Years go by, half a decade can pass, but your friendship and love always mean so much to me.

These past days I've begun to feel much better about everything. Partly because you've reappeared, but also, I feel, because I've come back to my hometown, because I've immersed myself in it as never before, and I'm seeing it more clearly now that it's ugly and so seriously wounded, this shitty hometown full of defects. I feel very well strolling its streets, talking, writing, and drawing again. Well, not really doing anything, but not doing it here—yes, here, where even the dead know me.

I think that with all this trouble we've been having there are lots of people missing, gone out of the country, or dead, and that other, new people have moved in who don't love us very much. But there's always some understanding.

Well, you're back, at least in these letters of ours which are the only things we own in common, and which have always made me feel that my friendship for you is as solid as the Rock of Gibraltar. Use that friendship for whatever you need. I like that "just for the pleasure of your company," as they say, because it fills me up so much. There aren't many people you find whose presence is so good, so satisfying, as yours.

I'm holding you in a tight, strong embrace.
Your Fernanda

P.S.: Rafael Dulanto came, with his delightful
Patricia. Something's wrong with him, and I fear it
may be something serious. He says he's fed up going
from gringo doctor to gringo doctor without anyone
being able to find anything. He looks thin and extremely pale to me. And now once again he's going
from doctor to doctor, but this time in Spanish. I
think he'd be delighted to get a letter from you. You
should write him. More to the point: write him,
please, because he's really depressed and never stops
saying how he's screwed, totally, and that someone
should bring him another whiskey and another cigar.

December 15, 1983

My friend and lover,
Today, so many things made me think about you
that it was only a miracle you didn't materialize in the
living room, sitting and smiling in the most comfortable chair.
First: Bing Crosby at Christmas has always made
me think about you, I have no idea why. It should be
Frank Sinatra, but it's Bing Crosby, I'm sorry.
Second: a sad trip to the coast, to the Dulantos'
family home, not to visit with a sick Rafael but to
attend his funeral. Rafael died two days ago. I think
you didn't get my last letter—or that it's taking a long

time to get to you—because I know you wouldn't have left him without the pleasure of a hello. Time is even crazier than we are and makes its own decisions.

Third: this morning I came upon your interview in the magazine of the University of Mexico, UNAM, as they call it. As usual, your words moved me, but I must confess that I nearly died of jealousy because of the girl standing next to you in the photo.

But today, even though I have you so present, the truth is that once again I don't know where or how you are, and it seems as if the globe has inflated in such a way that I can't reach you anymore. Is that what they mean by "worldwide inflation"?

At the same time, every word of your interview comes through so clearly and so well.

Please tell me where that interview took place. Pure feminine curiosity, I confess. And a certain unease, which I don't know whether to call feminine or merely human, very human, and common to both sexes, my elementary and beloved Watson. But in the end, so what? I'm a woman and with renewed spirit ever since a ferocious tonsillitis returned me to my ultrafeminine reality and stripped me of any whims about diving into the river every once in a while like Tarzan.

Tell me what's going on, you scoundrel! Or insist that all future interviews be published without photos.

And if this letter doesn't get to you, I'll feel very alone.

I'm hugging you still from the last time we hugged. Because hugs never fade.

Yours,

Fernanda

San Salvador, December 16, 1983

My so, so beloved Juan Manuel,

Just yesterday I sent you a letter and now look, one from you arrives today, and Patricia called to say that your deeply felt words didn't get to Rafael. It will break your heart to know he didn't receive them, but it's better you be told everything. Patricia read them and then read them to me over the telephone. Both of us were very moved.

I hug you with the wish that my hug will get to you by Christmas and bring you tenderness and joy. You'll see, the new year's going to be a good one. The moon tells me so, and she's usually so silent and, thank God, never gossips.

How tedious I am—aren't I? But I just have to be. Tell me who the girl from the interview is, because with every passing hour I see her getting younger and younger. I might even say too young for you. I'm tedious and a busybody, I know. But always your

Fernanda

The girl from the interview was Flor, and she was sitting next to me, and not very happy, I don't think, despite the fact that from the very start we had established our relationship as something quite free. We met as I was leaving a concert

I gave in Barcelona, and during the week I was singing in that city we saw each other every night. I was almost twice her age, true enough, but neither of us saw that as a problem, especially because our time together consisted only of extremely long walks through the city, interrupted by a dinner in some good restaurant and a drink in any bar or discotheque we might stumble on to before we went off to sleep, each one in his own bed. Thanks to Flor I got to know Barcelona, and the night I said good-bye to her at the entry to the building where she was living, I realized that while I got to know the city, I barely knew her at all.

"Only a few times have I run into a person as utterly silent as you," I said.

"It's true, I often don't say very much, but this time it was intentional. I restricted myself to asking you to sing a few of your songs. I don't know if you realize it, but you've given me a lot of pleasure. Or are you simply in the habit of wandering cities at night and singing without anyone asking you to sing?"

"It never occurred to me, no."

"Then I should thank you a million times over. You've given me a great deal, and I've really had a good time. That's why I was so silent—to listen to you in silence and be happy."

"I have to thank you in return for these beautiful walks through Barcelona."

"Juan Manuel, you're walking with another woman. Anyone could see that a mile off. And you sing about her, in addition to singing only to her."

"And what makes you so sure of this?"

"Because many times you called me Fernanda María. Actually you've hardly ever called me Flor."

"I'm so sorry. Please . . ."

"Forget it, it's not important. Anyway, it's just been the price I've had to pay for attending these private concerts."

"Take it any way you like, but I guess I've behaved like a jerk."

A few days later I called Flor from a bar—I still didn't have a telephone on the small farm I bought in Minorca, very near the port of Mahón but some distance from the sea, and surrounded by trees and thick vegetation. Gardening was Flor's specialty, and until that moment I hadn't taken the trouble to prune a single bush or take the slightest care of what could be a beautiful space full of flowers and climbing plants.

"Think it's possible, Flor?" I asked her by telephone.

"I love the idea, Juan Manuel. From time to time I need a rest from the city, and I've always liked Minorca."

"And I promise to call you by your own name. I promise."

"A million thanks, Mr. Juan Manuel Pavarotti."

"When do you think you can come?"

"I think that in two or three days I'll be able to find someone to replace me in my plant business. I don't want to leave any of my clients in the lurch. Do you have a telephone?"

"No, not yet, but you can leave messages for me at the Bar Bahía. That's where my mail goes, and they take calls for me. Let me give you the number . . ."

"Perfect. I'll call you then."

Everything around me flowered with the arrival of Just Flor, a name that sounds quite literary, like Brazilian fiction, or maybe like Antonio das Mortes, the bearded and sombreroed death-dealer in the celebrated *cangaceiro* film by Glauber Rocha, filled with all that violence and the miserable *sertão*, with shitty lives and slaughterhouse throat-slittings, total drought, Judgment Day sun, and an underdevelopment of hunger, tragic threats, apocalyptic revenge, and the like, but which in the case of the precious Just Flor hid tenderness and fragility, profound childhood traumas, night panics, and the dawns of a wounded little animal.

"So you'll never tell me your last name?" I asked her the summer morning she landed in Minorca as we drove from the airport in my car, heading for that country property where the only improvement I'd made until then was, of course, an homage to Fernanda María, a huge sign at the entrance:

VILLA TRINIDAD DEL MONTE MONTES

"In these parts, you say *can*, not *villa*, Juan Manuel Pavarotti."

"I know that, but, well, how to explain . . ."

"The letter you've got there on the dashboard explains everything. Didn't you notice? The return address says Fernanda María de la Trinidad del Monte Montes."

"So it does. I hadn't even realized. Maybe because I just picked it up at the Bar Bahía before coming to get you at the airport and . . ."

"And?"

"And, well . . . Let's just say that Fernanda Mía, excuse me, Fernanda María, who, ever since I first met her has never been sad a single morning, no matter what happens to her, aside from being a huge friend, is as brave and daring and healthy as Tarzan, though from time to time she comes down with a case of tonsillitis, as we all do sometimes, and then she's left with no voice and no shout in the asphalt jungle where she happens to live . . ."

"Stop right there, Pavarotti, you're breaking my heart."

"Okay, I'll stop, but I swear that the sign at the entryway is there because once the poor thing, with a husband and two kids to support, despite having been born an heiress, found herself painting signs for all sorts of shops, in all sorts of Californias . . ."

"Day and night and doing piecework, right?"

"Quite right: day and night and doing piecework. Couldn't have put it better myself.

"Really moving, Pavarotti."

"Okay, my last name is Pavarotti—but what about you? What the hell is yours?"

"Let's just leave it at Flor, Just Flor, in view of the fact that I don't have a last name that could even remotely compete with Doña Fernanda María de la Trinidad del Monte Montes, alias *Mía,* or *Tuya* . . . Oh well, I guess it all depends on the angle you see things from, or the point of view of the storyteller."

"Fine, just as you like, Just Flor, but here we are at the little house."

"*Home sweet home,* is that it?"

"Welcome . . . Welcome, really, and . . ."

"With all your heart?"

"Exactly. And it's true, even if it doesn't look it."

"I hope we get along, Pavarotti, because, really, there's a lot of work to be done here. It's been a long time since I've seen gardens so pitifully abandoned as these. Aren't you ashamed?"

"No more, because you'll make them bloom."

"That's why I'm here, right?"

"Absolutely. But now go put away your things, make yourself as comfortable as you can as quickly as you can, and let's go down to the port to have a drink and fill up on seafood, Just Flor."

"Your invitation is most welcome, Juan Manuel Carpio."

"What? What became of Pavarotti?"

"Well, let's say he had another engagement, and that I sincerely thank you for the invitation. And that I'm telling the truth, even though it doesn't look it. Does that sound okay?"

"Sounds perfect to me."

Of course I immediately opened Mía's letter and read it a hundred times, as usual, while Just Flor unpacked and put away her belongings and fixed herself up a bit.

San Salvador, February 1, 1984

Beloved Juan Manuel Carpio,

This year I've been slower than usual in sending you my year-end hugs and greetings, because here the whole family has been enveloped in great sadness because of the illness and death of my uncle Dick Mansfield, from the British company where I worked for so long, remember? More than an uncle, he was a second father and a guardian angel for all of us. He died on January 4, and only today was I able to summon up enough courage to pick up paper and pen and acknowledge the new year.

I'm sorry my greeting is slightly bitter, but very little that's good comes to mind. But even if my presence is sad, awkward, and ugly today, I still want you to have my tenderness and my best wishes for a beautiful year full of good things.

Happy, Happy New Year, and nothing more for the moment, my beloved artist.

Your

Fernanda

Moments later, I was surprised to find myself planted, as it were, in a most summery way, on the terrace of a bar that looked out on the port of Mahón and ordering two glasses of very dry, very cold white wine, if you would be so kind, sir, from beneath the brim of a canvas hat (ivory-colored, black ribbon included) that crowned, ever so carelessly, the costume of an English habitué of sun and surf, all of it shamelessly copied from Charlie Boston and at great risk (to me, that is) of looking like a ridiculous phony. I was also surprised to find myself raising my glass of white wine to toast Just Flor and her ever-so-welcome arrival. And toasting her in the phoniest, most insincere, and son-of-a-bitch way imaginable—and that's putting it nicely—blurting out the only thing it occurred to me to say, like a speech I'd memorized without understanding it: "To your health, Miss Gardner. And I do mean health. And I regret that my toast is slightly bitter, because very little that's good comes to mind. But even if my presence is sad, awkward, and ugly today, I still want you to have my tenderness and my best wishes for a beautiful summer in Minorca, overflowing with good things."

She could barely raise her glass, poor Flor. But, at the same time, she forced a lamentable trembling smile, which then spread to her hands, with the result that there was a little spilling of the white wine, followed by one of those moments of emotional crisis verging on an absolute upheaval of panic, and as she attempted, "T-t-to y-y-your h-h-health, Ju-Juan Ma- . . . ," the camera swinging slowly, in an interminable pan, the scene was so surreal it didn't need any special effects.

"Did you know that Mahón is the deepest port in the Mediterranean?" I asked, in a desperate attempt to change the script, since the first one—that is, my plagiarism of Fernanda's letter, which I'd just read—suddenly metamorphosed into a series of sentences that are among the most sincere and heartfelt I've ever spoken in my life, to this day. At which point, my recitation completely lost its source and its dishonest, thieving content through the power of feeling or "filin," as they say in the salsa Caribbean of Celia Cruz. As far as samples go, one will do: Fernanda María had written "full of good things," which, anyway, referred only to the year 1984, while I, on the other hand, had said "overflowing with good things," significantly changing the original script, and like any fish dying for not keeping its mouth shut, since besides everything else I'd been referring to the rest of life, not just 1984, so that, in reality, I was referring to the rest of *my* life, and in view of the fact that I was twice the age of the delightful Flor, who sat, in stunning fragility, at my side, staring with a trembling and moving distance in her big black eyes into the black waters of the deepest port in the Mediterranean, while the best that could be said is that the statistics didn't favor me at all, nor did they ever favor me, and why

193

should they, as everything became associated with Jorge Manrique's famous line about our lives being the rivers that empty into Mahón, which is death, and by then it wasn't only the statistical data that failed me while Just Flor persisted in gazing silently as even my vital signs began to fail me.

In sum, it was what people call *one of those moments,* and once it passed, we stuffed ourselves with seafood at the Marivent Restaurant, and Just Flor was the granddaughter of Jewish Anarchists shot in Barcelona and the daughter of parents who had fled to France when they were very young, who had met in a concentration camp, and who returned to Spain when Franco died, and things like that.

"What do you mean, *things like that,* Flor? Don't be such a dry flower, please."

"It's just that I was still a little girl, and my life was made up of my parents' memories, day and night, breakfast, lunch, and dinner, and my parents' memories were also those of my grandparents, and all day long it was death and horror in the civil war, here and in the resistance and Vichy, with changes of name, passport, and identity every so often, so it may well be true that my last name is Gotman, because that's what my father said when he was delirious on his deathbed, and my mother, damned if I understand her, still says nothing."

"You've already told me she's the quietest woman in the world."

"To the point that we don't even say hello to each other anymore."

"To the point that . . . Yes, I understand. Okay, then, a huge toast to your first day in Minorca, Flor."

"Just Flor. Never leave that part off, because I love having that name for you. Just for you, Juan Manuel Carpio."

"Thank you, thank you very much."

"Just for you and for no one else ever, understand what I'm saying, Juan Manuel Toastmaster?"

"I understand you profoundly, and I understand you horribly, and I understand you . . . Come here, come closer, and you'll understand exactly to what point I understand you."

I almost broke her ribs in a ferocious embrace, while Flor could barely manage to say, "Reality conquers fiction, Juan Manuel, because now it turns out that, suddenly, being named Just Flor with you, just with you, is the truth even if it seems a lie. It's really marvelous—even though you love some-one else and you're waiting for someone else, your Tarzan, and even though you may be wondering when I'll finish with my work here so you can invite her and receive her in my beautiful gardens . . ."

"Flor . . ."

"Let's get the hell out of here, singer."

But the dialogue continued a week later: "What I'm going to leave you with is lots of flowers, because I'm a professional in matters of gardening, because I already love your arid gar-dens, and because you're so afraid I'll wake up screaming and bathed in soaking nightmares, every night, that you slip, as a preventive measure, into my bed."

"Flor . . ."

"Thanks a million, Doctor, for your shock therapy."

"Flor . . ."

"The bad part, of course, is that the patient always falls in love, even with the couch."

"Flor . . ."

"Juan Manuel, excuse me for running on this way. I think I've spoken more in the days I've been here than I have in my entire life."

"That makes me very happy, Flor . . ."

"I won't say another word, my love. You talk now, a lot, and caress me as much as you can. Then I'll transmit each one of your words and cuddles to each and every one of your plants, your trees, and vines, and even to that bougainvillea, which, I don't know if you've noticed, is beginning to take root."

Just Flor made one miracle per day in the gardens surrounding the house, but of speech, what you'd call speaking and conversing, nothing at all, unless it was a matter of something absolutely indispensable. And then she'd say to me, for instance, that there was no more toilet paper, and I'd run out to get some—and a bottle of wine to toast the new roll.

"Juan Manuel, are you out of your mind? I told you *toilet paper*, not wine."

"And I understood you. But think of it as . . . an occasion."

"Nothing doing. Excuse me, but my work comes before anything else."

Things like that every so often, and I would receive letter after letter from Fernanda María, desperate, was I sick? was I seriously ill? had I died?, had I fallen in love with someone to the point of even forgetting to answer her letters? was it the girl in the photo, the one who could be my daughter? had I died? had I killed myself? had I died all over again? You could tell from a mile off that, if given the choice, Fernanda María would clearly rather I was dead than happily in the arms of a photo. And I, too, suffered because of that. And Just Flor became quieter and quieter every day, from one dawn to the next. So, with our lines hopelessly crossed, that is, "in the throes of a thousand contradictions" as they say, both on soap operas and in police reports—a curious case of cross-pollination—I opted for bribing an employee of the telephone company in Mahón, and no sooner did they install the telephone than I inaugurated it by declaiming long-distance a letter especially written to be shouted and listened to both in my house and in the house of Fernanda María de la Trinidad del Monte Montes, whose sign, by the way, I had repainted myself, replacing the Villa Trinidad del Monte and all that with *Can* Flor, and falling into a rage immediately because I would turn up in the gardens, which were more and more beautiful and complete with each passing day, of course, but also every day on the verge of I'm done, Juan Manuel, so you owe me this much and good-bye, it's been a great pleasure to work for you, yes, getting enraged immediately because I was standing there with that extremely heavy sign, and begging Flor to bring out a bottle of wine so we could declare ourselves on strike for an afternoon and toast the sign, and she mute, mute, mute.

"A fucking mute, damn it. A non-fucking mute on top of everything else. Like the bolero, you're a *Flor sin retoño,* a flower with no shoots."

. . .

"Know which bolero I'm talking about, or is it you don't even know that, you f-ing mute?"

. . .

And she went on watering and pruning and pruning and watering and fertilizing over here and over there and on the left and on the right, this Just Flor, while I, furious and hurt, sang (out of tune, of course), "Flor sin retoño," emphasizing the part where the poor devil of a gardener laments his head off and sings, *My friends told me, don't bother watering that flower, that flower will yield no shoots, its heart is dead.* But from Just Flor just nothing, so I had no other choice but to take my guitar and my sign elsewhere, actually, to the garage, because that's where I stored the paint and the brush with which my poor illusion of a house, in the throes of a thousand contradictions, ended up named "Canseco," which I think is very improper Catalan or Majorcan or Minorcan or whatever for "Can Just," though in Peru, Canseco is the very distinguished last name of a great friend of mine, so fuck off . . .

All of that led me, as I said, to bribe a high-level employee of the phone company in Mahón, meaning that the shouts in which I read my long- and short-distance letter so Fernanda María would hear me very very well there in El Salvador and Just Flor just as well here in her absolute muteness, and they both had my love, my shadows, my friendship, my palship, and a thousand contradictions, and an SOS, my tenderness and double love, though absolutely devoid of any hint of desire for a round bed or modern ideas of the third kind, and malice, and rage, and sorrow against the one over there and the one right here, because, well, because of one, life was shit, and because of the other, shit, that's what life is, and so on, finally, as Euripides would say, I had a good mind to kick their respective asses to Mars so they'd die of hunger in midair.

They both hung up on me while I was still reading the letter, Fernanda María with the telephone and Just Flor by uncorking a bottle of wine and leaving it there on the table in the living room with one single glass next to it, of course, and, with that, exiting the stage. And of that bottle did I drink, oh yes, and I composed and I sang until I'd composed an entire cassette with ninety minutes completely filled, one song after another with vanity and a thousand contradictions, which provoked the most glowing notices . . . for he has exchanged his sad style for a serious style charged with smoke in the eyes, hoarseness, bleakness, and finally pathos. And even today, there are critics who can't decipher the meaning of the song that gave the title to the cassette which brought me so much fame and money: "Canseco"? What did the already celebrated Peruvian singer want to express with the constant repetition of the word *canseco*? Because insofar as the artist himself is concerned, whenever he's asked about that oh-so-enigmatic title, he creates even more confusion when he smiles in his Indian fashion and answers:

Well, it's the last name of a great friend of mine. And a very well-known name down in Peru. And in Lima there are just plain Cansecos as well as Diez Cansecos, whose coat of arms, or so I'm told—I'm merely repeating this, because I know nothing about such things—is surrounded by ten dry dogs. Remember, in Latin "dog" is *can*.

And from that telephone blast to El Salvador and that open-wine-bottle-with-one-glass blast, I drank, composed, and sang, until the hope-against-hoped-for letter from Mía arrived. Although, of course, by then I no longer imitated Charlie Boston in anything. I was my own man and dressed completely in black, inside and out, you might say. And I wept quite often as I changed the lyrics of all the songs I began composing the very day Just Flor, monosyllabic and with that little tremor of the lips that was such a part of her—said, "Mission accomplished. I've even gotten someone to water, prune, and . . ."

"Does that mean you're leaving?"

"That's what it means, yes."

"When?"

"I've got my bag packed."

"Flor . . ."

"There's a flight leaving an hour from now."

"Flor . . ."

"I'll call a taxi in that case."

"No, please. I'll drive you."

"Okay, then let's leave right now."

"Flor, why don't you sit down a while so we can talk all this over?"

"In that case, I'll call a taxi."

"No, please, no. Let me drive you. Besides, I have to pay you."

"In that case, I'll call a taxi."

"I only want to know how much I owe you, Just Flor."

"Owe me? I've never heard of such a thing."

"You've been working here for months, and you need the money, I know that. So, as a farewell gift, I'm begging you to tell me how much . . ."

"In that case, I'll call a taxi."

"May I call you? May I see you when I pass through Barcelona?"

"You have my telephone number, don't you?"

"I do have your telephone number, Flor, yes . . ."

"In that case, let's get going."

On a curve, and not trying to hide it at all, because she looked at me, smiled, and told me she adored me, Just Flor opened the car door and threw herself out. I lost control while trying to catch her, and the old green Alfa Romeo, a collector's item, smashed against a wall. Just Flor was already dead when I recovered consciousness. I wasn't a relative, I wasn't anything, I wasn't anyone, and the few family members who came explained that sooner or later it had to happen, and that for her mother, this, in the last analysis, was going to be a liberation.

"She didn't even use that lady's last name. She didn't use anyone's last name," I told them.

"So by what name did you know her?"

"I called her Love, nothing more. Yes, Love, just Love, just as I'm telling you."

"You artists, of course, are different . . ."

"My arm hurts a lot. Would you mind . . . ?"

"But it seems you hadn't paid her. The body, in any case, had no money on it. Only her clothing and a plane ticket."

"How much do I owe you, gentlemen?"

"No need to behave offensively now . . ."

"It's just that my arm hurts so much."

"Well, you must know how much you owed the girl."

"Banknote by banknote, let's say from here to Lima, more or less."

"Calm down, sir. Our lawyer will get in touch with you, and with the police."

"Fine."

"Please don't misunderstand us. We know this wasn't your fault."

"That can never be known."

"What are you talking about? What about your broken arm, and all the damage?"

Life has those things. I mean that no sooner had I decided to go back to the house than my friend from the Bar Bahía turned up with this letter:

San Salvador, April 5, 1984

Adored Juan Manuel Carpio,

Just like that girl La Valentina in the Mexican song, *I'm prostrate at your feet,* and *If tomorrow I must die, let it be done in one fell swoop.* And hate me, please, I'm asking you to, because I much prefer hatred to indifference, since we only hate what we once loved. Or pray to God that I suffer a lot but never die. In sum, desire me and do with me everything suggested in the lyrics of those incredible Peruvian waltzes you once gave me, because of their ineffable words, and which I'm sure I'm remembering very inaccurately.

In sum, do whatever the hell you want with me, but first concede me the pardon—even if it's only for an instant—of reading the two brief paragraphs that follow.

How could I have reproached you for having found what all of us have searched for: love, a bit of happiness, and peace. And more: I know better than anyone just how honorable your search has been. You've never played the role of seducer. Actually it's you who's always been seduced by love, which reflects so clearly your untiring heart, just as you said to me once.

My love, we're like little dogs. We need petting. And like a faithful little dog, I thank you for the petting you gave me one day. Today, I wish you a marvelous spring, the best of all, and that your love be beautiful, as you are. If it is and if she loves you, I'll always love her as well.

I give you the tenderest hug I've ever given in my life.

Your Fernanda

P.S.: I have a good piece of news to give you as well. It's very likely that two of my books of children's stories will be published in Mexico, of all places. And, with luck, they'll also accept my illustrations. Meaning that I'm a hard, diligent worker.

My answer was a telephone call. A call that was so tender, so, so sincere, so everything. Of course, I incorporated into my words, into each one of them, the death of Just Flor. I think I talked to Mía for three or four hours. I'd have been able to pay for a flight to and from El Salvador for what I paid for that call. But that wasn't important. To hear Fernanda María's voice, which sounded so alive, so healthy, that after a good while, it again transmitted the sensation of being the voice of someone who feels like Tarzan at the moment he dives into the water, that was the important thing. Fernanda María was pulling me right out of the shit with the mere tone of her voice, the way she coated the desperation that led me to dial her number with words, to the point that she almost made that despair disappear.

And the things she said to me—the savage—doubtless only to make me feel deeply, forever, that life goes on, Juan Manuel Carpio. Unforgettable because they were so daring, the things you said to me that night, Fernanda María.

"Listen to me, Juan Manuel Carpio. And, naturally, you'll have to excuse me, but the truth is that through correspondence we live, or as you might say, 'at the end of the enormous distance.' I've just been asking your forgiveness, and still dying of jealousy, which seems incredible to me— over a love that has already died . . . Well, no, *died* isn't exactly the right word. Let's say that I've been asking your forgiveness over a love that's already killed itself. It sounds horrible, I know, but you understand me. And if you don't understand me, I beg you to make the effort to take note of the *Estimated Time of Arrival* of correspondence, meaning, put yourself in my skin. A person lives accustomed to certain ETAs, and the telephone seems a genuine qualitative and quantitative leap in time, and even in mores and customs, and even in the form in which a person like me was educated, if you push me a little. So, my love, my friend, if the ETA of life and letters has always behaved atrociously with us, the ETA of the telephone seems destined to make us go completely insane, at the very least. And if you add to that a tragedy in the meanwhile and a true mixup of letter ETAs and telephone ETAs, you tell me if it's my fault, even for having hung up when probably if I hadn't done it that night, we'd still be cursing each other out and probably Just Flor would still be alive. But, hell, I was thinking about your phone bill, too. Not only about my rage and jealousy. Calling me up . . . With the other woman sitting there, savoring everything . . ."

"Wrong, Mía. I can take anything from you except slander."

"Excuse me, my love. I thought I'd made you laugh a little bit, despite everything. And I took advantage of whatever was at hand. I made a terrible mistake and ask for your forgiveness."

"Go on, go on talking, Mía, please."

"But I'm worried about your phone bill, Juan Manuel Carpio. I know you've been making good money for a while now, but there's no sense in . . ."

"Then tell me something that will send me to bed, and to sleep, with this shitty broken arm."

"It must hurt a lot."

"And besides that, it itches under the cast. So tell me something, please, tell me that never in our lives have we ever argued. And make me believe it."

"Nothing would give me greater pleasure, my love. So listen now, carefully, very carefully, please: elephants, those mastodons, are extremely slow, secure creatures that D. H. Lawrence domesticated especially for us. Meaning that the day will come . . ."

"What day, Fernanda? Which day . . . ?"

"What a nice yawn Mr. Juan Manuel Carpio has made for us . . . Okay, then, I'll tell you soon. I'll explain it all better another day, because it would be the absolute limit if you were to fall asleep while I reasoned things out and explained them to you . . . Hello? . . . Juan Manuel? . . . My love, are you there? . . . Can you hear me, sweetheart?"

"Flor Mía . . . ?"

"That's right, Juan Manuel of my soul . . . That very thing . . . And a very good night, my adored elephant."

As if I had stayed asleep for more than a year, my correspondence with Mía did not begin again until July of 1985. We deserved to become reacquainted. At least that was what she'd decided, and I was willing.

New York, July 14, 1985

Dear Juan Manuel,

Your letter reached me today in New York. In the middle of so much moving around, so many of your road tours, God knows how and when that solitary meeting of the two of us will take place. I want so much for it to happen, and I think we both deserve it. Will it be with each of us standing on the wing of a different plane? In any case, I'll tell you where I'm going to be, and hope you can stop off before you go to Peru.

I leave New York for London on the 18th of July, and I'll be there a good while because Rodrigo has some problem with parasites that they can't treat in El Salvador, and I'm afraid I'm going to be dealing with doctors for a long time in England. I mean that you can call me, write me, or come see me at:

198 Old Bromston Road, London SW5
Tel: (01) 430 2825

In a separate package, I'm sending you my two books of childrens' stories, which just came out

206

in Mexico. I want you to give me your sincerest opinion.

My joy at knowing you're healthy and content is huge, immense. I hope to see you soon. Set aside a special, large, and beautiful space for me in your extremely tight agenda. Please accept the love of your

Fernanda

My commentaries were not slow in coming. And I've kept a copy of them, as I did of many of the letters I sent to Mía after so many of them were stolen that time in Oakland in 1981—or was it 1982?

Most beloved Fernanda,

Your stories: terrific! And thanks a thousand times over for having thought of me to read them and, even more, to give you an opinion of them. I'll sum up that opinion like this: each new sentence augments the charm and flexibility of these stories, which emerged one after another from your guts, with that eternal triumph, which was always in you, of joy over pain. Of that you certainly have the secret (or the secret has you).

A shame they didn't let you illustrate your own stories, because the little drawings can't hold a candle to your tales. But, well, asking that every note be a high C is like ordering up hoarseness for Pavarotti.

Once more, congratulations. This is becoming a litany, but believe me, the music comes from a good orchestra.

Take care of yourself. And lots of kisses and even greater *successes* (as we say in these parts). By the ton. From the top down and from the bottom up.

Allow me to daze you with hugs.

Juan Manuel

P.S.: I'll be going to Lima for a few weeks, but by the end of August I'll be back, and all for you— Minorca and environs included, along with your humble servant.

London, July 27, 1985

Beloved Juan Manuel,

How great it was to read your letter this morning! I only wish you'd call to tell me how your summer plans are going. Perhaps you're already in Lima. Your idea that we get together in Minorca seems very good to me. I think we'd be able to come toward the end of August or the beginning of September. During the first half of August we're going to be here, then in Paris, in the apartment you know, and we'll also go to Switzerland for a few days. Wherever I am, there's always room for you.

How I long to see you! How odd this acrobatic love is, jumping over years and places. I liked finding you so well in your last letter, and that it was delivered to me just when I arrived. Super remote control.

The kids are happy to see their cousin, and I'm very happy to be chatting with my sisters. Andrea's new house is pretty. I've even felt a desire to stay here and study something.

I expect news about Lima, if you're still there and the mail gets to you.

A big hug.

Your Fernanda

Why did I write these things about my trip to Lima? Was I hoping to keep Mía and her kids away from the Minorca house? Away from Just Flor's gardens? Knowing myself, I'd say it's very likely, but knowing Mía's enthusiasm, I also had no doubt she wouldn't pay the slightest attention to my efforts. And today I'm ashamed, I really repent and feel enormous chagrin for having written her things like these, a few days after returning from Lima to Minorca, to await her there with her sick little Rodrigo and her always pretty and smiling Mariana.

Minorca, August, 1985

Mía, Mía—though this is starting to sound like a cat—

In Lima, I spent almost all my time in the house of my friend La Leona, who's now in San Diego with her mother, brothers, little daughter, and brother-in-law. The dogs in Lima bite. Ergo, one attacked me, but thank God he didn't break the skin and only left a bruise. I ended up with some damage to my third nut (someone ascribed an unknown malady to me).

Effusions like whale spoutings. I miss you.

Juan Manuel

Fernanda María de la Trinidad del Monte Montes almost kills me with her elegant indifference and tender joy. Everything built up her hopes, despite the pestilence of my earlier letter.

London, August 13, 1985

Most beloved Juan Manuel Carpio,

It's great that you've made it to Minorca and that all this terrible running around is over, and that you've got a few clear days ahead of you. Your telegram with dates and addresses got here fine, and luckily everything will work out marvelously. Like you, I can't get there before September, because we're going to France and Switzerland with my aunt, and I can't leave her alone. She'll go back to London on September 2, and we'll leave then for Barcelona. So we can be at your house on the second or third of September.

The way to "Canseco" seems stupendous to me. Like a pirate treasure map. Don't give me any more hints, unless your friend from the Bar Bahía runs off to Río or something.

The idea of seeing you soon has me all worked up.

The summer here is horribly cold and rainy, but of course no one comes to London for the climate.

I embrace you, as we English say, "with my deepest love."

Fernanda

Crans-sur-Sierre, August 27, 1985

Most beloved Juan Manuel Carpio,

Pardon my silence, but I've been hysterical with Rodrigo's sickness, which the doctors seem unable to resolve. Finally, after four days in the hospital and thousands of tests, they've decided that it's a strong allergic reaction to the bite of a poisonous spider, which no one, not even Rodrigo, remembers ever having bitten him. They've already given him a million medicines, and here we are crossing our fingers in hope that he gets better quickly. We managed to leave London on Friday, and now we're in Switzerland, as you see, counting on the miraculous effect of the mountain air. We'll be here for about ten days. The weather isn't great, but, well, the air is the air.

From here we go back to Paris for a few days, which should take us to the 8th or 10th of September. Now don't get upset. We won't be coming back with my aunt. She's going on according to her own plan, but we're staying until December and perhaps even longer, which appears to be necessary if we want to get Rodrigo completely cured. That's more or less the time frame the London doctors gave. It seems the poor thing was hit with a really ferocious poison.

I beg you to forgive me for so many changes of plan and so much delay, but I promise you that as soon as I can, I'll call to give you an exact arrival date.

I love you deeply,

Your Fernanda

The one to make the biggest changes was, ultimately, me, but, well, I think anyone would understand the multiple levels of reasoning that made me do it. These changes have no logical order of priorities, like everything else we do, moved by very diverse and even contrary reasons of the heart, which reason doesn't understand, etc., meaning that, hell, again, "in the throes of a thousand contradictions." But there was one good, very good indeed, and very well-intentioned reason. My house and Just Flor's gardens were not very far from the port of Mahón, but they were far enough away from a good beach where the poor little tarantulized Rodrigo and *La* Mariana, as Mía always called her, could really enjoy the sun and sea, and also exempt me from a daily Canseco-beach commute, which would take me right by the *scene of the crime*—the saddest crime that ever happened or ever will happen to me, while my adored guest, seated at my side in the white Opel in favor of which our green Alfa Romeo collector's item, now doubly historic, had been discarded, to say the least, that is, my adored guest noted that so much Canseco-beach to-ing and fro-ing for the happiness of all and the health of poor little Rodrigo look how skinny and weak he is, and my God this kid never stops scratching, my love, I swear that if I could scratch myself even a little in his name and itch, Juan Manuel Carpio, meaning that so much Canseco-beach is making my beloved singer gloomier and gloomier, more and more wound up in himself, with the hope that we all come here, the hope that I above all came here with, and with the face of happiness mixed in with another reason of the heart with which he received us, as with his eyes jumping out of his head and probably even with the *sad pleasure of doing the things he did with her* as the poet wrote, more or less, although he also did them with me, I'm more than convinced, but okay, enough, *Don't say another word, let me imagine the past doesn't exist,* as Lucho Gatica sang, during the same years when the poet, it seems to me, but, well, what does it matter . . . Yes, enough, once and for all, Fernanda María de la Trinidad del Monte Montes, that you've got two children and even a husband in Chile, though the truth is that it's as if this Enrique fellow is fading away on us, the kids practically never mention him anymore, and it makes you sad that people grow dim that way, all alone, poor things, but well deserved in his case, I should say so, and although, well, of course, he goes on being married to me and me, as if nothing had happened, not even asking for a divorce, so, enough, then, how, once and for all, Fernanda María de la Trinidad del Monte Montes, so why, then, can't poor Juan Manuel Carpio have even a dead love, no matter how jealous it makes me and no matter how I'd really kill him, yes, I'd kill him . . .

It's true. It's incredible how well you can put yourself in the skin of the person you love, for all time, and despite how democratic and tolerant and understanding and how much of a good host we are to the reasons of the heart, etc., of our ever-so-expected guest, although Mía is once again operating with a terrible *Estimated Time of Arrival* and although all of that forces us to overcome the Hamlet we all have inside ourselves, that is, to overcome a *To be or not to be, but at the airport* in this specific instance, that is, an overwhelming and very comprehensible *To go or not to go, but to meet Fernanda at the airport,* and suppose we were to head for the hills, to vamoose? Impossible, impossible because in this instant I adore you, Mía, in this instant, and although it lasts only an instant, all the reasons of the heart, etc., have combined in the fact that I really do love you, my love, and in the fact that the poor little tarantulized boy, how is he to blame and how would the beautiful Mariana be to blame, in this instant that's prolonging itself, the stars have all lined up on your side, Mía, so that *Wait for me in heaven, Just Flor, my heart,* Lucho Gatica again, and you and your offspring at the airport, Fernanda Mía, wait for me because I'm racing there, I've got the pedal to the metal, flying, before other reasons and temptations of the heart, that, I'm more than sure, your reason certainly understands, red-haired Salvadoran of my soul . . .

The decision had been made, as you can well understand, especially now that guest and host had managed, in fractured interior monologues, to place themselves so reasonably within the heart of the other, although very grudgingly, and even I'd kill you at times. The decision had been made, also, because as long as I'm alive no other woman will trample the gardens where Just Flor, day by day, left her love for me in each plant, in each colorful vine, in the Lima bougainvillea I asked her to plant for me, and here I'd love to have some jasmines, you shitty mute, flower with no shoot . . .

And the decision had been made because that disgusting family of Just Flor absolutely refused to give me, or even sell me, the little urn with her cremated body inside, and, mind you, I begged and begged, I killed myself insisting and begging them, but there was nothing to be done, they loved her so little, they despised that girl so much, that girl whose father was so silent and whose mother was so sad, as my compatriot Abraham Valdelomar wrote one day, that no one knew how to teach her joy, and thus, they didn't even allow her to rest finally in floral peace at the Canseco, where I loved her and where oblivion had become impossible because of being so long and because of how traumatized I was about her absurd and atrocious death.

And the final decision, the sentence with no appeal, the sentence of that conscientious, sentimental, and tolerant jury was that I would rent a rather large and comfortable apartment on Cala Galdana, right on the beach and everything, in sum, what was right, most equitable and balanced, also, so that there no one would become overly self-preoccupied or become gloomy, no one would want to kill anyone else, in the happy and longed-for although delicate weeks we were going to be together, and so the pretty Mariana could spend all her time smiling and extremely affectionate, which she was, and, finally, so that all this vacationing next to so much Mediterranean coastline, the most extreme opposite of the ferocious Pacific coastline of his ocean at home, would work a miracle and the poor little tarantulized boy would stop scratching once and for all and let his mother live in peace in my arms.

But, truth be told, no sooner had Mía called to tell me the day, the hour, the flight that would bring them to Mahón, and no sooner had I told her about the apartment on the beach, with lots of rooms so that poor little Rodrigo and poor little us, etc., but I could no longer sleep at Canseco, thanks to Just Flor, or even in the hotel where I rented a room so I could sleep a little, although thanks this time to the fact that the days remaining before I could embrace Mía became eternal, just as, later, the hours became eternal, as did, in turn, the minutes and the seconds, and eternal the landing of the plane, and the picking up of baggage, then customs, both eternal because finally they arrived on an international flight and so after having lived a kind of *From Here to Eternity,* and completely "in the throes of a thousand contradictions," for the first time in such a long time, no sooner did I see my skinny, red-haired, freckled, and elegantly long-nosed Fernanda María de la Trinidad del Monte Montes, no sooner did I see her looking around for me anxiously, then see me and smile exactly as she always had, I turned her into the red-haired Deborah Kerr in the longest kiss in film and beach history, in *From Here to Eternity,* and I began to kiss her eternally on the beach at Cala Galdana, and I kissed her and kissed her just as I'd kissed her the days and their following nights, that is, until I transformed myself into the Burt Lancaster of that film that put its mark on my adolescence, so that you can imagine how, and how much, Mía and I kissed on the beach, and not on the beach, because she being so white-skinned and pretty and distinguished, as much, no, even more than Deborah Kerr, now that I think of it, but as far as I was concerned, as Burt, well, that was more difficult, owing to the fact that my paternal grandparents immigrated to Lima from Andahuaylas, still speaking more Quechua than Spanish, and my maternal grandparents immigrated in the same way, though from Puno, which explains the Indian features so apparent on my record jackets and the covers of my cassettes, especially in profile, which is the view of me my agent exploits most. Therefore, my chances of being taken for Burt Lancaster, who was also thin and athletic and in a bathing suit, on a U.S. beach to boot, were somewhere between small and nil. Nevertheless, our kisses achieved all of that. On the beach and not, with waves and without, in the sand and not, from here to eternity and not, and in our tender nights of love and search for lost time, and yes.

And how wonderful, how wonderful, how wonderful, and how wonderful was the comment I most heard Mía say, in public and in private, while Mariana and Rodrigo wandered off among some distant rocks, he scratching himself less and less, and she enjoying the summer more and more, and they would reappear only when it was time to eat, Mariana, now nine years old, enjoying her vacation as never before, and he scratching himself less and less, and now he's twelve years old, no, that's a lie, Juan Manuel . . .

"What's a lie, Mía? That he's twelve or that he scratches himself fewer and fewer times per minute?"

"Both things, Juan Manuel Carpio. How wonderful."

The little brother and sister brought us sea urchins for lunch and dinner, and they prepared them Chilean style, or at least that's what they called it, probably celebrating—without even realizing it, the little angels—the only contribution their father ever made to their education and culture. And we happily ate them and happily digested them, and happily moved on to dessert and after-dinner time with my lulling guitar as well, but the day came when, exceptionally, although I must confess that life is that way because that exception was repeated more than once, Fernanda did not say how wonderful when she awakened in the morning with me at her side, although she did smile and amiably wish me a good day with kisses on my forehead, and thanked me for the thousandth time for my invitation to the beachfront apartment with the many beautiful views, though most of them we never viewed, Juan Manuel Carpio.

But the always-adored bitch has never, to this day, told me why several times she did not say, in morning mode, naked, half-asleep, How wonderful it is to open my eyes beside you, with a view of the sea, my love, although I always suspected it was because, suddenly, in a flash, I must have stopped looking eternally like Burt Lancaster, and after having dreamed about Just Flor, out loud, I recovered completely my Indian mien and the not very slim look I have from both front and side, which I owe to the beings who brought me into the world, in Lima, by then the second urban generation, no matter that they managed to give me a completely white and coastal education, just as Western and Christian as the one my father had received, who rose to be a Supreme Court judge, when that still meant something in Peru. And, like my father in the field of law, I, too, stood out, but in the field of letters, with a major in literature at the University of San Marcos, the most ancient university in the Americas and my eternal alma mater, and I even won two poetry contests in a row, besides being unanimously declared the Young Poet of the Year before I took off for Europe, although the poet and student Carpio now sings rather than declaims, a bit like Brassens in France, although Carpio plays the guitar much better, and the music he composes, ladies and gentlemen of the jury, composes autodidactically . . . has, yes, has something of Atahualpa Yupanqui to it, and even a touch of Edith Piaf, I'd be so bold to say, if you were to force me to characterize . . .

"What he has, with your permission, Dean, is a great future in front of him. And he should travel, to Paris for example, because I think he needs a little more hunger, as was the case of our immortal César Vallejo, with his thunder-storm in the City of Light . . ."

"Restrict yourself to the business at hand, Mr. Secretary."

"Well, *as time goes by,* as the saying goes . . ."

But I should also say, out of simple respect to the truth, what I did not do after that first morning when Mía failed to say how wonderful, before and after giving me her *Thanks to life, which has given me so much.* I began, for example, finding everything how wonderful, even pretending I was still asleep and dreaming out loud about her and Burt Lancaster at her side, that is, *my* side and *my* self, but either Fernanda was the most intelligent and intuitive women in the world, or I was a terrible out-loud dreamer, because the more I dreamed and dreamed, even in the voice of my best performances, lulling her with unpublished love songs, doubtless the fruit of a long and profoundly in-love sleep, we awoke more and more In-dianized every day, or at least I did, and with a view of the sea. And I can remember playing some tricks, though I can't remember now the number or the order in which I used them, to make Fernanda say, once again, how wonderful, upon waking up in the morning, and I literally ended up try-ing to rape her while I was still asleep, like a log, although always imitating, in my dreams, the finest, most elegant and refined Burt Lancaster from *The Leopard,* but I fear that not only her thighs, as in García Lorca's poem, but all of Fer-nanda got away from me, like the most astonished fish. And we went along that way until one morning I not only got fed up with awakening as Indianized as usual, but that, like Burt Lancaster, furious in some film noir, my Indian side, as we say in Peru, leaped out and—"Damn it all!" I shouted. "Skinny bitch! I haven't spent a ton of money here renting this apartment just so you can start missing that drunk Enrique!"

Anyone can imagine the rest: *From Here to Eternity* turned into a reverse version of *Gilda,* with Mía as Glenn Ford and me as Rita Hayworth, and the slap from the movie was so loud on my cheek that in the huge bed in their bedroom Mariana and Rodrigo, upset and nervous, woke up; add to that an extremely overcast day, when the various vistas were opened, and beginning with a breakfast of false smiles, failed hugs, and little oh-well kisses, I could eat you up, Rodrigo, my darling bite victim, with no results whatsoever, the tarantulized lad began to scratch himself almost as much as he had the day he landed in Minorca, and that very night at dinnertime he was scratching himself almost as much as he had when he saw his first doctor in London, which made me so sorry that I was scratching my head for hours, thinking and rethinking a negotiated settlement for a crisis that was as serious as it was earthshaking. I should confess that Mía also scratched her head a great deal and that from time to time we both looked at each other as lovers and pals, and that, at certain moments, we were on the point of turning into thinking Rodin statues by virtue of scratching ourselves.

I have the immense honor and pleasure to have been the first to spy land, although, of course practically everyone knows, now that Fernanda and I have repeated it in a thousand and one interviews, at least in the Spanish-speaking *urbi et orbi,* how everything began that happy day at Cala Galdana when I shouted "Land! Land! I've just had a great idea, Mía!" setting into motion a complete literary and musical project that not only resolved Mía's economic problems forever, with the passing of years, but is also the essential reason why Rodrigo and Mariana are both cum laude graduates of Harvard and even own summer homes on the coast of El Salvador. He specializes in making money on the New York Stock Exchange and she in adoring a little boy whose first name is my full name, meaning that his first name is Juan Manuel Carpio, and his first *last* name is Monte Montes, and, well, in fact, no one remembers exactly what the child's *second*—Araucanian, of course—last name actually is.

But anyway, after having launched myself like some Jonathan Swift on "an universal censure unprovoked . . . I now happily resume my subject, to the infinite satisfaction, both of the reader and the author, After so wide a Compass as I have wandered, I do now gladly overtake, and close in with my Subject, and shall henceforth hold on with it an even Pace to the End of my Journey, except some beautiful Prospect appears within sight of my Way, . . ." the memory of the extremely successful future of the tarantulized boy and the ever-so-maternal tenderness that the always beautiful and smiling Mariana came to feel for my complete name, no matter that in some future letter Mía would write: "El Rodrigo and La Mariana get more and more eccentric every day."

Anyway, we were at the point where I shouted, "Land! Land!" and "I've just had a great idea, Mía!"

"I'm dying to hear it, brother. Tell me! Tell me!"

"Come on, Mía. Let's go to the beach and I'll tell you everything."

"Juan Manuel, how can you talk about beaches at a moment like this?"

"Let's go, Tarzan, a little dive into the sea, a little swim, *cheek to cheek,* and I'll tell you everything."

"No little swim, nothing, Juan Manuel, the time is not ripe, no, I'm warning you, I mean I've got acute tonsillitis today."

"Damn, I bring her all the way to Cala Galdana, but it turns out she's got a husband. Excuse me, that's what García Lorca would have said, Mía."

"Ve-ry fun-ny, asshole."

"And am-nes-i-ac to boot, ass . . ."

"Kindly explain what you mean by that."

"That I'm forgetting my great idea."

"All right. I'm not a whore, let's get that straight, but I will go to bed with you right now if you recover your memory."

Revenge, they say, is a dish best eaten cold, and it should be the truth, because Mía and I went to bed as we had since time immemorial, but for the first time, at least with her, the momentary son of a bitch I'd become had stopped smoking a month earlier, as in the tango, meaning zero, zero, and nothing, resulting in what psychiatrists call . . . a fiasco.

Meaning that—because Mía and I always had a frankly positive and optimistic side, even in our worst moments—we left the living room as if nothing had happened, went right to work, from the very instant when Mía said that that was the most wonderful thing anyone had ever proposed to her in her life, and that not only could it prove to be a most lovely idea, if she didn't let me down, of course, because, at the artistic level, although she did have two books of children's stories published, and in Mexico no less, and seven unpublished— that, too, of course—but also that I should get an agent or something, because in El Salvador there aren't even publishing companies, and in California they translate only things that have already been published, and in London, well, what with Rodrigo I didn't have time even to find out the names of the children's book publishers . . .

"You're drifting off the subject, Mía."

"It must be fear. And the reason is that, at the artistic level, even though I have two books published, and in Mexico no less . . ."

"You can't see the forest for the trees, Mía."

"Fuck! Excuse me, Juan Manuel Carpio, this is the most wonderful thing anyone ever proposed to me in my life, but artistically I feel like a dwarf next to you, and I'm *dying* of fear that I'll let both of us down."

"Mía . . ."

"Fuck! Juan Manuel Carpio, how wonderful and how wonderful, and how wonderful and how wonderful . . . And it really is a lovely idea."

"In that case, let's get to work. And let's begin with the words to this song, look here, read them. Composed by me, it is and will always be, no matter how hard I try, anything but a song that could interest a child."

"I'll infantilize it for you, my love."

"Now we're getting somewhere. You see, I'm dying to have among my records at least one for children. But I know I'll never be able to do it myself. So I'm going to give you themes, outlines, verses, maybe even an entire lyric, and then you'll see if you can take my dictator, let's say, and make him into some sort of big bad wolf, or if I'm talking about Mother Teresa, maybe you could get some Little Red Riding Hood action going for me, things like that . . . So what are you laughing at, if you don't mind my asking?"

"I'm laughing because it's true, my beloved Juan Manuel Carpio, you could never compose a song for children. What do you think, that they're idiots or something?"

"I understand, and, once again, that's the idea. I'll give you any theme, outline, idea, poem, and, as you put it so aptly, you'll infantilze it for me, and I'll supply the music."

"It's a deal, my adored partner."

"Wait one minute. A warning, so things are clear from the beginning."

"I'm all ears."

"That on more than one occasion, probably, you'll have to encounter a little girl named Luisa, and another named Just Flor, and probably even an Enrique."

"It's a deal, my adored son of a bitch."

We were a hit. It took a lot of work and a few years, but we were a hit. And, at least in the Spanish-speaking *urbi et orbi,* practically everyone recognizes the compact discs with photos of us on them. Underneath the pictures, it says: "Conception, music, and performance by Juan Manuel Carpio. Lyrics by Fernanda María de la Trinidad del Monte Montes."

Of course, there isn't a producer or album designer in the world who hasn't explained a thousand and one times to Mía that it's a lot of words for such a small space, and your whim may even turn out to be, shall we say, anticommercial, so I beg you to abbreviate all those names a bit, Doña Fernanda. Why don't we just make it simply, and very artistically, María Trinidad? And, of course, she and I had more than one argument on the subject, but let's just say that Mía is totally incapable of not honoring the memory of her deceased father, and of loving above all things in this world her adorable mother, meaning that the lyrics will always be by María de la Trinidad, etc., as her own sisters know her, even though they have had the odd argument about the matter, but as Mía herself writes me even today in her letters, which are becoming less and less frequent and more and more adorable: "My sisters are sometimes fine and sometimes fighting with me, as is normal, and I in the middle try at least to retain some composure. Sometimes I actually do." And, well, since we were always better by letter—in any case, I was—Mía also writes me, now almost thirty years after adoring each other for the first time and for always, such things as: "Maybe I'll go to San Salvador in July or August. It's hard for me to go since the death of my mother, without a doubt the one person in the world who enjoyed my letters most. No doubt that explains why I've stopped writing in these past years. Meaning that you should forgive me, my adored partner, my adored friend, my adored you, Juan Manuel Carpio, really I do beg your forgiveness for this secondhand silence that has fallen upon you."

That summer at Cala Galdana, Mía and I ended up working day and night on our first project. And of course one day we'd be laughing our heads off and the next we'd be at each other's throats, for no reason whatsoever, or because she wanted to stop working for at least a couple of hours and I accused her of not taking the project seriously, to which she would retort that I was a slave driver, to which I'd counter that what I knew was how to earn my living by the sweat of my brow, while you, you shitty oligarch, even when you're half-dead of hunger you go on being playing the little heiress and no-good landowner, all of which took us back to our Parisian youth, there in her apartment on rue Colombe, when everything for me was a lot of cold in winter, and hunger, even in summer, poor left-wing metro-entrance, café, and restaurant singer with his eternal cap, and thank you so much, *monsieur,* and everything for her, *le tout Paris* and UNESCO and a green Alfa Romeo, brand-spanking-new, and I loved to desperation the disappeared Luisa, oh how abandoned I was with my half-Andahuylino and half-Puneño Lima complex, and my Che Guevara-and-a-half haughtiness, which was when Mía gathered me to her clean, healthy, marvelous bosom, and later what happened was what had to happen, but here we are to celebrate it, partners, doddering lovers of Verona, friends before all else, delightful in bed, and buddies, my buddy, till death us do part, although, of course, with the way we arrange the business of our *Estimated Time of Arrival,* that is to say, badly, probably what we really need is to be dead so we can be completely together finally, and for insane and evil reality to leave us in peace, isn't that so, my adored Juan Manuel Carpio? What do you think—that would be our only hope, wouldn't it?—but let me give you a kiss and a hug the way I uselessly hugged you on rue Colombe, and even so, how beautiful all that was, even having fought like that is now a pleasure, my love, but okay, back to work and let's not fight anymore, because I've already noted that we fight for a while and then we're friends, delightfully, for a while, certainly, but poor Rodrigo is at the point where he scratches one day and doesn't the next.

It took a lot of work to produce a hit, for sure, and there were even people who wondered if Juan Manuel Carpio hadn't lost his touch. Why suddenly songs for children? Maybe the Peruvian artist has gone soft, with all these lullabies and all this lulling. And of course, since no one is a prophet in his own land, my first concert for children, in Lima, caused one of those perverse and envious critics—there's always one—to publish an article titled nothing less than "Juan Manuel Carpio, or the New Demon of the Andes," in which he compared me to Francisco de Carvajal, the savage Spanish conquistador who, at the age of eighty-three, still fought like mad, conquering half of Peru, and crossing, as if it were nothing, always greedy for more glory and for all the gold in Peru, the pugnacious octogenarian, again and again crossing the frozen peaks of the Andes on horseback. Until, finally, they nailed him, pistol in hand; they fell on him like a pack of dogs, the way they did to Juan Charrasqueado, shot in that Mexican song that has his name in the title, and reduced him to a mere package, tying him and tying him and folding him all up so he'd fit in a basket, and when they got him in, they tossed him, once and for all, into the next world. Well, that perfidious critic compared me to him, in part because the last words of the ferocious and proud Demon of the Andes, folded forever in his fatal basket, were: "Junior in bed, grandpa in bed—all content." "Well, something similar is happening nowadays with Juan Manuel Carpio," that damned scribbler concluded, no doubt inspired by the hatred and envy provoked by the fact that even though I may have been softened and finished, the immense tent where I sang was overflowing with children.

I'll never forget that tour. I flew directly from Lima to Santiago, the first stage of a long Chilean *tournée,* with a double intention. On the one hand, I did want to keep on promoting the new CD—"made by four hands," Mía and I liked to say. But I also wanted to pick up the trail that would take me to the location of the great Enrique, because the rapid transformation brought about in the affective life of Mía and her children nevertheless produced in me a great sorrow, proving to me once again just how complicated human emotions can be. Now that she back in El Salvador, having returned from Minorca and London a long time earlier, Mía was simply no longer concerned that Enrique showed no signs of life, and now that Mariana and Rodrigo never even mentioned him, now, the man who for so many years kept us apart, persistently, the man who could have been my great rival, the man I should have hated but who was becoming, in my memory, a close, unforgettable friend. Life had, no doubt, put each of us in the way of the other, but it turned out that when all was said and done, life had never made us opponents. Just the opposite, in fact, and during my Chilean tour, the first in which I had some success as a singer-composer— "by four hands"—of songs for children, I understood, slowly but surely, that this tour was turning into an intense and per-severing search for a beloved being. And it was in Valdivia where I finally learned that Enrique was living in Fuerte Cas-tro, on the island of Chiloé, something that his mother, in Santiago, either didn't want to tell me or didn't know.

I got to Fuerte Castro on a ferry, frozen stiff and carrying a cargo of Frank Sinatra. I asked for Enrique in a small book-store where, I'd been assured, everyone knew him. And I remember now that on the way from the hotel to that shop, I had the strong impression that I was searching for a friend, sometimes at the North Pole and sometimes on one of the thousand islands that make up Sweden, although from time to time I also thought I was in Norway. Anyway, every so often I'd meet up with a guy with the looks and clothing of a sea wolf from polar seas and faces that were sometimes Scandinavian and other times half-Eskimo.

I walked into the little bookstore and was both received and treated like a king, because the great Enrique's Peruvian friend, well, everyone knew him, as if for their entire lives. As a singer they knew practically nothing about me, but as a friend of Enrique, have another glass of wine, Juan Manuel, Enrique will turn up soon, and what a surprise you're going to give him, as soon as he gets off the next ferry and finds out that you've come looking for him all the way out here. Where was Enrique coming from? Oh, from the north, Juan Manuel. He had an accident and broke his arm and he's coming back from wherever it was they operated on him and put him in a cast.

Finally, an Enrique arrived, but one that almost made me start singing children's songs. Because the big Araucanian had shrunk to a normal-size version of himself, or is it that jealousy always makes you see and imagine your rivals as giants, or is it that I have the worst visual memory in the world, or is it that, in fact, the Peruvian singer-composer Juan Manuel Carpio has gone soft? Anyway, Enrique had shrunk, had lost a great deal of his Araucanian mane, and no longer had a sallow complexion, as he did back then when he split open Mía's head and adored her, all at the same time. No, now he'd been Norwegianized, or Swedishized, or something like that, because he was wearing a patriarchal beard and smoking a Protestant pastor's pipe. I mean, everything about him was really strange, except for his smile and the big hug, although his hug lacked its customary strength, but then there was the difficulty anyone would have hugging someone wearing a cast extending from shoulder to pinky.

"What happened to you, brother?"

"I fell off a cloud, little brother."

What I found was that Enrique was so serene and angelical these days that when he got drunk he didn't beat up Socorro or anything of that horrible sort but only tried to fly up to heaven, almost always without much of what you might call success. Socorro is the girl he was living with.

"Please meet my little friend, brother."

"At your service, sir."

That was the first and last thing I heard the humble and saintly Socorro say in the two days and nights that Enrique, she, and I spent together, staring at one another and smiling more than anything else, with me having to get as close to him as possible, my hand cupping my ear in hope of finally hearing what he was saying in that extremely low voice of his, which he muted to boot. Among the few things I understood was that Mía and the children would always be fine, unless they were already in heaven, little angels the three of them. And I understood very little else, although the ambience, shall we say, gave me to understand that Enrique was simply and plainly adored in that place, that he'd found peace, that Socorro was and would be his eternal life raft, and that in her and his friends from the bookstore, the ex-Araucanian had found a cushion of love and affection onto which he could land every time he fell off his cloud.

I didn't want to push him into drinking, so I held off giving him the Sinatra CDs until the last moment, and he didn't want to push himself into anything more than enjoying the pleasure of friendship; and because his latest crash landing was still giving him pain, he, too, held off giving me several cassettes by the pianist Roberto Bravo, one of those masters of music who, like Sinatra, simply makes you very thirsty.

I never saw Enrique again, though from time to time he has sent me a photo, with some poetic words written on the back along with some new address, and always mentioning Socorro with love and gratitude. Most definitely, things did not go completely ill for him, thanks to his being the extraordinary photographer everyone always recognized him to be. Two or three years ago, for example, I saw in the magazine *Ronda Iberia,* which is published by the Spanish airline, a wonderful article on Chiloé and the area around it, and all the marvelous photographs accompanying the text were by Enrique.

Actually, I've gotten ahead of myself here, because I still haven't mentioned how Mía left first Minorca and then London, at the end of 1985, with her adorable and adored Rodrigo completely detarantulized. As always, Mía's letters are the best medium, transmitting everything that summer in Minorca meant, as well as what its concrete results would be. So I'll stick to them, but above all because they're from the time when she still wrote me often. That was our epistolary golden age, which comes almost to an end with the death of her mother in El Salvador in 1992, the event that left her "unworded," to use her own expression, although neither she nor I is dumb enough to put all the blame for our long silences on the death by natural causes of a lady who was by then quite elderly.

There are, then, "other factors." But I'm not going to make another tremendous leap into the future as I did with Enrique and Chiloé, although in that future, from time to time, "some beautiful Prospect appear[ed] within sight of my way," as Swift wrote—I'm quoting him again because he's a real authority on the subject of digressions. One single thing remains clear after reading Mía's letters from those epistolary golden years. I was traveling a lot, and she went on fighting day after day, although sometimes it appeared that her tonsillitis was beginning to become chronic, and our success was still a long time coming.

London, November 9, 1985

My dear partner,

These first weeks in London have been extremely busy.

Aside from bringing Rodrigo to the hospital almost every day, we spend lots of time seeing if there are any possibilities for life here, some job, schools, a place to live, etc. But everything's turning out to be very difficult, and we've decided there's nothing to do but go back to El Salvador. I only hope that's a good decision. Here, the children as always are happy with their cousin, and there's lots of room in Andrea María's house. I'll also tell you that a couple of publishers have shown some interest in my little books. I only hope things move forward.

Today's the first day I've spent at home, with the kids and other things organized. Which is why it's only today I've been able to write you. Besides, I was a little afraid of this letter. I don't really know if we had a good time or not, if we fought or not, if there was the joy I dreamed of or not. Maybe a bit of everything, although I'll be thanking you the rest of my life for what you did for the children and for that so generous idea of making me into your partner.

Tomorrow I'm planning to go out looking for some courses at an art school. If things work out as well as they have until now, I'll be happy. I'd like to squeeze all the juice out of this time here. Maybe I can finally get a little education.

How was your trip to Madrid? And to think you'll soon have to go to Paris. I only hope you can find a little time to come here. I really like London a lot. I don't think I've ever enjoyed a place so much. But you know how forgetful love is. It's a real eraser. As far as right now is concerned, I've never seen a city as right as London.

Thinking over what I said about love and the eraser, that rule doesn't apply in your case, because you've got the most cumulative heart in the world. I felt that a lot in Minorca, where you have about a century's worth of love and tenderness stored up. The children felt it, too, and we all really enjoyed your music and your love right there on the surface in every corner. Right now I'm remembering your little apartment in Paris. There wasn't a single object that didn't get into your house except by love.

Seeing each other took a lot out of us. At least it took a lot out of me. It was painful for me not to feel a real joy in you that I'd arrived (at least that's the impression I still have, no matter how effusive and smiling and tender you might have been) and that you never wanted to bring me out to see "Canseco."

But I hope our friendship and that immense tenderness that never dies are as strong and brave as they've always been, because after all's said and done, as in every gesture and in each of the guitars surrounding you, there's a lot of love.

Take good care of yourself. I'll keep you right up to date on my work for your music. For now, at least, it seems to be going well.

A big hug,
Fernanda María

P.S.: Yours, or, if you like, Mía

San Salvador, February 28, 1986

Dearest partner,

Your letter arrived yesterday: open, with no envelope, torn, delivered by a child. That it wasn't lost was the purest of miracles. The mailman delivered it to the wrong house, and from there they sent it on to me in that sad state.

Coming back was hard for me. First, the initial shock, and then the early attempts to focus my eyes on a country that is as deteriorated or more deteriorated than yours. Leaving aside the fact that what could deteriorate was pretty ugly to start with, then there was getting used to being impotent in the face of events. With this government there isn't even the illusion of having a say in things. But I do know that we should stay here at least for this year. I'll try to take advantage of the time, which is the only wealth of underdevelopment, by working hard on your sketches and poems. I've also been painting and hope to keep on with it. Finally I see some progress.

The possibility of a recording "by four hands" really excites me. Today—right now—I'm going to start working, but I'm afraid you won't know anything until the end of March, when you come back. I think you'll perhaps only receive this letter then. You can see that the tropical forest becomes thicker every day. It's almost impenetrable. Maybe I'll get a post-office box.

I'll sign off, then, so I can send this letter today, and that way you can travel on the 7th with the reassuring knowledge that I'm still alive (though I am a bit muted, as if living in semidarkness), and that I commence, full of desire, work on our project. The small advances have raised me up, and I hope the energy bears fruit.

Your news and your confidence in me have given me my first joy since coming back here.

I hope you have a good trip.

I thank you and thank you a lot,

Your Fernanda and/or Mía

San Salvador, March 30, 1986

Dearest Juan Manuel Carpio,

Well, it's March, and I wonder how your life is, how your guitars (which made me so nervous) are sounding, and how your plans or preparations are going with regard to Peru, and how inclement the Minorca winter must seem to you.

Here in San Salvador, it's spring almost all year round, and a flock of green parrots has decided to use one of the trees in my garden as a motel. It's a tremendous racket at about six in the afternoon. The tropics have their charm. They also have other things.

It's taken me a long time to figure out the Minorca trip. With Rodrigo's sickness added to everything else, I came under what you could call extreme emotional circumstances. It's tough to reconcile the desire I've had for such a long time to make the trip with the impression I got from you at times—only at times— that we'd grown unexpectedly apart. Months have gone by, and I wish I could say that I've recovered. I wish I could.

Working for you, even from the other side of the ocean, makes me very happy. And how well you know it, you dog.

And now I feel completely yours,
Mía

San Salvador, April 19, 1986

My dearest partner,

Finally I have a way of sending you my words for your songs. Not all, of course, but some. A friend is leaving for Germany this weekend, and he can mail my letter from there. Frankly, the mail from here is extremely slow, and I'm afraid my letter won't get there by either Easter or Pentecost.

I really hope you like my words. I had such a good time writing them. If there's something you don't like, don't be afraid of tasting things and adding your own pinch of salt. Don't think you'll be offending me.

I haven't received your answer to my letter mailed from the United States by yet another traveler. Please don't stop writing. Although they're slow and have to travel the roads, letters do finally arrive, even to these remote spots. Anyway, many fewer arrive when none are sent, and I won't even bring up the matter of letters that are never written, as in the case of my mute sisters.

It would be a great thing for me if you could use my texts, and I hope you can convince your agent to have me mentioned as coauthor. It would be a lovely first step in the right direction. You'll tell me how this all works out.

How was your trip? And to think that right now you're probably very close to me here. Perhaps it will occur to you to telephone me. Too bad it was impossible for you to make a little detour from your itinerary. And now you'll only be in your house for such a short time before leaving for Lima. You know, you never stop. It's quite amazing, then, that of all the texts I sent you, of all those well-traveled travelers, not a single Ulysses is missing. I'm just dying to know your reactions. And I'm very curious to know what title you're going to give the album.

A big hug.

Fernanda María

P.S.: I taught a few classes at the high school. I don't like teaching anymore. I'm looking into maybe getting myself a little farm, so we can have someplace to walk when you come. Assuming you do come some-day, that is.

San Salvador, May 27, 1986

Thanks for writing by return mail when you received my letters. You can imagine how curious I was to know your opinion and to see what you'd do with my work. I'm really happy you liked it. Your opinion has the weight of the Supreme Court for me.

I wanted to write you in Lima, but a mail strike had us cut off from the rest of the world. Just this week they started working again, so I'm sending this letter to Minorca.

I changed jobs. Teaching bored me absolutely. Beyond belief. Meaning that very soon I'll be back in some office. As for that little farm project I told you about: it wasn't doable. With the little money I have, I can't get anything except a few barren acres.

I'm happy your singing went over so well in Cuba and that you'll be going back by invitation and in calmer fashion next year. Nothing less than the land of Pablo Milanés and Silvio Rodríguez. So I'm really happy that when you go back it'll be in a calmer fashion than it was this time, when you were probably very tired and returning from Peru.

What was Lima like? I wasn't with you, not even by letter. How's your mother doing? I hope the problems have been resolved. From the newspapers I see we're very cozy with your president. Who the hell knows what our Napoleón Duarte and your Alán García will cook up between them.

Your news was an immense joy for which I'll be thanking you forever.

A big hug from
Your Fernanda

P.S.: Or am I only my own Mía?

San Salvador, June 18, 1986

Dearest partner,

I received the letter where you tell me you'll be away from August to November or December. I hope you get something out of all that time.

I'm not at all well, Juan Manuel. Perhaps this is the first time you're hearing me talk this way, or it may well be I've forgotten that I've written to you before in this tone, which would actually aggravate the thing because it would mean the problem is beginning to become chronic. Everything, just everything, has failed since I came back. I don't know what's left to be done. No matter how much optimism I invent for myself, things here are just fucked up. Ever since I stopped teaching I haven't been able to find a job, and things are starting to get so tight I can't imagine any way of loosening them. If there's any profit from our first album, it would save me. I'm counting on you to do everything possible—and more.

I haven't heard any news from England. Not even from my sisters (now Ana Dolores is over there, too), not even from the publishers I visited, nothing at all. What a shitty deal! I'm even becoming foul-mouthed on this slippery slope where I'm currently standing.

Your letters and your tenderness are a blessing. As are the pure souls of Mariana and Rodrigo, who love me. Besides, he came back from Europe extremely healthy and plump, and, as you well know, you had a lot to do with it. Now they're on vacation.

If you were to get some money for me, please send it right away. I'll write all the information about my bank account on a separate sheet.

I'm sure there's got to be a way out, and maybe because I'm suffering so much I'm stumbling around without seeing it. I feel that every path is dangerous.

I hug you as I always do, except that today I've got the shakes. I know you'll understand me. I can't let you see me this way. I don't want to. Which is why I can't write any more.

A hug. Actually, I'm clinging to you.

Your Fernanda or Mine. Today I just don't know.

My agent was still not enthusiastic about our "four-handed" songs. Neither was the producer, or the company that brought out and promoted my recordings. If I sent Mía money, I'd be creating a false illusion for her, and besides, how was I going to trick her with a money order taken out of my own bank account? Besides, she'd instantly demand copies of the album to give to everyone in her family, not to mention her friends. So I kept on writing her and crushing her with more and more hugs. And when I did manage to give a few recitals for children—in Barcelona, Madrid, and Seville—the reaction of the critics was so negative that the halls where I usually sang began to empty out. Seeing which, my agent, my producers, and my promoters all began to doubt my project even more seriously. Since when songs for children? Since when do you stop singing your own songs? I always answered by quoting the words of some intellectual or newspaperman I'd recently read in a Madrid paper: "I prefer duets to arias and friendship to public relations."

And no sooner did I get back to Canseco than I ran to my desk to start crushing Fernanda María de la Trinidad del Monte Montes. Too bad it was only in writing, though I'd begun to get the feeling that she was starting to prefer it that way.

V

▲▲▲▲▲▲▲

Bob and I Are Fine

Happy memories taste much better mixed with grief.
So in fact I am not sad, but only greedy for pleasure.
                    Gustav Janouch, *Conversations with Kafka*

*I need everything these days, and I think it's this strange and long
winter that has me this way.*

*I wish I could have everyone near me. Meaning really near, in
person, because they're always in my thoughts. Uncle Dick playing
the harp, my dad with his smiling mustache and his big heart, my
five sisters, you and you and you, Charlie Boston, who just got
back from Rome, Rafael Dulanto, back from heaven, his Patricia
U.S.A., who loved him so much, the girlfriends I've had all my
life and their husbands, my buddies, I mean Charlotte and Jean
Charles, Silvia and her Richard, Susana and her Juan Carlos,
and of course my mother, who actually managed to die making
jokes with my dad about "Twenty years? That's nothing." The*

coquette died exactly twenty years after my dad. The exportation of beloved children, as you called it on your last solo album, has left us, the kids and me, really sad these days.

Which is why I'm leaving you for today. Enough nocturnal sadness. The sun will come back to its place and will find us Come piante novelle, rinovellate di novella fronda, *or at least more used to the old thorns.*

Another year is madly rushing to a conclusion, and I think about how little we've written to each other in recent times. Maybe two or three letters have made it out of my pen, even though I'm always thinking that I'm writing you. It must be one of the greatest hallucinations, but besides I'm also thinking that you constantly receive my letter, that you even answer it, and I read your answer every day. That way our old and immense tenderness and our eternal friendship go forward full speed ahead, and that is eternally marvelous. It's always one the greatest surprises of the day.

So everything is perfectly fine, and perhaps it isn't necessary to fill the mailboxes with paper that comes and goes. If the letters manage to get to you so well this way, and your answers also reach me, it's better to avoid that mess of stamps and having to bother the mailmen on every continent. Although, of course, all of this is nothing but a rotten lie, because it's superwonderful to actually receive one of your letters, and it certainly must be the same for you.

—Extracts from two letters from Mía, from 1995 and 1998.

Sausalito, October 4, 1988

My always beloved Juan Manuel Carpio,
How suddenly time passes. After months of anguish when I tried to set myself up again, I now feel, luckily, better, more adapted. Quite an accomplish-

ment, believe me. Basically, it's because I'm finally working at something more stable, something, also, that I like. The business of translation and interpretation is too unstable for me in my situation. It pays well enough, but without a secure support I feel really nervous about not knowing if I'm going to have work the next day. So I went through all this time scared out of my wits. Now I'm working with a writer who publishes a biweekly magazine about finance. The subject is not my usual kind of thing, but, well, I try to understand something and to put it in words, at least in the editorial work. My job is to polish the language, do the layout, help in production. It's quite wonderful. Besides, the place is near home, in a nearby town.

I think that someday you're going to work up the energy to see me again on this continent. I really haven't had luck with your visits, since they've always taken place in someone else's house, and that's hard for both of us. I'd love to have the pleasure of receiving you on my home turf. I haven't abandoned the hope of exploring this part of the country with you, the way we did last year, enjoying the vineyards and mountains, which really are spectacular.

How are things going for you? I got your letter from Minorca, where you talk about your plans for going back to Peru, but always keeping your island house for the months that are winter in Lima but the heart of summer there. Thanks for writing me, as always. The kids never forget the summer we spent with you there. It was a beautiful time for them because neither in the U.S. nor in El Salvador had they ever been at the beach for such a long time. Here we live near the sea, meaning the bay, and our view is terrific. But it's impossible even to put a finger in that water. To begin with, the bay isn't what you'd call clean, and besides, it's terribly cold. But in Minorca you can swim all day. I hope you've had a good season.

I can't see any way of even thinking about visiting you, and I don't know for how long. Even if the trip is much cheaper from here than it is from El Salvador. Also, the money doesn't work against us so much. When you're in San Salvador you think buying an ice-cream cone in another country costs a fortune. As you do in Peru.

I send you all my affection. I send you lots of hugs. I only wish I could spend an afternoon chatting with you. Please send me magazine articles, ideas, things you find interesting, but most of all your new songs. I really need to chat. We always remember you, and your place at the table awaits you day after day, even though the last time you had to get a room in a hotel. How embarrassing, my God, but we simply didn't all fit in the house of the good friends who were putting us up then.

Hugs and kisses,
Fernanda María

Sausalito, October 26, 1989

Dearest Juan Manuel Carpio,

What a pleasure it was to receive your letter after so long, a letter full of news and enthusiasm about your new life in Lima, your new house, your old friends, and your favorite places from before. There's no doubt about it, our moves are never definitive, and it makes me happy you think not even this one was the last.

My move to this coast hasn't been easy, as you can remember from your last visit, when I still didn't even have a bed. But I'm convinced it was necessary. Life in El Salvador, where we were surrounded by injustice and misery we couldn't do anything about, was unacceptable, both for the kids and for me. There are no paradises, and if there were, they probably wouldn't be here, but at least there are more alternatives here for living than there are in El Salvador. And as far as Mariana and Rodrigo are concerned— they're happy. I'm beginning to be happier, after long months like a sail with no wind in it. I think I told you I'm working for a financial publication, as an assistant editor.

I'd really like you to come back, to have you near. I really need my friends. If you come this way, it would be the most wonderful thing for me. I read and reread your letter, and just seeing your handwriting makes me happy.

This week I spoke with your friend Raúl Hernández, the Stanford prof. I want to use his name in a job application as an editor of publications related to the teaching of Spanish, which I think would be much better for me than finance. If it goes through, I'll be happy.

Raúl told me he saw you in Lima, though he didn't have the chance to party with you at all because he was so sick. He's back in Stanford with his two daughters, and he still has his professorship even though he doesn't teach full-time.

How I wish I could be talking to you. I really thank you for your letter, because it pulled me out of the silence, and besides it coincided with my applying for that job it would be so great to get. The good thing is that here, if that doesn't go through, there will be other things. Like moves, it's always good to know this one isn't the last.

Don't disappear, please, because I always love you a lot and every so often need you here.

Mía but yours,
Fernanda María

California, May 13, 1990

Dearest Juan Manuel Carpio,

Now it's our turn to tell you we've moved. We're living in Berkeley, and I really hope you'll visit me someday soon—very soon.

New address: 1492 Sundance Drive, Berkeley, CA 94701. Tel: (415) 867-5743.

We have trees, a good view, and more space, though it's also true the place needs lots and lots of work. I owe all this to you, my dear dear partner. The good sales of our first two albums and that 50% our agent has sent on to me: I spent it all paying for this rather run-down house. Run-down it may be, still it belongs to me and my children. A million thanks for everything. For the agent, for the money, for all the promotional work you've done with the albums. The kids, huge, healthy as can be, and happy.

I include the text I sent to our agent, a kind of c.v.-prologue he wanted for the new catalogues and reissues, which, he tells me, will be coming out soon, and maybe if they're as generous with the money as they were the first time, I'll be able to make those terrifying but totally necessary repairs. Okay, then, here's what I wrote, let's see what you think. I'd be delighted if you liked it:

"I've been asked to tell you something about myself. The first thing I should tell you is that I've always liked stories, poems, songs, and children.

"I know it's going to seem very long and even unbelievable, but my name really is Fernanda María de la Trinidad del Monte Montes. I was born in San Salvador on September 27, 1944, in a small neighborhood that winds around the Primera Calle Levante, near the Hermitage and behind the Aqueduct. I say 'small' because the whole neighborhood consists of three blocks, which all the children who lived there used to crisscross every day. But I just as easily could have said 'huge,' because those of us who were

neighbors there are still friends even today, no matter how far apart we are.

"I worked on many of the songs on these four albums in a 'four-hands style' with the extraordinary singer-composer Juan Manuel Carpio, and they have to do with the subject of our childhood neighborhood, to which we always return, a place where we played, laughed, ran around, and sang when we were children with our friends, a place we never really abandoned, no matter how much we traveled and no matter how far we've moved from it. And God knows the travels through the world that life has sent us on, sometimes without our wishing to, both Juan Manuel Carpio and me.

"That's why I'm so happy these songs were composed in 'four hands,' together with one of my best friends in the world, Juan Manuel Carpio. As if we were playing a children's game, Juan Manuel and I wove these songs together until his music and my words found a common language to sing to you about our countries, cities, neighborhoods, friends, and trips, which is really the story of a marvelous friendship."

I was holding back my tears, because Mía's text had really moved me with its naïve realism, and because I'd just decided the moment had come to say to her: "Okay, my love, come to Lima with your children, and we'll get married as soon as possible. And when we're eighty we'll still be happy for having finally managed to do it," when my eyes slipped down to the following sentence and the farewell:

Bob and I are fine. Receive all my tenderness, my friendship, and my eternal gratitude, in a million kisses and hugs.

Fernanda María de la Trinidad Etc.

Bob? Who the hell was Bob? *What* Bob? Where do you find a man, a Bob, with whom you're just "fine"? At what point did Mía's naïve realism become pure and hard realism? Either you're happy with a man or forget about it. Therefore: Was I going to kill myself, or was I going to kill him and her after having sent the children off to a good boarding school until the time, not so far off, really, when they'd want to go to college? All this is real, and it really transpired inside me, not just in my mind. Yes, it transpired with all its brute force, deep within the essence of my body and soul, my entire nervous system. And, of course yes, logically as well, in my entire sentimental system. And I lost the true path, lost my calmness. But when a decent period of time had gone by, and when, all on their own, the waters receded, I also remembered that my entire organism and—how to put it?—my complete organization, the man in his own sauce, as it were, had already lived through a terrible situation and a terrible sensation, very—and I mean *very*—similar, when Mía told me she'd left Chile feeling sad after saying good-bye to Enrique and her in-laws instead of happy, which was what I expected, because two and two make four. But it was as if two and two made five, and I took it badly that time, though I also took it really terribly again because it brought my time with Just Flor back to me, in the tremendous perpetual-motion machine life is, a whirlpool so voracious that you really have to live clinging to something in the present, something that at least also represents the past in order to perpetuate ourselves in some way and be tolerant and faithful and patient and lasting, or, to put it clearly for a change, so we aren't forgotten, not even when we forget ourselves. Meaning that, no sooner had I finished rereading the letter from my adored Fernanda María de la Trinidad del Monte Montes, than I calmly walked over to the telephone, dialed American Airlines, and booked a ticket to San Francisco. Of course, after that I called her, and told her she could expect me there on Thursday, my love, on American Airlines flight whatever the number was, the one that gets there at 8:00 P.M, *Estimated Time of Arrival.* And I didn't even have to say anything to her about Bob, because, well, the poor guy in all likelihood would have vanished forever thanks to my pure and hard realism.

But despite his presence—a huge and very laconic guest—it was Bob who slept in Mía's bed every day I was in Berkeley, so there was no way I could avoid reaching the conclusion that I was the guest, and that I would probably remain the guest forever. Besides, Bob, the man with whom it was possible to be fine and that's that, turned out to be a highly pacific and penetrating person and, no doubt about it, with nerves that could withstand Fernanda María del Monte Montes and her Juan Manuel Carpio, who never stopped adoring each other from breakfast until the postprandial chat and music session in the evening, sometimes in Mía's house, which would soon collapse, sometimes in a restaurant in Berkeley or San Francisco. Besides, Bob had the special ability to disappear for a long time every night so she and I could peer out a window, hold hands, and speak, for instance, about the incredible way in which we still loved each other and would go on loving each other forever.

"That being the case: *Bob?* . . . What is this Bob doing here, my love?"

"He's the ideal companion, for a million reasons. To begin with, he knows just how much you and I love each other, and he respects it immensely. And then there's that peace that characterizes him, which is contagious. And he adores the kids, who also adore him, and every so often he travels, because the company he works for is capable of sending him to Paraguay one month and the next month to Senegal."

"Forgive me for sticking my nose into your personal life, Mía, but I really have the impression that what Bob most resembles is a rest cure for someone who is in absolutely no way tired."

"I don't see it that way, Juan Manuel. Bob loves me a lot, and I love him, and it's as if he accompanies me in my not living with you. And, if I do say so myself, I also know that I'm excellent company for him."

I stayed for ten days, which passed in a holy and contagious peace, and since on the morning of my departure the house had still not fallen down, and since another of our albums was about to come out, Mía accepted an advance from me so she could, at least, shore up the facade and the side and rear walls of that ancient house in which she'd discovered, no doubt thanks to Bob (to this day I don't know his last name, I swear, though it gives me great pleasure to call him Bob Fine, or Bob Peace, and my wit bothers neither Mía nor Bob, really), a tranquility that she'd been in need of for a long time. And that was the beginning of a series of visits I made to Berkeley, which became more frequent after Rodrigo (first) and Mariana (three years later) entered Harvard, and especially after our music "in four hands" allowed us a series of luxuries and expenses, among which the most important for Mía was the acquisition of a very nice house on Telegraph Avenue in Berkeley. When Bob's there, Mía and I always appear at a window, as if the subject seriously mattered, to Bob or to God, and we spend hours there, completely involved in the importance, historical by now, of our love, tightly holding hands under the moonlight, or whatever kind of light there happens to be. And then I return, deeply infected with peace, to Lima or Minorca. When Bob's away, it's as if God, too, were not around, meaning that we don't appear at any window, just in case the subject does in fact matter to Bob or God this time, in which case of course it does also matter to us because neither you nor I, Juan Manuel Carpio, have ever been able to harm anyone.

"That's the truth, my love."

"Perhaps that was our greatest mistake, don't you think?"

"Yes, it was a very big mistake, Mía, but it hardly compares to the constant failure of our respective ETAs."

"Let's go into the dining room, Juan Manuel. Mariana and Rodrigo are dying of hunger."

"Ladies first, madame."

Berkeley, October 16, 1991

My dearest Juan Manuel Carpio,

Even your moody letter brought me joy. Thank you for timing it to meet me with your presence on my return. Life, of course, is not easy, and we're not spring chickens anymore—luckily. How boring we'd be as spring chickens.

My trip to San Salvador was beautiful because I met up with three of my sisters who were also visiting, and my spirits really picked up when I felt the genuine warmth of my friends. My mother's health is very good, although her mind wanders. Ana Dolores and Andrea get younger every day. Now they look like teenagers. We enjoyed our time together. Susy was there, too, of course, but now she's going out with a new painter boyfriend who does nothing but paint her all day long. He'd already done about seven portraits when I got there. And to think, I couldn't even inspire Enrique to take my photo for a passport . . . Could it be I don't have any muse potential? Maybe I'd be better as a moose.

How I want to see you. But it looks like it won't be for quite a while. Let's at least write each other a lot.

Bob and I are fine, as usual, and understand this, sir, that's no joke.

I love you in enormous quantities. Your
Fernanda

Berkeley, December 23, 1991

My dear, dear Juan Manuel,

Since there's no hope this letter will get to you in time for Christmas, I'll rest my hopes on the thought that my words will somehow manage to communicate my tenderness and my thankfulness to you for your friendship, which has been a treasured gift over the years. At every turn in the road, and now in this damn *mezzo* of the road in the sometimes extremely dark forest, the quality of your friendship has been a light.

Of late I've been missing your letters, and I'm worried about your absence. I worry about you because I think perhaps you're not well. And I worry about myself, because your presence in my life has, for more than twenty years now, been an indispensable pillar. I've tried again and again to get your Lima telephone number, but with no success. Send it to me, please, when you write, so I don't have to go around saying to myself again and again: These fucking friends! They get famous, and then I can't even find them! Besides, we have an agent, as common to us both as he is implacable, because he won't even give your damned Lima number to me, and here I am your partner in four albums. Would you mind telling him, please, that I'm much more than some fan, in addition to being extremely discreet?

Lately I've only been able to find you in your music. The music you write alone, the music that, because it's of an earlier vintage, I like more. You said something like that once about something I sent you. But what's surprising in your songs, year after year, is the grace and flexibility of some melodies and some lyrics that really do come from your guts, with that painful joy for which you really have the secret. Or maybe it's the secret that has you.

I have very little news. After a few months of house repairs, and depression, and being dispirited about how many crazy roads I've run while I ran, as if in a panic through the forest, and also because I saw myself so alone this Christmas with you disappeared and with the company's having literally stolen Bob from me and dropped him on the other side of the world, suddenly it's as if I've made my peace with that bitch solitude, and therefore I feel better.

I live committed, body and soul, to my work, which isn't always lyrics for our songs, so it isn't always fun, now that the run-down house I managed to buy—and which you know so well—is completely redone.

I don't see many possibilities for traveling toward your neck of the woods this coming year, but I certainly wish I could.

Please write.

I wish you all the best for the new year.

With much, much love,

Fernanda

Berkeley, July 11, 1994

Juan Manuel Carpio, my dear brother,

No matter how blind we are, it seems it's harder for us to be seen than to see. Sometimes we think someone's really seen us and fallen in love with the person we really are. But suddenly we discover it's not true. Even worse, our presence doesn't help. At least in my case I've been loved more from a distance. Is it possible to be any more inept than we are?

Just look. You've always written beautiful love letters full of joy, but then our extremely unpunctual *Estimated Time of Arrival* does the rest. Bob

Fine never stops sending me faxes full of the purest and sincerest tenderness. And don't laugh, please. He's laconic, and his style is the fax. Even when we're both illuminated by the same little candle of domestic love, and under the same roof, which is to say not so very often, because his company is always arranging for him to love me from Patagonia or Australia.

I'll have to go back to San Salvador again at the end of the month, and I'll be staying for several weeks. Now that my mother's dead, it doesn't make much sense to keep up my little house there, and I'm going to try to sell it. Now that this house is almost completely redone, and our agent is talking about "strong income," why shouldn't I dream about one more move and a place to which Mariana and Rodrigo can happily return whenever they get a decent vacation from the university?

Why would you ever think you could offend me with your by-now-legendary visit to Enrique on Chiloé? I'm very happy to know that the three of us still love one another. I only hope these three blind mice can escape from the farmer's wife. If my letters slacked off, it's because I wrote to practically no one for two years, something I really can't explain to myself, and which makes me enraged with myself. But I hope I've recovered my senses and can get back on the job.

I've already received my share of the profits from the sale of our albums in Mexico. How great that they're selling so well there.

Write me here or in San Salvador.

I hug you hard and with all my immense tenderness.

Fernanda María

Sometimes I feel the force with which time passes and
scatters everything. And the damned wind of distance also
ends up scattering everything, little by little; but firmly, and
with a certain sadness, I see that all by themselves the years
are piling up and that we can't even know where we should
build our nests. Perhaps in a gesture, when we smile, perhaps
in a grimace that because we always shave in front of a mirror
in which we don't even see ourselves anymore, we'll never
notice. What's all this going to be like when thirty years have
gone by? And later, when it's forty, now that Mía has found
calm, a true and lasting tenderness, and respect in a good
man named Bob Peace? Of course she can go on loving me,
adoring me, but I reread her letters and see clearly that little
by little I'm being planted along a thousand roads in one or
another letter, always tenderly and lovingly, sure, but sometimes as a plant called *Love,* another called *Brother,* most of
the time called *Friend.* Of course, none of this is bad, and
seen this way it actually seems logical. Although I must confess that it doesn't always turn out logical and that sometimes it's as absurd as weeping for Just Flor, one night in
Minorca, and then in some hotel in Paris or Madrid, Mexico
City, or Buenos Aires, where you turn out the light, so sleepy
and tired you can't stand it anymore after a concert and the
big dinner afterward and in the darkness of the room there
reappears a boy paralyzed at a Paris stoplight and an old
green Alfa Romeo. Twenty-five years? At the wheel of that car

there seems to sit, paused and blind forever, a beautiful, long-nosed girl with red hair, eternal freckles.

It may seem incredible to you, Mía, someone says to no one in the darkness of that hotel room, but I've just had the profound joy, the emotion, the honor of weeping some huge tears for you. It happens to me quite often, Red.

Berkeley, September 9, 1996

Dear Juan Manuel,

It seems as if decades have passed without my knowing anything about you and without my writing you. It happens that I always think you're nearby and that all I have to do is cross the river. What river? I don't know what river, because here in Berkeley it would have to be the bay and one of its bridges. Even so, many moons have passed without crossing that river and being able to visit you. Also, I miss your letters and your news, although it's true I owe you at least two calls and three letters.

You do know it. Now I have a very good house and a luxurious room for when you come to visit us.

I'm the same me, perhaps even more the same recently, something that will make you happy. At least it makes me happy.

What can I tell you about myself? That I'm going to be many years old on September 27, and that I'd like to have a beautiful party with so many friends but they're all scattered.

I don't write much, but that doesn't mean I don't have you present in my mind.

I imagine it's the same for you, though it's true you write a lot more.

Doesn't it sadden and shame you that we communicate more through our agent than from your pen to mine and mine to yours?

Life, the main event, as Frank Sinatra said, so old now the poor guy. Remember?

I hug you.

Fernanda María

Now do you see, Juan Manuel, sans Carpio? This time you've been planted, you might say, in a desert, and your new name has been shortened until it fits with *Dear.* You're like a Just Juan Manuel now yourself. But it isn't really true. A letter from Mía received in Minorca almost a year later resolved practically everything. To the degree that was possible, of course.

Berkeley, September 7, 1997

Juan Manuel Carpio, always most beloved,

Don't worry. I didn't get lost. And, like you, I always have you present in my mind. Without ever forgetting.

Bob and I are on our way to London at the end of the month. We'll be at Andrea María's on September 26, just in time to celebrate my birthday the next day. The address and telephone number are still the same, so I'm begging you to leave your island, where I hope you've spent a beautiful season of rest.

I'm begging you to be in London on the 27th, to

toast my first gray hairs (and lots of them, the bastards), and because I really believe I deserve some
tangos or mariachis.

After that, Bob Fine and I are going to go on to
Ireland, though I have persuaded him that we won't
abandon London until you show up.

Receive my usual love and the immense enthusiasm with which I'm preparing this ever-so-hoped-for
journey to my always favorite *London town*.

And since London also has windows to peer out of at a
moonlit night, or any other kind of night, and since Bob dis-
tilled all his peace, his smiling laconism, and his tranquility
for Andrea María, her husband, and her child, Mía's birthday
was a true super-success in holy peace, no matter how many
mariachis and Carlos Gardels sang out, and no matter how
many hours Mía and I spent holding hands, as if we were getting even, like people returning to the world and to love after
a well-deserved rest. They all even sang *Happy Birthday, dear
Mía,* with us peering on like the most abstracted of observers,
and the most anyone in the apartment said, though who
knows whether it was in the living room or the dining room,
was "What a pair of nuts."

"It's just that they haven't seen each other in such a long
time," Bob Peace moderated, really very, very well, almost
professionally.

And ever since, thanks to Bob, certainly, our *Estimated
Time of Arrival* has never let Mía and me down. It's as if that
excellent friend arranged everything and kept her or me from
sticking our big noses into the subject. As long as there are
nights and windows, and as long as the moon or whatever

matters not a thing to us, there will always be punctual meetings. And quite wonderful and happy, I'd say. Besides, like that encounter in the nocturnal London window on September 27, 1997, when in some room in the apartment a small chorus intoned a long "Happy Birthday," there could also be encounters that, besides being happy, successful, pacific, and tranquil, like that one, could also be tremendously clarifying, even explanatory, with regard to so many, many things, Fernanda Mía.

"Sometimes, in some hotel after a concert somewhere, anywhere, I swear I still spill big tears for you, even now that I'm pushing sixty, Mía. But it makes me happy to do it, because in the depth of that silent sadness, those big tears also contain their dose of profound joy. And the dose will no doubt be greater from this night on, when I bless the moment that I decided to come to see you in London, for the first time since we met. And it really makes me happy to confirm, once again, to what an extent you've found peace, Fernanda María . . ."

"Believe me, peace is nothing more than a very deep manifestation of nostalgia, Juan Manuel Carpio. Peace, deep down, is a nostalgia, my old and beloved boy . . ."

Montpellier, Madrid, Las Palmas de Gran Canaria,
January 1997–April 1998.